CHEDDAR
OFF
DEAD

CHEDDAR OFF DEAD

A Cheese Shop Mystery

BY

KORINA MOSS

St. Martin's Paperbacks

For my boy Harrison

This is a work of fiction. All of the characters, organizations, and events portrayed in this novel are either products of the author's imagination or are used fictitiously.

First published in the United States by St. Martin's Paperbacks, an imprint of St. Martin's Publishing Group.

CHEDDAR OFF DEAD

Copyright © 2022 by Korina Moss.

For information, address St. Martin's Publishing Group, 120 Broadway, New York, NY 10271.

www.stmartins.com

ISBN: 978-1-250-79519-9

Our books may be purchased in bulk for promotional, educational, or business use. Please contact your local bookseller or the Macmillan Corporate and Premium Sales Department at 1-800-221-7945, ext. 5442, or by email at MacmillanSpecialMarkets@macmillan.com.

Printed in the United States of America

St. Martin's Paperbacks edition / April 2022

10 9 8 7 6 5 4 3 2 1

ACKNOWLEDGMENTS

Every person who guided and supported me along the way has a part in making my author dream come true.

My gratitude goes to my amazing agent Jill Marsal and my terrific editor Madeline Houpt for giving me this opportunity; to Danielle Christopher and Alan Ayers who designed and illustrated, respectively, my gorgeous book cover; to copy editor John Simko—I'm in awe of what you do; and to everybody at St. Martin's who had a hand in bringing this book to life. #TeamCheese!

Thanks to Eileen Pearce, Janet Lomba, and all the members of the Christie Capers book club at the Windsor Locks Public Library for cheering me on since the early years; and to the Wicked Authors I met at a book signing—Liz Mugavero, Barbara Ross, and Edith Maxwell—plus Jane Haertel, who were so generous in answering all my questions as a new cozy mystery writer. You pushed me forward. I have immense gratitude for editor and author Barb Goffman for her expertise, support, and belief in me at a pivotal time in my life.

I'm grateful for Mystery Writers of America New York Chapter who honored me with the Leon B. Burstein/MWA-NY Scholarship for Mystery Writing to support my writing endeavor; for Sisters in Crime, an organization that has been an invaluable resource and community for me; and for my Writers Who Kill colleagues and all the mystery authors I've become acquainted with who inspire me. I love the friendships I've made with my fellow writers, especially my talented agent-sister Bella who rode the tough times by my side even though she lives half a world away.

I humbly thank all the devoted cozy mystery readers who are giving this series a chance, and my friends who bought this book in support of me. I hope you enjoy it the same way I've delighted in reading mysteries all my life. Thanks again to Liz Mugavero and to Carolyn Haines and Bree Baker for agreeing to read my book in advance—I'm thrilled to have the endorsement of three authors I admire.

Lastly, a full heart goes to David and to my extended family who believed in me all these years and never once said I should give up, even when life got in the way. Extra shout-out to my sibs Kim, Kari, Kelly, Kris, and Ron.

I firmly believe most of life's problems can be solved with cheese.

—Willa Bauer

CHAPTER 1

"Taleggio." I presented the younger couple with a sample of the dense, pale yellow cheese with its orange edible rind. I watched for their reaction, knowing they'd sense a pudding silkiness on their tongue just a moment before delighting in its mellow sweetness and lingering earthy aftertaste.

When their smiles told me I was right, I handed them a recipe card. "This artichoke risotto is amazing with Taleggio cheese. It's very easy to make, but sure to impress."

The newly married couple would be hosting their parents for the first time and were relieved to get help with dinner ideas. I could've kept them in my shop for hours sampling cheeses that would elevate even the most basic recipes, but I'd learned in my years training in cheese shops all over the country not to overwhelm the customer on their first visit. They agreed to the Taleggio.

I cut a portion from the refrigerated glass case by the checkout counter. My co-worker, Mrs. Schultz—"smack-dab" in her sixties, as she liked to say—was cutting and wrapping their charcuterie selections. Deluged by the choices upon entering the shop, they'd homed in on the day's highlighted varieties, which were advertised on chalkboards hung on the raised panel wall behind the counter. In their panic, they'd ordered "one of each." Instead, I spent time with the couple at our sampling counter so they could make a more informed choice about their cheese purchases. It was the very reason I made sure we always had a glass-covered platter of soft and aged cheeses to be tasted with accompaniments like crispy baguettes or chewy dried apricots. I never want anyone to be intimidated by cheese.

While Mrs. Schultz was finishing up their order, I scanned the shop to make sure Guy Lippinger from *All Things Sonoma* hadn't arrived without my noticing. I'd been open barely two weeks, but somehow the magazine critic discovered my French-inspired cheese shop in the small town of Yarrow Glen. His review could determine whether my shop prospered or died—no biggie.

I also had my fingers crossed that a good review would be published in time for the Sonoma's Choice awards next month. I could use all the publicity I could get. I'd sunk every dime I'd made the last eight years into Curds & Whey, and signed for a hefty loan on top of that. Receiving the most votes for Best New Business would give my shop a boost, so I needed to get Curds & Whey noticed pronto.

I smoothed the wheat-colored shop apron I was wearing over my white blouse and khakis, which were cuffed above my ankles. I had a hard time finding pants to fit both my short stature and my cottage-cheese thighs. Hey, at least I came by them honestly. I reconsidered my shoes. I'd chosen my fanciest Keds this morning from the eight pairs in my closet. Did striped navy triple platforms properly represent me as a certified cheesemonger?

Mr. Lippinger still hadn't arrived, leaving my nerves

cranked on high. I stood at the door to glimpse my shop as he might when he walked in. There was no denying my French-inspired design. The textured orange-gold walls resembled rich wallpaper above raised panel wainscoting the color of light butterscotch. It was offset by a full antique oak-paneled wall behind the counters. But the real star of the shop was the cheese. Distressed turned-leg tables held stacked wheels of aged cheeses in wax casings and wrapped wedges from all over the world, so they towered over jars of relishes, olives, and jams. Reclaimed wood shelves lined one wall, crowded with more hard cheeses. Related items, such as picnic baskets and floral tablecloths, along with pairing snacks like nuts, dried fruits, and cured meats, were scattered throughout the shop. Snug in the rear corner was a kitchenette. Everything looked perfect to my eye, but it didn't calm my nerves.

I went to one of the front windows to fuss with the display. I rearranged some of the well-known Italian wedges—Asiago, Romano, Pecorino Locatelli, Parmigiano-Reggiano—to entice passersby who couldn't smell their heady aroma until they stepped inside. It was meditative, tweaking each cheese wedge so it sat in harmony with the others—not too aligned like soldiers, but not too chaotic as to look messy. It was a quiet skill to achieve a measured disorder of cheeses.

Mrs. Schultz finished ringing up the couple's purchase. I'd suggested when she started working here that she dress comfortably under her Curds & Whey apron, especially because she rode her bike to work. However, she insisted on wearing her usual attire, which was a fit and flare dress paired with a loose scarf. She looked like an updated Lucy Ricardo, but with the curly blonde hair of her sidekick, Ethel.

The newlyweds thanked us as they left and I returned the sentiment perhaps a little too aggressively as I followed them out the door, repeating "Thank you" and "Come again" multiple times. I couldn't help but be grateful for every customer.

"They're going to have strange dreams tonight," Mrs. Schultz declared after they left.

"Oh? Why do you say that?"

"Everyone knows eating cheese at night gives you strange dreams."

Mrs. Schultz was a lot like her statements—very matter-of-fact, but also a little out there. When she applied for the job, she let me know she preferred to be addressed as "Mrs. Schultz," thank you. Perhaps her background as a high school drama teacher explained her unconventionality.

The squeal of metal upon metal brought our attention outside, where a delivery truck braked to a stop in front of the shop. I took a detour to the sampling counter, then hurried to the sidewalk.

The driver hopped out of the box truck he'd double-parked. "You Willa Bauer?"

"I am," I said.

He opened the back of the truck, then took a second look at Curds & Whey. "That your shop?"

I nodded and looked at it, too, beaming with pride like a new mom. The façade was encased in wide cream-colored molding with Curds & Whey painted in teal in a sweeping font. Beneath the name, the matching teal front door with a six-paneled window was kept open in the pleasant April weather for customers to wander in. On either side of the door, plate-glass windows displayed shelves of aged cheeses in differing shapes and sizes, their wheels cut open to reveal their speckled textures and varying white and yellow coloring. On the top tier of the wire shelves were brightly painted milk jugs and metal sheep and cow sculptures beside a stack of cheese-lovers' cookbooks. It was a feast for the eyes.

I knew my cheese shop would have to compete for attention with the dozen other wonderful stores on Pleasant Avenue, directly perpendicular to the busier Main Street in the center of town. The street was a hodgepodge of mostly older flat-roofed buildings, which were renovated into shops and cafés with second-story offices or cozy apartments. Shoppers strolled the wide brick-lined sidewalks dotted with crepe myrtle trees awakening for spring. Curds & Whey was adjoined on one side by Carl's Hardware and abutted on the other by an alley, separating it from the next pair of shops.

"It's new, huh?" the driver noted.

"Brand spankin'," I answered. "Here." I handed him a cocktail napkin with the last square of cheese from the sampling platter.

"What is it?" He took it from me.

"Aged goat Gouda."

His eyes squinted skeptically at the unfamiliar offering. "Never heard of it."

"I promise you'll like it."

He put it up to his nose. The crease between his brows disappeared. "Smells kind of like . . ."

"Butter pecan ice cream?"

"That might be an exaggeration."

I laughed. "Try it."

He popped the nugget of cheese into his mouth, then nodded in approval. "It's not butter pecan ice cream, but I like it."

I smiled. There were few things more satisfying than introducing people to flavors and textures they'd never experienced before. "Come in anytime. We've got lots more."

"I think I just might." He returned his attention to his clipboard. "It's just the one box, otherwise I'd have pulled into the alley."

"This'll do."

I rubbed my arms over my rolled-sleeved blouse to ward off a chill. April weather in Sonoma Valley was warm when the sun was high, but as soon as it dipped behind the mountains in the late afternoon, the temperature followed suit.

Nineteen-year-old Archie, my other store clerk, came to meet us at the truck. His affable smile was as ever present as his freckles and the port-wine stain birthmark across his left cheek. His board shorts mostly hid his knobby knees, but he didn't seem chilled in the least under his T-shirt and Curds & Whey apron. The driver passed his clipboard to me. I checked the sheet carefully. This was a custom order and I wanted to be sure it was right before I signed it.

"Willa, where do you want this?" Archie's strained voice matched his reddening face as he cradled the heavy wooden box of cheese in his skinny arms. He staggered from the truck through the doorway of the shop. I hastily passed the clipboard to the driver, shouted a thank-you, and raced to the checkout counter ahead of Archie. I cleared off the corner, helping him lift the round box onto it. He shook his arms and squeezed his nonexistent biceps, probably trying to get the blood flowing through his rangy limbs again.

"You should've let me help you," I said.

"It didn't look that heavy. I was excited to get it inside. It's what we've been waiting for, isn't it?"

What my new clerk lacked in cheese knowledge, he made up for in enthusiasm. I thanked him and walked behind the counter to remove the aged artisan cheddar from its box. Even though I bought my clothes in the petite section, I was used to pulling palettes and heaving cheese wheels during my decade working in cheese shops across the country, so I was able to lift this particularly heavy custom wheel on my own.

"So this is the secret cheddar wheel we've been expecting?" Mrs. Schultz asked.

"It is. We'll be encouraging the customers to guess its weight. We'll put a jar next to it where they can put in their written guess along with their email address. At the end of the month, whoever comes closest without going over will win a sample of it, delivered if they choose. It'll be fun. Hopefully we'll get enough addresses to start sending out a newsletter."

"It's gotta be over a hundred pounds," Archie ventured his own guess.

I didn't want to correct him and bruise his ego. "Cheese wheels are usually standard weights, so I had it custom made so nobody can find the answer on the internet."

"So how much does it weigh?"

"It might be easier to keep it a secret if I don't tell you."

Archie looked dejected, but Mrs. Schultz nodded.

"Mr. Schultz had a tell whenever we played poker," Mrs. Schultz told us, which left me wondering about her poker-playing days. "His left ear would burn red if he had a really good hand. No one else seemed to catch on to it but me."

She often interjected her late husband into conversations. It was understandable—I was still occasionally reminded of my ex-fiancé, and we'd only been together a few years. After forty years together as the Schultzes had been, I imagined pretty much everything would be a reminder of him.

"Should I take a picture for the website?" Archie pulled out his phone.

"Good idea." I turned the cheese wheel one way and then the other, futilely looking for its best angle.

I was able to get Curds & Whey on the California cheese trail, an online list of creameries and cheese shops for cheese-loving travelers to visit, so our linked website was important. All tourists had to do was venture off the beaten path to this nook of northern California's Sonoma Valley, and I knew they'd fall in love with our small town of Yarrow Glen, as I had. Hopefully, they'd fall in love with my cheese shop, too.

"The chalkboard signs I made for it are in the back," I told Archie. "Check my office for them."

He nodded and went to retrieve them.

"I'm glad it got here before Mr. Lippinger." I eyed the wall clock. "It's only two hours until closing, so he's got to be coming soon, right?" I pressed my hair behind my ears, a nervous habit I'd developed since getting it cut short. It hadn't quite grown enough to pull it into a ponytail.

Mrs. Schultz obviously sensed my jitters. "There's an exercise I used to do with my drama students when they'd get nervous right before a performance."

"Oh, that's okay, I—"

"Breathe in from the diaphragm, Willa." She inhaled audibly to demonstrate.

It was a few moments before I realized she was still holding her breath, waiting for me to follow her lead, so I quickly inhaled to keep her from passing out.

"Exhale through the mouth." She exhaled like she was blowing up a stubborn balloon.

I did as I was told.

"Now we're going to project our voices from the back of our throat."

"Um, why?"

"It pushes the tension out of the body."

"Maybe we should stick with the breathing?"

A guttural sound came from Mrs. Schultz, long and loud like an angry moose. No one was in the shop, but I looked out the front windows to make sure we weren't scaring anybody away.

She stopped only long enough to say, "Do it with me, Willa." And then the low moan began again.

It seemed the only way to stop her was to do it, too, so I joined her in making moose noises.

Archie came running out from the stockroom. "Are you two all right?"

Thankfully, this ended Mrs. Schultz's lesson.

"How do you feel now?" she asked.

I assessed myself quickly. Surprisingly, I did feel better. "I actually feel pretty good."

A man close to Mrs. Schultz's age walked in, and my newly relaxed state vanished.

"Welcome to Curds and Whey," I announced, unintentionally sounding like a circus ringmaster welcoming him to the greatest show on earth. I was about to ask if he was Mr. Lippinger when he inquired about a restroom. Thoroughly deflated, I pointed out where our sole bathroom was, and he hurried to it.

I directed Archie where to place the chalkboard signs alerting our customers to guess the cheddar's weight.

"When he *does* get here, he's going to love your shop," Mrs. Schultz said. "How could he not?"

I appreciated her assurances. "It's nice to have a calm and supportive voice to drown out my anxious one. I bet you were the most popular teacher at your school."

She smiled. "All my students had their share of talent. What separated them was their level of confidence. I felt my job was to build their belief in themselves so they could perform to their potential."

"Have you always been so self-assured, Mrs. Schultz?"

"More so when I was younger. When Mr. Schultz passed, I was already retired and I found myself becoming scared of almost everything. That's why I applied for this job. I needed to get out of my . . . what do you call it? My comfort zone."

"I'm thrilled you applied, then. I have to say, you covered your nervousness well in your interview. I wouldn't have known it."

"You just have to pinpoint one or two things about yourself that will secretly give you confidence for a particular situation."

I could already list many things Mrs. Schultz was good at. "I recall you said you were a quick learner and a people person, both very true."

"Those were standard interview answers, but they weren't my confidence boosters."

I laughed at her savvy. "May I ask what they are, then?"

"I have distinct taste buds and good ankles."

"Even better!"

I looked at my shop, chock-full of cheese, but empty of customers. "I'm confident in my cheese, but I'd feel better with a few more customers milling about when he comes."

"Will I do?" Roman Massey sauntered in, his voice

as chill as his gait. I'd only met him once before at his Golden Glen Meadery across the street.

You'll do just fine. I immediately rebuked myself for the unbidden thought.

"What—uh, what brings you in?" I stammered.

"I forgot what time you said the cheesemaking class will be tonight."

"It's at seven. You're still able to come, I hope?"

"Wouldn't miss it." His lips formed a slow crooked smile. The dimple in his cheek wasn't hidden by his close-shaven beard.

Gosh, he was cute—in an approachable way, not like a Chris Hemsworth way. He looked about my age, a few years over thirty. His manner seemed as laid back as his T-shirt, jeans, and cowboy boots. I was determined not to let his easy charm get to me, though. I wasn't about to let myself get sidetracked by another man. I'd keep my butterflies about Roman in check.

"Care to take a guess, Roman?" Mrs. Schultz indicated the new cheddar wheel.

"It's a monster," Archie offered, subconsciously massaging his arm again.

Before Roman ventured a guess, a woman in her early forties entered the shop with a warm smile and two laden paper bags. We all recognized Vivian, the bangs of her unnaturally vivid red hair stuck out underneath a bandana. The apron that hugged her full-figured curves was the same bright blue as the awning on Rise and Shine Bakery.

"I come bearing bread." She transferred the larger bag to me, the warmth of the fresh loaves seeping through. She handed the other to Mrs. Schultz.

I thanked her, inhaling the aroma as I unpacked two

crispy loaves of sturdy French bread and a fragrant rye for my soft cheese tastings. My creamier cheeses like Camembert and Brie coated all the nooks and crannies in her crispy baguettes. The deep-flavored, chewy rye loaf was perfect for the more pungent, buttery-textured blue cheeses. I wanted to be sure to have the freshest breads possible on hand today.

"Thanks for bringing mine by. I could've picked up my rolls before you closed," Mrs. Schultz said to Vivian.

"I was afraid we'd run out before you got there. I don't mind getting out of the kitchen. I had to bring the extra order for Willa, anyway. By the way, Archie, Hope's saving you a cinnamon roll. For some reason, she didn't want me to bring it over." Vivian's lighthearted bewilderment indicated she knew exactly the reason.

A pink flush crawled up Archie's neck and rosied his cheeks. I hadn't yet met Vivian's niece, and had no clue before now that she and Archie might have a thing for each other.

"Nothing for me, Vivian?" Roman splayed his empty hands.

"I didn't expect to see you here. Are you already starting in on the new girl?" She elbowed him playfully.

He seemed to take the ribbing in stride, but I was wide-eyed. What did she mean by that?

"Give her time to settle in, at least," she continued. Then to me, "Watch out for him. He's gone through all the single women in Yarrow Glen."

"I haven't dated *you* yet, Vivian," Roman retorted just as good naturedly, adding a wink.

"If I decide to become a cougar, I'll let you know."

I chuckled at the exchange, but kept that piece of information in my mental file. There was always some truth to jokes, and Roman's charm was evident.

"Sorry I was running late with the extra bread you ordered," Vivian said to me.

"It's actually good timing," I assured her. "It'll be nice and fresh when the critic from *All Things Sonoma* gets here. If he ever does. He's supposed to review my shop for his magazine today."

"Guy Lippinger's coming here?" Vivian said, suddenly slack-jawed. She whipped her head around, as if he might be hiding behind the wedges of Manchego.

"You know of him? Has he reviewed your bakery?" I said.

"No, I got off the hook."

"Off the hook? Won't it be good publicity?" I surveyed their faces, every one of them apparent with anxiety.

"You told me some critic was coming," Archie said to me. "You didn't say it was Guy Lippinger."

"What's the difference? What do you all know that I don't?"

Nobody was willing to speak up.

Vivian said, "I've got to get back to the bakery. You'll be fine, Willa. I'll lend you my motto: 'Take one problem at a time.'"

"Does that mean Guy Lippinger's going to be a problem?"

"I mean, don't worry about things until they happen. I'll see you at your class tonight." She scurried away, calling out "Good luck" as she left.

That didn't make me feel better. "Okay, what's going on?" I looked the three culprits right in the eyes.

"You know I used to work at Apricot Grille before I started here," Archie said.

"Yes."

"Archie . . ." Mrs. Schultz's tone appeared to be a warning.

"Tell me, Archie," I insisted.

Archie reluctantly continued, "He gave the manager Derrick a pretty scathing review. I didn't read it, but Derrick sued him for defamation because of it."

"It was that bad, huh?" This was the last thing I needed to hear right before his visit.

Archie tried to soften the blow. "Lippinger ended up settling, so . . . if he slams the shop, maybe you can sue?"

"Great."

I went behind the counter where I took out the special cheese sampler I'd prepared for his visit. I was torn between needing to scarf down some soothing cheese and not wanting to disturb the beautiful platter I'd spent an hour meticulously arranging this morning. I'd included some varieties that would likely be new to the critic. I loved getting lost in the stories behind each one, like the firm Swiss I'd chosen, Kaltbach Le Crémeux. It's named for the river that runs through the twenty-two-million-year-old sandstone caves near Lucerne where it's aged.

What did it matter? I could probably eat ten pounds off that giant artisan cheddar wheel and still not feel calm. I left the cheese board alone and paced the wood floor instead.

"I told you not to tell her," Mrs. Schultz admonished Archie in a whisper I still heard.

"It's okay," I said, trying to reassure myself as much as them. "We do our best and we don't get upset." Oh boy, now I was repeating my parents' sayings.

I spent quite a bit of time as a kid trying to get out of mucking stalls and carrying grain and water buckets on our dairy farm. I didn't love farming the way my younger brother Grayson did. My parents finally relented when I was a teenager and allowed me to trade off farm chores on the weekends for selling our cheese on my own at the farmer's markets. I was thrilled with the arrangement at first, and not just because I wouldn't be ankle-deep in cow manure. People actually listened to me and believed in my expertise about our product. I didn't realize then that I was experiencing a glimpse into my future, connecting with others through cheese. It was my first taste of independence with a dash of success thrown in, which only heightened my desire to prove to my parents that I could contribute in my own way.

However, as my expectations for myself rose, the pressure began to weigh on me. My father would say that was life's way of keeping us humble. I could practically hear his voice now—*"It's not about the outcome, it's about the work."* I started to feel guilty that my parents had given in to my complaints, seeing as how they never voiced their own. In the Bauer family, you didn't brag and you especially didn't complain. *"We do our best and we don't get upset."*

So I couldn't be giddy about the days I sold every wedge or grouse about the times I didn't. Not to my parents, anyway. Grayson, still barely in middle school, would high-five me when I returned from the farmer's market with an empty cooler. Even if he understood the dairy cows more than he did my adolescent worries about being my own person, he listened. My parents supported my desire for something more than just an honest day's work, but they didn't understand it. They wouldn't appreciate my apprehension about the opinion of Guy Lippinger, a stranger. They would say his judgment didn't change what I knew about cheese or the work I'd put into my shop. And they'd be right.

I stopped pacing, but my craving for cheese remained.

A rapid pair of dings sounded. All of us checked our cell phones—except for Mrs. Schultz, that is. She had an aversion to them and didn't keep her phone on her, even though the full-skirt dresses she wore tended to have enviable pockets.

The text was Roman's. He checked it briefly, then said, "I have to get back to the meadery." He stepped closer to me and trapped my gaze with his. "You're going to do great. Don't doubt yourself. I'll see you tonight." He threw a wave to Archie and Mrs. Schultz, then left the shop, leaving me with a tingly sensation I didn't approve of.

I had to admit, though, he was right. Maybe I still had some lingering doubts about moving to a new town where I knew no one, but I never doubted myself when I was in my element—I know cheese the way a vintner knows wine. There's no way Guy Lippinger would be anything less than impressed.

"One critic's opinion either way is not going to change how incredible our shop is." I was really channeling my parents now.

"That's the spirit," Mrs. Schultz said.

I went back to the samples board and lifted the glass dome. "Let's toast to our hard work." We each plucked a toothpicked piece of cheese off the board, gathered in a circle, and held them aloft, as if we were knights raising our swords in alliance.

"To Curds and Whey," we toasted, and enjoyed the bite.

"There's almost nothing an exceptional piece of cheese can't fix," I said afterward. "I'm feeling better already."

The customer I'd forgotten about came out of the restroom. Before I could offer him a cheese sample, he said,

"By the way, your toilet's stopped up. Sorry." He hustled out of the shop.

I looked at Archie and Mrs. Schultz and turned back to the cheese board. "I think it might take more than one piece."

CHAPTER 2

꧁❦꧂

The comforting give of warm mozzarella between my fingers was the elixir to my anxiety that I sorely needed. I'd kept the shop open an extra thirty minutes, but Guy Lippinger never showed. I had to stop obsessing about it and what it possibly meant, and focus on my present situation instead.

Four of my fellow small-business owners were gathered after hours around the island in my cheese shop's kitchenette. Tonight I was teaching them the magic of turning curds into cheese. It was actually chemistry, but I found most people were intimidated by that word.

I recalled my excitement while creating this small space in the rear corner of my shop so that it would be perfect for giving classes. I'd had a simple kitchenette installed with a backsplash of shiny white subway tiles behind the pale teal cabinets and white quartz countertop. I liked the convenience of being near a stove and a sink, where I could also occasionally make some cheese-based recipes for customers to sample, like a decadent mac 'n cheese made with an herbaceous fontina instead of the usual cheddar. The long farm table with benches was to be for future cheesemaking students to sit around appreciating their creations, partnered with perhaps some rustic Italian garlic bread, savory prosciutto, or salty olives.

Tonight's basic cheesemaking class was a way to introduce my new neighbors to my shop, and more important, to me. Growing up, I was a bit of an outsider. I didn't fit in with the future farmers clubs, but to everyone else, I was still known as *the farm girl*. So I fell somewhere in between friend groups, leaving me with none. But here, with others who ran small businesses, I was one of them. I needed to be embraced by them for my shop to flourish, but on a personal level, I secretly hoped we'd become more than merely business acquaintances. This was the first place I'd ever put down roots since leaving Oregon almost ten years ago. I wanted to be accepted.

However, much like the whey in my bowl, so far the evening had been lukewarm. Several people I'd invited couldn't make it. I was surprised Derrick, the manager of Apricot Grille, had agreed to come, since he wasn't too friendly when we'd initially met. Unfortunately, his demeanor wasn't much different tonight either. He must've figured networking was networking, even if it meant putting on an apron and wrangling curds. He was a tall, lean guy, probably entering his forties, and a little intimidating. His buzz cut and perfectly fitted black button-up and slacks indicated to me that he liked things to be just so. I had the sense he was used to giving directions, not taking them.

I was bursting to ask him about Guy Lippinger, since Archie had told me about the bad review and Derrick's lawsuit. But seeing that he was already a little sour, I decided against saying anything for now. That was, until Vivian spoke up.

"So how did your visit go with Guy Lippinger?" she

asked, manhandling the mozzarella like bread dough. So much for keeping Guy's visit under wraps. She'd freshened up since I saw her earlier, donning a clingy blouse printed with lemons. The color competed with her bright red hair, which was no longer confined by a bandana but hung in waves to her shoulders. The red lipstick she wore was as bold as the rest of her. She vaguely reminded me of one of those Hollywood bombshells from the fifties, in Technicolor.

Guy Lippinger's name brought about the same response it had earlier in the day. Birdie, the owner of Smiling Goats dairy farm, and Derrick both popped to attention.

"He never showed," I replied.

"The man's a weasel," was all Derrick said, before returning his annoyance to his curds.

"How long have you been with the restaurant?" I asked him, attempting to soften his reserve with a little conversation. Men tended to like it when they got to talk about themselves.

"It'll be a year this August. And doing very well under the circumstances," he added, defensively.

"I've only heard good things about it," I assured him.

"It's a great place," Roman chimed in.

"Lippinger single-handedly put the last two restaurants that had been in that space out of business," Derrick said.

My stomach dropped. I'd heard of the magazine, but I didn't realize it had that much influence.

"You can't know that for sure," Roman said to Derrick.

"Granted, most restaurants fold within the first year anyway, but I'm sure his horrible early reviews didn't help."

"If he's awful about every place, why would he have such influence?" I asked.

"He's not awful to everyone, just the places in Yarrow Glen. Except for Roman's meadery, that is." He glared at Roman. "Roman got a glowing write-up."

"Did he?" I said, happily surprised.

Instead of looking proud, Roman kept his head lowered and said nothing. Was that for Derrick's sake?

"There was no reason for him to come after me—I won't be working here for much longer—but he seems to have some kind of vendetta for this town," Derrick continued.

"What do you mean? You're not leaving because of him, are you?"

"No way. I'm not afraid of Guy Lippinger. He should be afraid of me, if anything. I don't work permanently anywhere. Owners hire me to get their restaurants up and running and off to a successful start, to make sure they don't fall into the percentage that fail. And then I hire and train a permanent manager and go where I'm needed next."

"Oh, I see. So you're an expert at opening restaurants."

"Yes, and I can't have my reputation ruined because the guy has it in for Yarrow Glen."

I cleared my throat and said carefully, "I heard you sued him."

"Darn right."

"I also heard he settled."

"You'd better believe it. The magazine printed a retraction, too. His ego was more damaged than his wallet, believe me."

"He didn't lose his job over it?"

"He's got the best job security possible—his family owns the magazine."

"I didn't know that."

"They have old friends in the publishing industry, so

his reviews get picked up by other outlets. That's why a bad review from him can be so damaging."

"It's probably a good thing he didn't show up to your shop today," Vivian said to me.

I felt like I'd dodged a bullet, but for how long? Would I get a rain check on the visit when I was least expecting it? One of my parents' chipper mottos wasn't going to ease my mind this time.

"Are we almost done here? I've got a big party coming in at nine," Derrick said. "I need to make sure we're set up for them."

What little enthusiasm he might've had at the start of class was now extinguished, not that I blamed him. I was sorry I'd pursued my questions about Guy Lippinger. Sometimes the best thing to do was to keep your head in the sand—or in this case, in the cheese. I would not let my first cheesemaking class be a bust. I stuck a smile on my face and brightened my voice.

"So has everyone formed their curds together?" I looked around to see they had. "Now we get to the fun part—the stretching."

"Oh, good. I've been on my feet all day and my back's killing me," Vivian said. She pulled her shoulders back for relief.

"Not that kind of stretching. Stretching the mozzarella." I demonstrated by gently pulling just an inch or two at a time continuously and letting gravity cascade it back into the bowl.

Their faces lit up as they saw it becoming more like the cheese they recognized. Maybe this was going to work out, after all.

"This was a great idea, Willa," Roman said, probably more enthusiastically than he felt. I could sense he was trying to help me out, and I appreciated his support.

All evening, he'd been giving this cheesemaking thing his all. "I was excited to see you move in. Your shop, I mean," he clarified promptly. "I'm looking forward to pairing your cheeses with my mead."

"We'll definitely have a conversation about doing some tastings at your meadery," I told him.

"Have you ever tried mead before?" he asked.

"No, I don't think I have."

"Isn't that what the Vikings used to drink?" Vivian's cheese was stretched and draped back in her bowl.

"It's come a long way," Roman replied. "Vivian, I can't believe you haven't tried it. I've been here for four years."

"Where were you before you came to Yarrow Glen?" I asked him.

"I've been around," he answered vaguely.

"You can say that again," Vivian mumbled with a cheeky smile, then elbowed him with friendly affection.

Outwardly, I ignored the comment, although I fully remembered what she'd said earlier about Roman being a ladies' man. But this was business, strictly business, as I had to keep reminding myself.

"What about you, Willa? When did you decide cheese was your passion?" Roman asked.

Why did I get the feeling he wanted to change the subject? I made a mental note to ask Mrs. Schultz if she knew anything more about him. Not that I was interested in him—merely for curiosity's sake.

"I always had an affinity for it growing up on our dairy farm, but it really solidified in college when I earned a scholarship to study abroad in France for a semester. I found a little cheese shop outside of Lyon and I was hooked."

"France! That sounds like a dream," Vivian said. She closed her eyes for a moment and sighed deeply. "I feel like George Bailey, never having gotten to go anywhere. Maybe someday."

"Remember, George Bailey had a wonderful life," Roman said.

Vivian sighed again. "Still . . ."

"I hope you get to go," I said. "I imagine you'd want to see how the French make their bread."

"To be honest, I'd be more interested in their wine."

Bursts of laughter broke out. I was glad for Vivian's good humor—the mood was starting to improve.

Vivian surveyed the kitchenette's counters. "No wine accompaniment, Willa?"

"I knew our time was short tonight, so I thought it best we stick with just the cheese."

"You're in Sonoma Valley. There's always time for wine. Roman sells a nice local brand of Chardonnay—Enora's has become my favorite."

"Expensive taste," Derrick commented, although his tone seemed to indicate he approved.

"The Chardonnay I carry *is* one of the best local labels," Roman concurred. "But mead is my specialty. I brew it myself."

"Meaderies are just starting to pop up around the country. You're getting in early," Derrick said. "That's a good thing if you want to branch out."

"I'm hoping to, eventually. I was finally able to add a tasting room last year."

"Is it considered a beer or a wine, Roman?" I kept my focus on the cheese even as I asked, determined not to get caught up in those speckled green eyes of his.

"Neither, really. I'll tell you all about it when you come by. You *are* going to try it, aren't you?"

"I'll need to in order to choose the cheese pairings. It's a rough job, but someone's gotta do it."

The others laughed. I think I might've even seen the corner of Derrick's mouth inch up. Okay, things were definitely starting to improve.

Sleeves pushed up, Birdie was carefully rolling up the mozzarella she'd just stretched. I noticed she had barely said a thing the whole hour. She was the only one here without a business on Pleasant Avenue, but that was why I specifically wanted to invite her. She was a fellow farm girl. She and her husband's goat farm supplied me with chèvre—the creamy goat cheese with a fresh, lemony tang most people were familiar with. I also liked to introduce my customers who had more timid palates to other types of goat milk cheeses, like the wine-washed Queso de Murcia al Vino from Spain with its mildly fruity flavor. Why have your wine separate when you can eat cheese that's been cured in it? But there was something to be said for a classic, local goat cheese.

"I'm excited for you to be speaking here Friday about your goat farm," I said to her.

"I'm a little nervous about it. I've given talks to kids at the elementary school, but never to a room of adults," she said.

"I'm sure you'll do great. We're going to have a bunch of hors d'oeuvres to highlight your goat cheese. I think it'll be good publicity for you."

She smiled shyly, crinkling the freckles sprinkled across her nose. They gave her a youthful appearance, although I knew she was about Vivian's age, a decade older than me. She looked pretty much as she did when I'd driven out to her farm—she was a fit woman with chestnut brown hair pulled back in a ponytail and wearing only a hint of makeup. However, the confident, sociable person who had shown me their small, hands-on production wasn't present tonight.

"What's your farm called?" Roman asked her.

"Smiling Goats," Birdie replied.

"I like that," he said with a nod.

It drew an authentic smile from her. If anyone could break someone out of their shell, I suspected it would be Roman.

"I've been thinking of adding fried goat cheese balls to the appetizer menu. We like to use as many farm-to-table ingredients as we can. We'll have to talk later," Derrick said.

"Sure." Birdie perked up some.

"It looks like everyone's got their cheese stretched. Now let's roll it up the way Birdie's doing, like so." I demonstrated. "It'll end up looking like a croissant, but then you form it into a ball." I gathered it at the bottom as if holding a balloon. "As long as you stretched the mozzarella slowly and didn't break the protcins, you'll get glossy cheese, like this." I held up my cheese ball and was happy to see everyone's looked quite good. "Beautiful! Now there's nothing left to do but try it."

"Do we do anything special to eat it?" Vivian asked.

"Nope, just pinch off a piece and savor your creation."

We were finally all in harmony with appreciative *mmmm*s and *ooooh*s. I plucked a dollop off of my own smooth ball and rolled it around in my mouth, tasting the creamy cloud of milky cheese.

An insistent banging from the front of the shop interrupted my zen.

"Did I forget to put the Closed sign on the door?"

I wiped my hands and left the others, hustling around the island toward the front door. Whoever was banging must've really had a hankering for cheese—the pounding was ceaseless.

"I'm sorry. We're closed." I tried to shout in a singsong

way so as to not peeve a potential future customer, but it might've been too late for that.

I passed the refrigerated case, the tables of aged cheeses, and the checkout and sampling counters on my way to the door. The front windows were being rattled by the incessant banging.

I repeated to the impatient customer, "I'm sorry, we're closed." It was just after eight o'clock—most of the locally owned retail shops in Yarrow Glen were closed at this time of night. I wasn't the anomaly.

I turned my key in the lock and assessed the persistent man through the six glass panes of the front door for a moment before opening it. The streetlight shown on a bespectacled man possibly in his forties with wavy, disheveled hair and a receding side part. His style was neat if not trendy—a sweater vest over a collared shirt, and beige pants. He stopped knocking when he saw me and allowed me to open the door.

"Is there an emergency?" I asked.

The man pushed past me, the odor of hard liquor following him like a kite.

"You're closed at an inconvenient time," he declared.

He headed to one of the tables and began handling and sniffing the various wrapped cheeses.

"I'm sorry, but the hours are clearly posted on the door. Now that you know what they are, you can come back tomorrow."

He scoffed and allowed a wedge to drop from his grasp onto the table.

"Hey!" Looks like this guy wasn't going to respond to manners. "Excuse me!" This time I put my fists on my hips to let him know I meant business. "You can't come in here after hours and start . . . *fondling* my cheese!" I trailed him, trying to keep up with recreating my impeccable displays as he now picked through the cheddars.

"You don't know who I am?" His voice took on a haughty air.

I looked a second time at the man. I thought maybe his black-framed rectangular glasses were hiding his identity from me, but I still couldn't place him. Nobody had told me there was a well-dressed town drunk to watch out for.

Derrick stepped out from the rear of the store. "Guy Lippinger."

CHAPTER 3

I felt the blood drain from my face. I was probably as pale as the mozzarella I'd just made. My hands went from my hips to a praying position. "Mr. Lippinger. I'm so sorry. I was expecting you earlier."

His previous look of disdain seemed to harden on his face when he noticed the others. "What are they doing here?"

"I-I'm teaching a cheesemaking class. Would you like to join in?"

"No," he said before I could even coax him to the rear of the store. "I have no desire to stay." He was now at the refrigerated case. He picked up a stick of soft cheese, took one look at it, and dropped it back in. "I don't like where you get your cheese. And your customer service leaves something to be desired."

"Guy, come on," Roman tried, but Guy paid him no attention.

"You caught me off guard," I explained. "My class is just about done, so give me ten minutes to finish up, then I can walk you through my shop and tell you all about our international and local cheeses. I'll give you tastings—"

I barely noticed another rap on the door until everyone's attention was pulled by the college-aged girl with a pixie-style haircut who strode in. Her floral yoga pants and slippers indicated she hadn't planned to be out. She pulled her unzipped sweatshirt closed over her T-shirt.

"Oh good, you're still here. You weren't answering my texts," she said, facing the group.

"Hope, now's not the time," Vivian answered.

"Sorry to interrupt," she said with a snarky tone, indicating she wasn't. "I just wanted to tell you before you left to go home that there's no way I'm getting that spreadsheet done tonight. It's too confusing."

Vivian's embarrassed glance brushed all of us before it landed on her niece. "I'll come to your apartment and help you with it as soon as I leave here."

"Can't you just do it on your own? You know what you're doing. I'll learn it eventually." Hope leaned on the sample counter, pushing aside with her elbow one of the four gift baskets I'd made for the class participants, as if even talking about it was too much effort.

This time Vivian shot a look at Guy only, surely wishing the critic wasn't hearing this. I sympathized, but I had my own worries. I had to convince him to give my shop a chance before he left.

"Mr. Lippinger, is it possible you can come back tomorrow when we're open? You'll get a much better idea of what my shop's all about."

"That won't be necessary. I know enough."

"But you can't write a review based on two minutes in the store."

"I won't be back. I don't like the company you keep." He was suddenly calm. "You have to be careful who you associate with, Ms. Bauer. People aren't always who they seem to be." He looked at the others when he said it, his stare unwavering from the foursome. "Especially the ones who have something to hide."

"Whoa," Hope murmured from behind us, straightening her posture in attention.

"You're one to talk," Derrick countered.

"You're right, I am. So now I'm talking. Does everyone want to know a secret? Should I tell it?" Guy asked.

Roman had drifted nearer to Guy and gave his shoulder a firm but friendly squeeze. "I think it's best if you go now, Guy. Maybe you've had a little too much to drink."

At that moment, the front door swung open and another man barreled in, this one carrying a toolbox.

"Where's Willa Bauer?" He came straight toward me, even before he got any confirmation. He might've been about my age, with a stocky build and an open face. "Sorry, I'm late. I'm the guy you called to fix your clogged toilet."

I cringed.

"So this is the new place in town. The *fromagerie*?" He exaggerated the *aaa*. "Nice." He nodded in approval as he looked around. "Hey, guys," he said to the others with a smile before noting our silence. "Uh, sorry, did I interrupt something?"

"Guy was just leaving," Derrick said.

Guy didn't budge at first, then started to allow himself to be shown the door, apparently changing his mind about revealing secrets. Maybe he would change his mind about my shop, too.

"Please, Mr. Lippinger—" I pleaded once more.

"Lippinger?" the toilet guy repeated. "Dippy Lippy, is that you?"

Guy Lippinger's eyes narrowed.

"I didn't know you still graced our town with your presence," he continued.

Guy ignored him and walked out on his own accord, leaving an uncomfortable silence in his wake.

CHAPTER 4

I left the kitchenette sparkling clean, as if I could wipe away what had happened. Well past when I should've given up, I'd continued begging Guy for another chance, even following him to his car around the corner like a spurned lover. It was no wonder the others, obviously embarrassed for me, had been in a rush to leave and didn't even take their freshly made mozzarella with them. I noticed the gift baskets that I'd so carefully filled with my favorite hard cheeses, a small cutting board, and a matching cheese knife that had the C&W shop initials engraved in the wooden handle were still sitting on the sample counter. With the commotion that ended the class, I'd forgotten to give them out. Great.

It was days like this when I tended to question giving up my nomad life. The more you had to love, the more you had to lose. Unfortunately, I knew that as much as anyone.

I puttered around Curds & Whey trying to shake off the bad juju Guy Lippinger had brought into my shop, my haven, but it was no use. This was going to require something more than the meditation of aligning cheese wedges. I surveyed the refrigerated case. I was in need of a thick slice of . . . Challerhocker—a Swiss unlike any other. The deep flavors of peanuts and buttery caramel was such a satisfying bite, only heightened by a lingering salty finish. I stopped myself after one slice of the smooth, dense Swiss, feeling better already. Who needs Xanax when you've got cheese?

I yawned. I guess six weeks of eighteen-hour days getting Curds & Whey up and running were catching up with me. The late work nights also meant I hadn't spoken to my parents in over a week. I pulled out my phone to call them, but it was after ten—too late to call. Farmers notoriously started their day at the crack of dawn and my parents were no exception.

I took a last look at the room before dimming the lights. Thirteen years ago, the seed of this dream was planted in a small shop in France. I'd been exhilarated by the idea of being in a city like Lyon, completely different from the farm. But three weeks in, I found myself searching out the quieter areas that might feel more like home. One excursion to a nearby village led me to a small cheese shop and to its owner, Genevieve, a stoic, even-tempered woman who reminded me of my mother. I began taking frequent jaunts out to her shop, learning about cheese, and eventually I worked out a sort of apprenticeship with her. She expected a lot from me, but she was patient and caring, also like my mother. Returning home was bittersweet. I knew when it came to opening my own shop one day, I wanted it to transport me back to my time in France with Genevieve. I'd been through a lot since then to get here. I certainly wasn't going to let Guy Lippinger rip it from me. I'd find a way to make it better tomorrow.

I went to the back room where cardboard boxes seemed

to multiply on their own, mocking me by the back door. I took as many with me as I could carry and staggered outside to the side alley dumpster, tossing them above my head to make it into the recycle bin. As much as I told myself to not think about the awful magazine critic, questions about him still ran around my mind. Did he really have a vendetta against Yarrow Glen like Derrick said he did? And if so, why?

I shivered without a coat in the cold April night. About to rush upstairs to my apartment, I was surprised to see a car parked at the end by the road. It was unusual to see any cars at night on this part of the block, I'd come to learn. Derrick's restaurant and The Cellar at Yarrow Glen's inn were the only two places nearby that were open this time of night. They were well up Pleasant Avenue, past Main Street, and had parking lots.

Guy had been parked there earlier. Was that still his car? The streetlights in the alley produced concentric circles on the pavement, leaving the area around them dark, but a Mercedes Benz G-Class was easy to distinguish, even in shadow. I started toward the car. Was the dim light playing tricks on me or was he sitting in it? I wouldn't mind getting some answers. Maybe I wouldn't have to wait until tomorrow to turn my bad luck around.

As I approached, my hunch was confirmed—he was slumped against the driver's side door, passed out, no doubt. His night of drinking must've caught up with him.

I wrestled with whether to leave him there. Regardless of what happened earlier, I didn't want him waking up and driving home in a bad condition. I thought I should probably take his keys and call him an Uber.

I rapped on his window when I reached the car. His

glasses askew, he didn't stir. I tried the driver's side door and pulled it open. I was ready to catch him as he began to spill out, but I automatically leapt back when I saw the knife in his neck. Guy Lippinger fell to the ground, dead.

CHAPTER 5

I'm not sure if my screams alone brought the cops or if they were called by the guy who fixed my toilet earlier and seemed to suddenly appear by my side. He stayed with me until they arrived. After I pointed to the body, the police left me sitting on the front sidewalk under the splash of a streetlight wrapped in one of those shiny Mylar thermal blankets like a baked potato.

The toilet guy sat down next to me. He shook his head slowly. "What the huckleberry?"

I stared at him, confused. "What the what?" *Could I no longer understand sentences? Was I going into shock?*

"Sorry, old habit. What the huckleberry—my mother used to make my dad say it instead of swearing in front of us kids. It's something we all kind of picked up."

"Oh."

"You okay?"

"I don't think so. Did you see him too?"

He nodded.

I squeezed my eyes shut, but the scene was still encased in my memory. "How'd you get here so fast?"

"I heard you scream. I live upstairs."

"Wait a minute, *I* live upstairs."

"Above the hardware store."

"Oh, of course." The hardware store was next to mine, in the same building as my shop.

"What do you think happened?" he asked me.

"I'm Detective Heath," a mellow voice interrupted before I could answer. I looked up to see him standing before us, presenting a badge before snapping the case shut and sticking it back in his suit pocket. "Which one of you found the body?"

I stuck my hand through an opening in the crinkly wrap and raised it.

Detective Heath asked the toilet guy to leave us and directed another officer to take his statement.

"You going to be okay?" he asked before leaving with the officer.

"Sure." It was a rote answer. I'd never been in this situation before. How did I know if I'd be okay? I gave a weak thanks as he walked away.

Detective Heath squatted in front of me, his face blocking out the rest of the street, so that all I could focus on were his dark eyes. I caught a hint of cologne, intoxicating notes of citrus and wood. He flattened his tie to his chest so it wouldn't dangle in front of him.

"What's your name?"

"Willa Bauer." Okay, so I remembered my name. This was a good sign.

"What were you doing here, Ms. Bauer?"

"I was about to go to my apartment. It's above my shop. I just finished work."

The detective's eyes left mine for the first time and looked to my right.

"Is this your shop?" He read the exterior. "Curds and Whey?"

I nodded. The mention of my shop, like a familiar face,

brought me out of my initial shock. I clumsily stood, my blanket crinkling, and got my bearings.

Detective Heath stood with me and produced a pen and a spiral notebook a little larger than the palm of his hand from his suit jacket and asked me to tell him how I discovered the body.

There wasn't much to tell. Dumpster. Car. Dead man.

When I finished going over the ordeal, he wanted to know about me. I fumbled over my words. Merely being questioned by police made me somehow feel guilty, but he seemed satisfied enough with my responses.

"Did you recognize the deceased?" he asked.

I nodded.

"You knew him?"

"I met him once."

"When was that?"

"About two hours ago."

If he was surprised, he didn't show it. "Why don't you tell me about that? Go slow. Don't leave anything out."

The jumbled mess of an evening began to unreel itself the longer I talked. By the time I got to Guy Lippinger bursting into my shop, I recalled the threat he'd made about revealing someone's secret. I shared it with Detective Heath.

When I'd finished recounting the evening, he made me tell him everything again. He jotted down things in his notepad without giving anything away. I bet he didn't have a tell in poker like Mr. Schultz had.

"Do you mind if we go inside your place of business?" he asked when I'd finished my story for the second time.

I was happy to. My feet were cold and my legs were starting to cramp from standing in place. Without thought, I turned around toward the alley to go back the way I'd come, but it was cordoned off with police tape and officers milling about. The piercing red police car lights were attracting a crowd. I felt for my keys in the pocket of my cuffed khakis and led him to the front door instead.

Detective Heath took his time looking around as if he were a browsing customer. I brightened the lights for him. He was certainly more polite than Guy Lippinger had been. I immediately felt guilty for still harboring bad thoughts against the man now that he was dead.

"How long have you been open?" he asked, looking closely at the baskets of recipe cards and folded cheese-cloths but not at me.

"Almost two weeks." I sat on the stool behind the counter then hopped off again, too agitated to sit still. I didn't like the detective's interest in my shop. "Do you think what happened here earlier had something to do with his death?"

Detective Heath ignored my question.

"Don't you think it could've been someone who was trying to carjack him or something? That Mercedes is pretty flashy," I pointed out.

"We'll be looking into all possibilities."

I shrugged off the thermal blanket, feeling suddenly overheated.

"I heard Yarrow Glen was safe," I said.

"It's a very safe town, but murder can happen any-where."

"Apparently," I muttered. "I just moved here. Well, you know that already."

He was on my turf, but I'd never felt more vulnerable. He knew all the basics about me and I knew nothing about him, like a lopsided blind date. Was he good at his job? Did he think I was guilty of something?

I pressed my lips shut and considered him more closely

as his taut body moved about the room. His tailored suit traced his broad shoulders and tapered to slim-fit trousers. He was the only officer here I'd seen who wasn't in uniform. He was perhaps older than me, closer to forty than thirty. His black hair was thick and wavy, but without a hair out of place. His sharp jawline was enhanced by a five-o'clock shadow. I wondered if he was as precise as his style. All I knew was that his calm demeanor was unnerving.

"Have you always worked in Yarrow Glen?" I didn't expect a response; I just couldn't keep quiet any longer.

He surprised me. "I'm pretty new to town too."

"How long have you been a police officer?"

"An officer for thirteen years, a detective for the last three."

So he had some experience behind him. Shouldn't he know, then, that there was nothing to be discovered here? Shouldn't he be checking out the murder scene again or asking people if they saw something?

He made his way around the shop to the sampling counter where I was.

I couldn't take it anymore. "Is there a reason we're in here? He was murdered out there."

Detective Heath was now checking out the four gift baskets on the counter I'd forgotten to hand out after class. A line etched itself between his dark brows, like he disapproved.

"Those are gift baskets I made," I said impatiently, hoping an explanation would move him along.

"May I?" he asked as he made to reach into one.

"Be my guest." Why was he asking me? He was the police detective.

He reached into one of the baskets and took out the pronged cheese knife, engraved with C&W for Curds &

Whey. He held it up and pulled the protective sheathing off the blade.

"Do you use these solely for gift baskets or do you sell them here?" he asked.

"I plan to do both. So far these four are the only gift baskets I've made."

"Did you put the exact same items in all four baskets?"

"Yes." Now I was really getting impatient. "Why are you so interested in my shop? The man was killed in his car on the corner. He was here earlier in the evening, but I didn't even know him before tonight. There are five other people he may have threatened who were here. This has nothing to do with me."

"One of your gift baskets is missing a knife. And a knife identical to this one was found in the victim's neck. Your shop supplied the murder weapon."

I swallowed hard. This had everything to do with me.

CHAPTER 6

I slept fitfully. My closed eyes sensed the room becoming tinted with light, and I awoke before my alarm. I laid there for a while trying to get back to sleep, but I couldn't hit the Stop button on my mind's replay of last night. I finally had enough. I threw the covers off and wiggled into my yoga pants, slipped an oversized University of Oregon sweatshirt over my head, and shuffled to the bathroom.

Oh, I looked rough. When I rubbed the dark rings under my eyes, I was relieved to see it was mostly smudged mascara from the day before. I washed my face and pushed my bangs back and forth in some kind of attempt to make myself look better than I felt. If I didn't find a hairstylist soon, my bangs would be hanging over my eyes like a sheepdog. Those two wiry gray strands I'd found yesterday had the nerve to still be there. Against my black hair, they were as noticeable as a neon sign. It crossed my mind to pluck them, but I wasn't that invested. It seemed a silly thing to be concerned about after yesterday. So did making the bed, but my mother's edict that "a made bed is the first task of an accomplished day" remained in my head and wouldn't allow me to keep it rumpled. I did my daily duty of straightening the quilt and fluffing the pillows. Today it was more like punching than fluffing, if I were to be honest, and it felt pretty good.

I padded to the living room and pressed the remote for the TV. My iridescent red and blue betta fish, Loretta, began wiggling excitedly around her bowl the minute the TV started streaming the Food Network. Some people tried to tell me she was just reacting to the colors or the movement on the screen, but I knew she had a preference for Ted Allen.

My two-bedroom, one-bath apartment was what realtors liked to describe as cozy. My kitchen and living room mirrored each other in one open space, the areas delineated by a butcher block island with a trio of stools tucked under two sides. The kitchen had a great east-facing view of the mountains with a matching tall, arched window in the living room. The apartment was charming if you ignored the slight slant of the hardwood floor.

My fish continued to wave her red crown tail like a flamenco dancer.

"Loretta, you're entirely too active for this early in the morning."

I sprinkled fish food in her bowl and let her enjoy breakfast watching Chopped while I made my cappuccino. The milk looked so lonely in my practically empty fridge. Since moving to Yarrow Glen, I'd been more concerned about filling the shop rather than my apartment with everything it needed. My own pantry came in a distant second, save for the cheese I always stocked for emergencies, like late-night stress eating. I'd been bummed to find there was no inside staircase from my apartment to my shop, but in hindsight, not having easy access to that much cheese would probably save me an extra three inches on my hips.

My living room was pretty much in place, thanks to the vintage furniture from my grandmother's farmhouse: the console I used for my TV, the tall metal stool which served as Loretta's island, and a wide bench I used as a coffee table. My comfortable couch had to be relocated to my office downstairs, since it was too big for my current living room. My love seat and chairs once again made the move with me, their transformation from shabby chic to shabby shabby almost complete after so many times relocating. Luckily, I also had my grandmother's knitted throw blanket to drape across the back of the love seat.

My worth-every-penny coffee/espresso/latte machine was unpacked, but a couple of corners of the apartment were still crowded with boxes. If I didn't get around to unpacking them this month, maybe I'd go minimalist and decide I didn't need them at all.

I opened the flap to a box by my feet. Two shiny black dots stared up at me. *Oh, Hoot!* I grabbed the stuffed owl from the box and gave him a hug. He'd been with me since I was seven. No minimalism for me.

Hoot got the place of honor on my reading chair. I considered taking advantage of my early start to the day by unpacking some more things. But that mountain view sunrise called to me. I stuck a woolen hat on my head, retrieved my cappuccino, and went out my front door, which was actually in the rear of the building.

I stepped onto my postage-stamp-sized deck. I'd stuck a lone side table out there just large enough to hold a drink and a dessert plate of cheese. The space got crowded when I unfolded my single camping chair next to it, so I kept it propped against the stone building.

The warm mug kept my fingers from stiffening in the crisp morning air as I leaned on the creaky wooden railing overlooking sixteen acres of preserved land. I could see part of the walking trail that looped through the mature oaks and opened onto the park behind town hall. The park lawns were used for events like the April outdoor market on Thursdays, a prelude to the summer's farmer's market.

The fog had settled into the distant mountains. The sunrise brushed its yellow, red, and orange palette across the sky, slowly chasing the shadows from the rolling hills and vineyards. How could the ugliness of last night happen when there was so much beauty right here?

A purposeful cough sounded from over my shoulder and startled me into almost dropping my cappuccino. There was someone sitting on the adjoining deck behind the privacy trellis. I looked through the smattering of last year's dying brown vines that still clung to it. It was the toilet guy again.

"It's you!" I said.

"Hey, neighbor. Willa, right?"

"That's right. And you're . . ."

"Baz. Baz Tooney."

"Baz." Thank goodness, I wouldn't have to keep thinking of him as the toilet guy. "I forgot you said you lived here. I didn't get a chance to thank you for last night—staying with me until the police came. So, thank you."

"No problem."

"You must work for Carl's Hardware, then, since you came to snake my toilet." Mrs. Schultz had said she'd contacted the hardware store.

"I self-contract for them as a handyman—any job you need."

"A jack-of-all-trades. I envy you. I'm handy on a farm,

but fixing things in my apartment or my shop? Not so much."

"A farm girl, huh? My dad's a home builder—I learned everything when I worked for him, but it wasn't for me. Too much pressure. I like helping people out by doing the smaller jobs, so they have someone they can trust when something goes wrong or needs replacing. You get to know people instead of just working all day to the sound of buzzsaws and drills."

"That must've been why Mrs. Schultz knew to call you. I'll remember that. Are you normally an early riser, then? Up and out?"

"Not sunrise early, but it was kind of hard to sleep after last night. It's not every day you see a—well . . ."

"Yeah." My mind's eye flashed the picture of a dead Guy Lippinger with a knife in his neck—*my* knife—and I shook it away. "You knew him, right? Last night when you came into my shop, you called him . . ."

"Dippy Lippy. It was a stupid nickname he had in high school. I didn't really know him, though. He was a lot older. It was my brother or maybe one of my sisters who overlapped him in school."

"How many sisters do you have?"

"Three sisters. My brother and I bookend—he's the oldest and I'm the youngest. Anyway, I knew *of* him. Everyone knew Guy."

"Because he was a food critic?"

"Ha! No. His family's pretty infamous in this town. They were what you call land barons in this area for a long time. Greedy ones. They made life tough for a lot of folks before they sold up and left. Guy got the brunt of the loathing even though he was only a kid. That's probably why he's a lousy adult. Was. Jeez." He dropped his head.

So that's why Guy didn't want anybody to succeed in this town.

"Since we're neighbors and all, I want to tell you something so that you're not freaked out," I said.

"Freaked out more than I was last night? Try me."

I took another sip of my cappuccino before I laid it on him. "I think I'm a suspect in Guy's murder."

"Because you found him? I don't think a murderer would scream like that. My ears are still ringing."

"Sorry about that. I'm glad you believe I didn't do it, but they found one of my cheese knives in his neck."

"That doesn't prove anything. Anybody could've taken one."

I leaned against the trellis between us. "Before you came to my shop last night, Guy was in a mood. He was a little drunk, but it was more than that. He was agitated about something, and I don't think it had to do with me."

"What was it about?" Baz leaned in his chair against his side of the trellis, too, so we were barely a foot apart.

"He was just being rude when he first got there, but then when he saw the others, he changed." I quieted my voice further, even though the closest apartment was an alley away. "I think he wanted to warn one of them that he was going to tell their secret."

"What do you mean?"

"There were four of them—Derrick from the restaurant, Vivian from the bakery, Birdie from the goat farm, and Roman from the meadery. Vivian's niece Hope was there, too, but she was standing behind him. He was looking at the other four when he said it."

"Said what? Come on, don't keep me in suspense."

I already felt a bond with Baz—seeing a dead body with someone can have that effect. And there was also something about him that reminded me of my brother. He had that easy way about him.

"Did you ever play pranks on your brother or sisters when you were kids?" I asked him.

"Sure. When you're the youngest, it's the only leverage you've got. What does that have to do with anything?"

Yup, just like Grayson. "It's nothing." I decided to trust him. "Guy said one of them had a secret. And he was about to tell it before you came in. Then I guess he changed his mind."

"Whoa." Baz was quiet for a moment.

"The knife that was used was taken from one of the gift baskets I'd made for the four of them. I made them after I'd closed up the shop—so no one else could've taken it except someone who was there last night."

Baz seemed to be considering what I'd told him. "A secret, huh? You think one of them killed him to shut him up?"

I didn't want to be the one to say it. I was the new girl in town and I was just getting to know everybody. But that's exactly what I thought. "What do *you* think?" I said diplomatically.

"I only know all of them through work. Derrick's got a temper, but . . . I don't know if I see any of them being a murderer."

"Yeah, you're probably right. There must be another explanation."

He thought about it a few moments more and reconsidered. "But I guess we can't be sure. You never know what people are hiding."

"That's why they're called secrets." I found myself getting excited that I had someone who believed in me, just like my brother always did. Plus, this was Baz's hometown—he could be a good ally. "You said your brother or one of your sisters went to school with him. I wonder what they know about him."

"I don't see them too much anymore, but I'll ask. I'm kind of the black sheep of the family."

"Oh, I'm sorry."

"It's no big deal. They all went to college and work for my dad's company. I was the only one who didn't want to do it. It wasn't the work, don't think I'm lazy or anything."

"I don't."

"It was the pressure of working for my family. There's no getting out from under it."

"I can kind of relate. I think my parents would still love for me to come back to their dairy farm."

"Yeah. Parents are like that, I guess. I don't regret my decision. I'd rather have freedom than money. They think turning thirty's gonna change my mind, but it won't. Anyway, I can ask them for you, see what they remember about him, but it was a long time ago. What are you hoping to find out?"

"Honestly? I have no idea." I sipped my forgotten cappuccino, but the chilly air had already made it tepid. "So you've never seen Guy in town all these years? You didn't seem to recognize him last night until someone said his name."

"He moved away a good twenty years ago when his parents sold the land. I was a kid, so I didn't know anything about it until years later when I started hearing the stories over and over. They tried selling their land to a research company instead of keeping it sustainable, which made them even more hated. Luckily, it fell through. Can you imagine? Yarrow Glen would be the blight of Sonoma Valley."

"When did he come back?"

"Just a couple of years ago. He wanted my dad's company to build his house, but my dad wanted to stay far away from the Lippinger name. Guy had a place built on the outskirts of the glen. It's supposed to have an amazing view, but still, I can't believe a great view would be enough for him to want to come home. Why come back to a place where you were despised? The only reason I know anything about him is because I hear the gossip when I'm working. People still hold a grudge."

"Do you think that could be the reason he was murdered? Somebody with a grudge?" I unfolded my camp chair and sat down next to the trellis to consider the information Baz was giving me.

"That's a long time to wait to exact revenge, but I suppose anything's possible. It was really his parents who screwed people over, though, not him, but he still wasn't going to be welcomed back to town. Maybe that's why his wife wasn't seen around much either."

"He's married?" I didn't consider that. "Does he have kids?"

"No kids. Nobody's seen the wife around since they first moved here."

It made me too sad to think of him as someone with a soft side who'd fall in love and get married. I'd prefer to remember him as the jerk who stormed into my shop. My heart sank again. Thinking of what happened in my shop last night didn't help either.

"Everyone heard me begging him to give me another chance. As far as that goes, I've got motive—he was going to give my shop a bad review. And the Curds and Whey knife in his neck incriminates me." Chills snuck under my sweatshirt. "It doesn't look good for me."

"So we need to do something about it," Baz declared. "You're obviously not a murderer."

"I appreciate the vote of confidence, but how come you're so sure?"

"You're the cheese lady, right?"

"Cheesemonger, yes."

"Cheesemonger. The point is, nobody whose life's work is cheese could be a bad person."

"I think we're going to be good friends, Baz. I already feel like I can tell you anything."

"Maybe because talking to you through this trellis feels like a confessional."

A hearty laugh burst from me. It felt good.

CHAPTER 7

I brought out a cappuccino for Baz after offering to make him one. I had to rummage in my box labeled "Kitchen" for the extra sugar he requested in it. I handed it to him around the trellis.

"Thanks a bunch," he said.

"My pleasure."

"So what's up first? How are we going to prove you didn't murder Lippinger?"

"I'm not sure. This is new territory for me." I thought about it some more. "You don't happen to be friends with Detective Heath, do you?"

"Sorry, no."

"That's right, he said he's new to town. I was thinking if we knew what he's discovered about the body and the crime scene, we'd have some more to go on." That gave me a thought. "Do you think they took Guy's car away last night?"

"I don't know. Why? Oh, wait. Are you thinking . . . ?"

"If they don't have anybody stationed next to the car, we should check it out."

"And put our prints and DNA at the crime scene?"

"My prints are already at the crime scene. But you're

right. We don't want to mess with evidence." I didn't like feeling so powerless. I stood up, suddenly feeling trapped on my cramped deck. "I want to check the front of my shop and make sure it's not taped off so my customers and I can get in." I looked at the stairs, not moving toward them even as I said it. The thought of seeing the alley again had me shook.

Baz must've sensed my hesitancy. "You want me to come with you?"

"No, don't be silly. I'm fine."

I took a fortifying sip of my cold cappuccino, wishing I'd made a double espresso instead. I needed the boost.

I left Baz and my drink, and descended the steps lining the back wall of the building. I was rounding the corner when police tape halted me. They'd cordoned off the entire alley. There, on the far end, was the pricey Mercedes Benz SUV. A shudder went through me. Then just like last night, Baz was by my side. His brownish-blond hair was uncombed and he had a night's worth of stubble on his doughy cheeks that I hadn't noticed through the dead vines of the trellis. He was dressed more appropriately than I was—he had work boots on rather than slippers and was wearing a short jacket. His hands were stuffed in his jeans pockets.

"I needed some exercise," he said.

I accepted his lame excuse to join me. As much of a blow as it was to my pride at being self-sufficient, I was glad he was there.

"We're going to have to go the other way," I said.

I wasn't sorry not to be making the walk down the alley. Instead, we strode across the strip of blacktop that ran the length of the building, past the single row of parking spaces, four of which were allocated for

Baz and me as residents. Cars could only access the lot through the alley on the other side of Carl's Hardware. The narrower alley on my side, where my dumpster and the shop's back entrance were located, was for delivery trucks only. Guy had parked there illegally. We took the alley by Carl's Hardware to the sidewalk of Pleasant Avenue.

The sun was now fully above the mountains, but the street was still empty. It was too early for any place to be open, even the bakery. I could immediately see they hadn't cordoned off my shop, thank goodness. The police tape started at the corner where the back of Guy's SUV was visible. A man stood just outside of the tape, peering at the car.

I threw my arm in front of Baz and backed us up against the front of Carl's Hardware to try to hide us from the man's view.

"There's a man looking at the car," I whispered. He wasn't wearing a police uniform and there was no cruiser in sight. "You think he's trying to steal evidence?"

Baz squinted. "I know that guy."

"Who is he?"

Baz didn't answer. He left our hiding spot and walked toward him. I had no choice but to follow.

"Hey, Richie," Baz called when he neared him.

"Baz," Richie greeted. They did the half-hug, half-handshake bro greeting. Underneath Richie's tight polo shirt, he was all muscles, like he'd been blown up with a bicycle pump.

"Are you here to tow the Mercedes?" Baz asked him.

I belatedly noticed a tow truck parked up the street.

"Yup, I'm just waiting for the final okay from the sergeant. They want it in custody. Shep went to get coffee and I told him I'd keep watch. The car's lit, huh?"

"Who's Shep?" I asked, sidling up beside Baz.

Richie looked me up and down and a grin formed. "Officer Shepherd. We go way back." Then he looked at Baz with raised eyebrows and nodded toward me. The unseemly grin grew.

"Come on, Richie, get real. She's just my neighbor," Baz said, emphatically.

Not that I thought of Baz romantically either, but I self-consciously tugged my hat farther down on my rumpled hair and crossed my arms over my baggy sweatshirt.

"She was the one who found the guy dead," Baz continued.

The grin was wiped off Richie's face. "Ugh. Sorry. I bet you don't want to see this anymore. I'll have it towed as soon as Shep gets word from the sergeant."

"So if they're towing it, does that mean they didn't find anything?" I asked.

"No. They probably want to do more forensics on it. It's more protected in custody than leaving it out here. I've done it for them before when a car's involved in a criminal case. But they already found something this time. Shep let slip that they were pretty excited about a business card stuck in the passenger seat."

"Whose business card?" I could hardly contain my own excitement.

"It was for some nail salon."

"A nail salon. Did it have an appointment date on the card?"

"No writing on it." Richie's cell phone rang. He answered it and stepped away from us to talk.

"What are the chances a manicurist killed him?" Baz said.

"More likely, it's someone who visited the shop. Or it could be Guy's. I wonder if he got mani-pedis."

"Did you happen to look at his hands?"

"No. I suppose the coroner will get a good look at them or his wife would know. It could be hers—it could've slipped from her jacket or purse, and that might've happened at any time."

"If she's been around."

"If it wasn't hers, you think it was accidentally left by one of our suspects?"

"It's something, anyway. We could ask around."

"We have to go about it carefully. I don't want any of them knowing I suspect them. I just got to town—I can't afford to make enemies and end up being as hated as Guy was."

"I gotcha."

"It might be easier to ask about him and learn more about his relationships with the four who were in my shop last night—Derrick, Vivian, Birdie, and Roman."

"And Hope."

"You're right. I guess we have to include her too."

"And I'll keep my ears open. When I'm working, people tend to forget I'm there."

"That could be helpful. Maybe we'll be able to figure out who had a secret worth killing for."

CHAPTER 8

By the time I opened my shop, Richie Muscles had towed the SUV, but several officers were still scouring the taped-in area. Unfortunately, their police cars were parked conspicuously in front of the alley and my shop.

I'd called Mrs. Schultz and Archie to let them know what had happened and to make sure they were still comfortable coming to work. Somehow, word had already spread, and they seemed eager to come in.

Mrs. Schultz stepped outside for the eighth time in as many minutes to keep an eye on the goings-on at the corner. She'd just cut and wrapped a pound of Cheshire cheese for an online request for a vegetarian order and was still absently holding onto the dense, aromatic British wedge.

I didn't blame her; it was impossible to concentrate on work. I'd told her and Archie the details of the murder as soon as they came in. I thought it was only right to disclose that I was a person of interest in the police investigation.

"How long do you think the police will be out there?" Mrs. Schultz came back in and joined me at the sample counter.

"Who knows? It stinks that we still haven't gotten permission to have a table at the park yet. Today would've been a perfect day to sell at the lunchtime outdoor market instead of here. We're not going to be getting any votes for the Sonoma's Choice awards if people are afraid even to stop by."

Every other year the free community newspapers in Sonoma County sponsored a write-in contest for the favorite locally owned businesses in different categories. I was probably putting too much pressure on my little shop, seeing as how we'd just opened, but I'd been told that those who won Best New Business invariably ended up becoming one of Yarrow Glen's staples. I wanted my cheese—and my shop—to be on the lips of everybody in town.

"We still have the cheese hunt on Saturday," Archie said. "Did you see the flyers I printed up for it?"

"I sure did. They look great. We're going to have to find some time to distribute them in the next couple of days." We'd brainstormed a fun interactive event for customers involving cheese trivia questions. "Hopefully that will get us some attention—the kind that we want."

Mrs. Schultz wasn't done with the topic of the murder. "The police can't really think you did this, can they? It's outlandish."

I shrugged. According to the evidence they had so far, it wasn't as outlandish as it would initially appear. I tried to focus on prepping a sampler cheese tray. I chose a smoked assortment from Germany, Spain, and Vermont. I gave a piece to Mrs. Schultz and offered one to Archie. "This one's smoked Ammerlander. It was first produced by Trappist Monks in an abbey in Bavaria. It's still made using a traditional German recipe, naturally smoked over a beechwood fire until it forms that brown rind you see there. You can go ahead and eat the rind, too."

Mrs. Schultz put the piece I offered under her nose before popping it in her mouth. "Mmm. Smooth, smoky . . ."

"A little nutty," Archie offered, tasting his piece. "It's stupid, too. Not the cheese. The—what is it? Smoked Ammerlander? It's good. Thinking you killed him is stupid. Like you'd be dumb enough to leave your Curds and Whey knife as evidence. I think someone was trying to set you up."

"Who would do that?" Mrs. Schultz said. "She just moved here. She can't have made any enemies yet, have you, Willa?"

"I sure hope not." I ate another square myself, this time the Grafton Village smoked cheddar from Vermont. After its aging period, it lingers over smoldering hard maple wood, giving it a slightly sweet finish. If this murder wasn't solved quickly, I'd be eating all my profits.

"Can one of those forked cheese knives even kill someone?" Archie asked.

I saw it lodged in his neck pretty well before I knew what it was, and Guy was definitely dead, so my answer was yes.

"I suppose if it hit the carotid artery, it wouldn't need to go in that far," Mrs. Schultz said.

"If it wasn't a setup, then it was a way to put suspicion on you," Archie conceded. "Which means it was planned ahead of time."

"Premeditated, they call it," Mrs. Schultz said. "I directed a production of *Twelve Angry Men* one year. I learned all the legal lingo."

"I think it was planned, too," I agreed, "but how far ahead, I'm not sure."

I had a good guess. Even though I already felt quite close to Mrs. Schultz and Archie, I still wasn't sure where their loyalties would lie, especially since Archie had a crush on Hope. I didn't think it would be wise to let on that I suspected our Yarrow Glen neighbors. I had told them what happened with Guy in the shop last night, but I wanted to let them come to their own conclusions. Luckily for me, our deductions aligned.

"Derrick hated him," Archie let on. "It's one of the reasons I quit working in his restaurant. He was already a tough boss, but after the review Guy Lippinger wrote, he was enraged every day and he took it out on us."

"So Derrick has a temper," I said. Baz had told me as much.

"Oh, yeah. He used to say it all the time, that he was going to kill him for writing that review. I never thought he was being literal, but now? My money's on him being the murderer."

"That's something you ought to tell Detective Heath."

Archie's face turned an extra shade of pale, highlighting his freckles. "I-I guess I should. I don't want to point the finger. I mean, I feel okay talking about it with you, sure, but to the police?"

His final words were interrupted by a customer, a middle-aged woman in a flowy dress and an oversized pocketbook slung over her shoulder. We immediately clammed up and I greeted her, thrilled to finally have our first customer of the day.

"Hi. Is one of you Willa Bauer, the owner here?" She looked at me and Mrs. Schultz with a wide smile.

"I am. Can I help you?"

"I've been meaning to come in and talk to you since you opened." She rummaged through her purse and pulled out a business card, which she handed to me.

"Deandra Patterson. I write for the *Glen Gazette,* Yarrow Glen's free newspaper."

Free publicity! Maybe things were starting to turn around today. "It's so nice to meet you. I'm happy to speak with you."

"Great. I'd like to get your statement about the murder of Guy Lippinger."

CHAPTER 9

I sensed my mouth opening and closing silently like a ventriloquist's dummy, but I couldn't form a response.

"What happened exactly? What did you see?" Her smile didn't falter, as if she'd just asked about a queso recipe and not a murder.

"I have no comment," I finally spit out. Thank goodness there weren't any customers in the shop.

"But you did discover the body right outside your shop, didn't you?"

"I . . . uh, I—"

"She has no comment." Detective Heath stood in the doorway. It was the first time I was happy to see him.

"Detective, perhaps you'd like to shed some light on what happened. It's better our community hears what's going on straight from the source," she said.

"Our department will issue a formal statement later today. I'll make sure you get a copy. Have a nice day."

The woman shrugged and looked back at me. "My number's on there if you want to be quoted in tomorrow's story," she said, referring to the business card she'd handed me.

She left, not seeming too broken up about not getting

a scoop, but I did see her dodging the occasional car in the middle of the street to take a picture of the shop. Curds & Whey was going to get its first free publicity, but not how I wanted. Great.

"Thanks for running her off," I said to him.

"Please don't talk to her," he said.

"I don't plan to." When Detective Heath remained, I asked, "Are you here to ask me more questions?"

"I wanted to speak to your employees." The Curds & Whey aprons Archie and Mrs. Schultz wore gave them away as such.

"They weren't at the shop at all last night," I explained.

He nodded. "I'd still like to speak with them. Do you mind?"

It got under my skin that he was so darn deliberate and polite. I knew my good feelings about seeing him wouldn't last long.

"Of course not," I said unnecessarily. He was going to do it whether I gave my consent or not.

He gestured to Archie. "How about you first?"

I was about to ask Detective Heath not to talk to him in the shop, but he was already leading a nervous Archie out the door.

"What do you think he wants with us?" Mrs. Schultz said after he and Archie left.

I could tell Archie's skittishness about the police showing up was starting to rub off on her.

She continued, "I don't know much about Guy Lippinger these days, except for what I hear around town. When I knew him, he was my student. That had to be twenty-five years ago. Surely, the police don't care about that."

"He was one of your students?"

"Yeah. He never tried out for our plays, but he was

in the English composition class I taught. I used to have them write stories or poems or essays at home in journals and hand them in weekly. I found they were more expressive than when they were asked to write in class. He was quite sensitive underneath that angry exterior that made it hard for most people to like him, even the adults. We had a bit of a rapport because I knew that vulnerable side of him through his writing."

"What kind of things did he write?"

"The year I had him, it was mostly love poems."

"He had a crush on you, Mrs. Schultz?"

I pictured Mrs. Schultz in her heyday, her contagious enthusiasm coupled with her bright hazel eyes and toothy smile. I imagined most of her students felt a connection with her.

She guffawed. "No, not me. By his descriptions, it was one of his classmates."

"Do you know if his wife was his high school sweetheart?"

"No, he wasn't married until later in life from what I heard. His family left Yarrow Glen somctime after he graduated college, and then he was gone for good up until a couple of years ago."

"Did you hear why he came back? By most accounts, it couldn't be because he was homesick."

She shook her head in thought and seemed about to answer when Detective Heath returned with Archie, who traded places with Mrs. Schultz. I waited until they walked out of the shop and down the sidewalk out of sight before grilling Archie.

"What did he ask?"

"Uh . . . well, I told him what Derrick said." Archie seemed to be speaking to his sneakers.

"That's good. You don't have to be nervous about it.

I'm sure they won't mention your name when they talk to Derrick."

"It's not that. He mostly . . . well, he mostly asked about you." Then he added hurriedly, "But I didn't say anything bad."

"Oh, Archie, I'm sure you didn't." It wasn't a surprise to me that I was the focus of his inquiries, but hearing it aloud made me more than a little nervous. Did it make Archie question who he was working for?

"That knife is only circumstantial evidence," Archie tried reassuring me.

"Except they also have my fingerprints on his car."

"Oh, yeah. Right."

I really wished I'd just gone straight up to my apartment last night. "Are you having second thoughts about working here, Archie?"

"No way. I know you didn't kill him."

Relief and gratitude spilled over me. I tried not to cry—the kid was freaked out enough. "I appreciate your support, especially since we haven't known each other very long."

"I know you're a good person," Archie said. "This is the first place I've been excited to come to work. Everybody's been telling me since I graduated high school last year that I'm supposed to know what I want to do with my life. Nothing ever really interested me that much. But since getting this job, you've taken so much time with me, teaching me all about cheese, plus everything I learned helping you open the place. I love it here. I think I might want to be a cheesemonger, too."

My heart was a melted puddle. I'd assumed Baz and I would be trying to solve this murder on our own, but clearing my name was no longer just for my sake. It would also keep Curds & Whey in business, which meant a lot more to Archie than I'd realized.

"Besides, it's not logical that you would kill him," he continued. "A bad review would've been better publicity than having a man murdered outside your door. I'm just saying, if you stabbed someone, you would be a lot smarter about it."

I chuckled. "Thanks for the vote of confidence . . . I think. But you're right about the bad publicity this might generate. We haven't had a single customer come in all morning. Hopefully once the police are done in the alley, things will go back to normal." It was hard to think about anything else besides the murder, but I still had a business to run.

Mrs. Schultz returned, but she avoided looking at me, just as Archie had.

"It's okay, Mrs. Schultz. I know they wanted to know about me."

She seemed relieved that I knew, suddenly becoming vehement. "It's a waste of time asking about you, and I told the detective exactly that. If he wants to pin it on someone who was here last night, what about Derrick? He never lives in one place for long. Does anybody really know him?"

"I told Detective Heath what he said about Guy," Archie said.

"Well, that detective didn't seem too concerned by it when I brought it up." Mrs. Schultz said, pursing her lips.

"He's got a good poker face," I interjected. "Maybe he didn't want to let on where the case was headed."

"I hope you're right. How much do you trust him?" Mrs. Schultz asked me.

I thought about it for a moment. "Do I trust him to

do the right thing? Yes. He seems aboveboard, but that could work against me, too. This is a small town where everyone is only a few degrees of separation from each other, at most. Nobody's going to confide anything to him. Even Archie hesitated to tell him about Derrick. No offense, Archie. I completely understand, which is the same reason no one else will tell him the things he'll need to hear to solve this case. No one wants to point fingers at their neighbors. Who wants to get ratted out for implicating someone who might be innocent and then still have to work down the street from them?"

"You're right about that," Mrs. Schultz said. "People in this community are going to stick together. The others in town don't know you yet like we do. If another suspect doesn't come along soon, even if you're eventually acquitted . . ." She shook her head, leaving the rest of her thought unspoken.

"I'll be forever linked with this murder. Is that what you think?"

"That's what I fear, anyway. I could be wrong."

I could tell she was only saying that last part for my benefit. We both knew she wasn't wrong.

"Oh, I'm sorry, Willa. I shouldn't have said that. I don't mean to scare you."

"You're not saying anything I didn't already suspect. I trust Detective Heath to do the right thing, but not to clear my name soon enough. I'm going to have to figure out a way to find out information on my own."

"People will talk to me," Mrs. Schultz offered. "I hear gossip all the time."

"I can help, too. I'm pretty stealthy," Archie said.

First Baz, and now Mrs. Schultz and Archie were willing to stick their necks out for me. Over the last eight years, I had gotten used to doing everything for myself, but I didn't think I could do this on my own.

"I love that you want to help me. Thank you both. But I don't want anything negative coming down on you two on my behalf."

"It's on behalf of what's right," Mrs. Schultz insisted. "Besides, I have a selfish reason too. Without Mr. Schultz, I was getting depressed, being retired and alone. This cheese shop has saved me at a difficult time in my life. I don't want it taken from us."

"You know how I feel about the place," Archie added.

I swallowed the lump forming in my throat. I used to feel my brother was the only one I could count on, and without him I'd always be alone. But Mrs. Schultz, Archie, and Baz had already shown me I was wrong. "All right, keep your eyes and ears open, but be discreet. And promise me you won't do anything dangerous."

"Done," Mrs. Schultz said.

"Ditto," Archie followed.

"I feel better already," Mrs. Schultz said. "How about you, Willa?"

"I'd feel better if I knew what Detective Heath's next move was. Hold down the fort for me, will you?"

I strode outside, determined to take matters into my own hands and defend myself. I understood that the police couldn't move the crime scene, but why wasn't Detective Heath talking to any of the others who were here last night? One of them had a secret Guy wanted to reveal. I shouldn't be the only person the detective asked questions about.

Detective Heath was speaking to another officer near the crime scene. The police car and the yellow Do Not Cross tape were attracting the lookie-loos, but the public's interest didn't extend to my shop. My freedom and my livelihood were being threatened, all because a man was murdered in the adjacent alley. Now that I knew Mrs. Schultz and Archie had an emotional investment in Curds & Whey too, I was more determined than ever to steer Detective Heath in the right direction to solve this case.

He shooed the officer away as I marched up to him. I told myself not to be intimidated, even though I had to literally look up to him.

"When do you plan to take all this away?" I demanded. "It's keeping customers from coming into my shop."

"Hello again, Ms. Bauer." His tone was once again irritatingly calm and friendly, and threw me off guard.

"Wha—? Oh. Hello."

"What was the question?"

Darn him. It was hard to play tough in the face of politeness. I got my bearings.

"I was wondering when you'll be finished here so customers won't feel like they're going through a checkpoint to buy some cheese."

"We'll be finished when we're done doing our job."

"Isn't it your job to investigate *all* the persons of interest? Derrick, for example. He was one of the people Guy was looking at when he threatened to reveal that secret. Derrick also sued Guy for giving him a bad review in his magazine, and Archie just told me that Derrick said on multiple occasions that he would kill Guy."

"Yes, I have all that information."

Did nothing ruffle this man?

"So then why aren't you at Apricot Grille asking *Derrick's* employees questions about *him*? Shouldn't he be your number one suspect?"

"Ms. Bauer—"

"Willa. I'm Willa, I'm a real person, not just a surname on your suspect list." I could hear my voice rising and feel my face warming, but I couldn't contain my frustration any longer.

"I'm aware of that, Willa. Nobody is our number one suspect yet. We're gathering information right now."

"So why does it feel like you're targeting me?"

"I can assure you, we're not. This is our standard procedure."

"Then why aren't you at Apricot Grille?" I said.

"We've already been there."

"For a beet salad or to arrest Derrick? He had means, motive, and opportunity."

"He also has an alibi, Ms.—Willa."

That stopped me mid-rant. "Are you sure?"

He tilted his head and raised his eyebrows like, *seriously*? "We can pinpoint the time of death between the time Guy was seen leaving The Cellar about nine p.m. and when you found him at ten fifteen."

"The Cellar? That's the bar at the Inn at Yarrow Glen, isn't it?" I'd heard of it, but hadn't had occasion to go for a drink, although it was looking more likely by the day. Now I was stumped. "So Derrick's got a corroborated alibi. Huh. I was sure it was him," I said mostly to myself.

"That's why you need to let us do our job. We don't go by assumptions."

"Good, then I hope you're not assuming that I had anything to do with Guy Lippinger's death."

Detective Heath put a hand on my back to lead me farther away from the police officers. "It's my job to get a complete picture so I can read the evidence properly. I've spoken with the people who were in your shop with the victim last night. I'll proceed accordingly." He looked behind him, then leaned closer to me, although no one was listening in. His dark eyes stared into mine. "Willa, we're not out to get you. Please, trust me."

His earnestness surprised me. I wanted to trust him. Wouldn't that be easier than trying to investigate on my own, all without creating suspicion while still attempting to make new friends in the process? But how could I trust that he wasn't targeting me? Maybe this was his way of keeping me at ease, hoping I'd slip up. Even if he was as much of a fair-minded good guy as he seemed to be, he wasn't going to stop me from finding my own clues to clear my name.

"Okay, I'll trust you," I said, mostly to appease him, although the look of trust on his own face after I said it gave me a pang of guilt.

"Now let me get back to work so we can clear out of here as soon as possible," he said.

"I'd appreciate that."

He almost smiled, but not quite, just directed a head nod my way as well as a second gaze before I dropped my own. My face was feeling warm again, but not out of frustration this time. He walked toward the crime scene and I walked away from it.

So Derrick had an alibi for the time of the murder. Drat. That left Vivian and possibly Hope, Birdie, and Roman. I didn't like to think any of them could do this. I had some event flyers to hand out, and I could always use the excuse that I needed an extra loaf of Vivian's bread. Rise and Shine Bakery would be my first stop.

CHAPTER 10

❧

I followed the sidewalk past Carl's Hardware, Lou's Market, and Read More Bookstore & Café to cross at the T intersection where Rise and Shine Bakery was located on the corner. I was happy to be on the same block as the Yarrow Glen staple, as its reputation enticed tourists from the busier Main Street area all the way down to our end of Pleasant Avenue, which was the last block of commercial businesses.

The shops along Pleasant Avenue were uniformly connected in pairs. Alleys in between the buildings separated them from the next pair of shops. Rise and Shine was the exception. It was located in a single-story cottage with faded clapboards. The bright blue awning as well as the two oversized six-over-six paned windows to the right of the entrance shaded the door. I wondered if it had been someone's home at one time. It was the perfect dwelling for a cozy bakery.

As soon as I entered the snug shop, I was enfolded in the sweet, buttery aroma of baked goods. I didn't get more than a few steps in since a throng of customers were clustered in front of the narrow space between the entrance and the counter. I got the sense that most of them were regulars, as nobody seemed confused by not having a single line to order. Unlike my shop this morning, Rise and Shine was hopping.

I hung back and caught a glimpse of a woman about Hope's age in a bright blue apron ringing up orders at the wraparound counter. I spotted Hope serving up fruit-topped pastries and fat muffins coated with sparkling sugar from the glass display cases flanking the register. Behind the counter were baskets filled with fresh bagels and at least seven types of bread, by my count. The letter board above listed their items and prices. I also noticed several Sonoma's Choice awards from years past mounted on their wall.

I didn't see Vivian, so I waited my turn as I surveyed the luscious bakery items. I wasn't much for sweets, but spending time in here might change my mind. The cinnamon rolls were going fast. I remember Vivian mentioning yesterday how Hope had been saving one for Archie.

By the time it was my turn, there was a lull, and I was the sole remaining customer.

The dark-haired cashier eagerly awaited my order. She had a sleeve of tattoos and was wearing a nose ring, which instinctively made my own nose twitch.

"I was hoping to speak to Hope?" I said, making an effort not to rub my nose.

Hope was now straightening the baked goods and looked up as soon as I said her name. Today she wore a band of petite flowers in her pixie-styled blonde hair, which was streaked with turquoise to match the overalls she wore under her apron. The polish on her clawlike nails also matched, and I wondered how she worked with them.

Her eyes widened upon seeing me and she immediately

came over to stand across from me at the wraparound counter. "Can you believe what happened last night? You know about it, right? I mean, you must, he was practically killed on your doorstep. You want some coffee? I need some coffee."

I didn't think she needed some coffee. She seemed pretty amped up already.

"Jasmine, you've got this, right?" she said to her co-worker.

Hope didn't wait for Jasmine's confirmation as she poured coffee into two paper cups and handed one to me. She nodded for me to follow her around the bend of the counter where the cream and sugar were kept. She poured plenty of both into her own cup, but I declined. If it wasn't a latte or a cappuccino, I took my caffeine straight up, especially during work hours.

"I was freaked out enough last night after how weird that man was in your shop, but when the police came to the bakery first thing this morning and told us he was murdered . . ." She exaggerated a shudder.

"Can you maybe not keep saying that out loud? It's probably best to keep it on the down low." I said quietly, hoping she'd mimic the low volume of my voice.

"Oh, right, right," Hope said in a hushed voice.

"Did they question you too?" I asked.

"Yeah, they did. Aunt Vivian's been complaining that her whole schedule's backed up now because she had to talk to them. I'll be hearing about it all day." Hope rolled her eyes.

"Archie picked up our bread order on time this morning, so she must be doing all right."

"Yeah, I saw him. He talks about you all the time, you know."

"Good things, I hope?"

"Oh yeah, he thinks you're so cool. I was even starting to feel a little jealous until he told me you were old."

"He must've been talking about Mrs. Schultz. She works there too."

"The one who used to be a teacher? No, she's really old."

Maybe I *should've* plucked those gray hairs this morning.

"Did you happen to hear anything last night after you got home?" I said, wanting to get back to the reason I was here.

"Not until I saw the flashing lights through my window, but I thought maybe a car had gotten broken into or something. I didn't think for a second someone was murdered. Stuff like that doesn't happen here. Last year, Aunt Vivian's condo was broken into. That was bad enough."

"How awful."

"She said they didn't take much, just made a mess. They went to the wrong condo if they were looking for jewelry or something expensive." Hope chuckled, then became serious again. "Luckily, she wasn't home. We were at my grandparents' in Oakland for Thanksgiving."

"Is that where you're from?"

"No, that's where my aunt's from. And my mom. Where are you from?"

"Oregon."

"So you just decided to come here to start your business or did you know someone here?"

"The town just kind of . . . spoke to me."

It was hard to describe. Yarrow Glen was the first place I'd considered staying put. There was a comfort about it I hadn't felt anywhere else. Maybe it was because the mountains reminded me of Oregon. Or maybe it was because it was close to my parents, but full of possibilities instead of heartache.

"Wow. That's what happened with my mom," Hope said. "At least, that's what people tell me. I never thought to talk to her about it when she was alive. My mom discovered Yarrow Glen and up and moved here, then took over the bakery when she was like twenty-two. Without knowing a soul here. It takes some guts to do what you and she did."

"I never really thought about it that way, but I guess it does." I'd never given myself much credit for becoming a cheesemonger and opening my own shop. When I left the farm, it felt like I was running away from something, but I believe I would've come around to owning a cheese shop one way or another.

"Aunt Vivian moved here to help us out after my mom got cancer, because I was only thirteen and my mom couldn't keep doing everything by herself. Then she died." Hope stared at her coffee and swirled it with the stir stick hypnotically.

"I'm sorry. I had no idea."

She shrugged. "How would you? It sucks. I miss her. I talk to Archie about her all the time. He's a good listener."

I agreed—Archie was a gem.

"Since my dad went back to Alaska after my mom got pregnant, Aunt Vivian was the only one who could help, so it's been me and her for eight years now."

"I'm sorry. He never came back even after she got sick?"

"He's a deep-sea fisherman, so he's on a fishing boat most of the time. He used to write me nice letters, but my mom didn't want me shipped off to Alaska. Literally. Someday I want to go up there and meet him, but I want to live here and stay at the bakery. It's all I've got left of my mom." She shook herself out of her gloom. "I can't wait until I can put my own personality into it. . . . Wait here." She held up a finger to pause our conversation and snatched something from one of the display cases with a square of wax paper. She stuck a napkin under it and slid it onto the counter in front of me. "It's my newest creation, the ultimate cinnamon roll. Try it."

I pulled apart the yeasty dough smeared with a thick coating of white icing. I could smell the cinnamon streaked within its layers. It practically dissolved on my tongue without having to chew it, the promised flavors melding in my mouth.

"This is incredible," I said honestly.

Hope's face lit up. "It's been a big hit, even if Aunt Vivian doesn't want to admit it. We do a steady bread business, but we're a bakery. I want us to have cakes and pies and fancy French pastries. Aunt Vivian says I don't have the training and we don't have the money to hire the right bakers, but I think she's just set in her ways. I mean, she wouldn't even paint the walls a different color. We had to repaint after the roof leak last fall, and I told her we should paint it pink. Nothing says bakery like pink, right? But she wanted to repaint it this boring white. At least I got my apartment painted the color I wanted." She stuck a thumb toward the rear of the bakery. I'd noticed the second entrance in the recessed part of the house, but hadn't known it was Hope's apartment.

"My apartment's attached to my shop too. I love it. It's very convenient," I said.

"A little too convenient if you ask me. I'm expected to be the first one here in the morning since she has to drive in. Just because I only have to walk from my door to this one doesn't mean I want to get up at four a.m.

You hire people for that, right? I even had to convince her to hire Jasmine last month, but she doesn't want her to open or close the place by herself. Maybe *you* should talk to Aunt Vivian. We probably wouldn't argue so much if she understood the perks of being the owner."

Luckily I had a mouth full of cinnamon roll to cover my laughter. The perks of being the owner was that you had to do *all* the jobs, including the early morning ones.

The kitchen door swung open and Vivian came through with an armload of fresh baked baguettes. I noticed the front area was crowding again with customers, and she must've too. She looked around.

"Hope, help Jasmine with the customers, please."

Hope looked at me and did another eye roll, as if her aunt was being unreasonable. "Say hi to Archie for me," she said to me before following Vivian's order to get back to work.

Vivian slid the baguettes into a tall basket before coming over to me. "Hi, Willa. Don't tell me you didn't get your order this morning."

"Oh, no, Archie picked it up just fine. I came by to make sure you're doing all right. I heard you spoke with the police."

Okay, so maybe I didn't hear about it until after I came to the bakery, but she didn't need to know that. She had her arms crossed under her ample bosom, allowing me to check out her nails. Her fingers were reddened from kneading so much raw dough, no doubt, and her nails were short and serviceable. It didn't look like she bothered with a manicurist. If the salon business card was a clue, it wasn't Vivian's. It occurred to me that Hope's nails, however, were perfectly polished.

"They asked me some routine questions. There wasn't much I could tell them except for how weird Guy acted last night at your shop. It's not like I knew the man personally."

"You told me yesterday you got 'off the hook' because he didn't review the bakery. You must've known something about him."

"Sure, what everyone else around town says about him. Plus, I've read his reviews. Looks like I wasn't wrong by the way he acted at your shop last night. What about you—have the police questioned you?"

You could say that. "Yeah, I was the one who found his body."

"Oh, wow."

"Did you happen to hear anything last night?"

"My condo's on the other side of town."

Vivian didn't know Guy, she wasn't around last night when he was killed, and she most likely didn't frequent a nail salon. Looks like I was down to three suspects.

"The hour at the police station this morning was enough to set me back. So I hope you don't think I'm rude if I get back to work," she said.

"Of course not. Oh, here." I handed Vivian a few flyers, remembering the excuse I was using to be here, although it was a legitimate one. "We're doing a cheese hunt on Saturday. I'll need some extra afternoon bread for it too. I'd love for you and Hope to stop by if it's possible."

"What's a cheese hunt?" She squinted at the flyer, extending her arm to read it.

"We'll be giving clues to customers, and they have to figure out which type of cheese the clue describes. And if they find the cheese, they get a discount. We'll also be giving away prizes and doing some other fun things."

"That's so creative. I don't know if Hope will be able to make it, but I'll certainly try."

"Great. Would you mind putting around a couple of these flyers for it too?"

"No problem. Give them to Hope. She can tape one to the front window. I'll see you Saturday." She disappeared behind the swinging door to the kitchen.

I took my time finishing the gooey cinnamon roll until the line of customers had receded, then I told Hope about the flyer and our cheese hunt. While I accompanied her to the front window, I made a point of complimenting her nails.

"I haven't found a hair or nail salon in town yet. Where do you go to get them done?" I asked, feigning interest.

"I do them myself. I don't have forty bucks to lay out for acrylics. That's the thing Aunt Vivian doesn't understand. She wanted me to do that inventory stuff last night, but I needed to color my hair and do my nails. How am I supposed to get everything done?"

Now I recalled why Hope had come into the shop last night. "Did Vivian end up helping you with those spreadsheets last night?"

"She made me do them with her until like nine thirty, so I had to stay up late to do my hair and nails. And she wonders why I'm so tired in the morning."

Vivian didn't mention going to Hope's when I asked her about last night.

When Hope finished taping up the flyer, I bought a few cookies to take back to Archie and Mrs. Schultz and thanked her when I left.

According to the police, Derrick had an alibi for the hour between Guy leaving the hotel bar and when I found him dead in his car, but it didn't look like the same could be said for Vivian. She left Hope's apartment after Guy had left The Cellar, even though she implied to me that she went straight home after my cheesemaking class. I suppose spending some time at Hope's could've slipped her mind. Or maybe she was purposefully keeping it from me. Hope seemed like an open book, but it left her without an alibi too.

Roman seemed pretty chummy with Vivian. Maybe he could fill me in. I had to remind myself that he was also on my suspect list. It was time to take him up on that mead tasting.

CHAPTER 11

❧

When I returned from the bakery, only one officer remained, but that awful yellow tape stretched across the alley still drew attention wiggling in the breeze. I stepped into a quiet Curds & Whey feeling low.

"Any customers while I was gone?" I asked Mrs. Schultz.

"Only one, but he asked more about what was going on with the police than about cheese."

I glanced at the wall clock. "The lunchtime outdoor market's started, so there won't be too much sidewalk traffic either. Where's Archie? Did he leave for his break? I brought cookies from the bakery for both of you."

"We have a surprise for you too."

"A surprise?" I tried to match Mrs. Schultz's expectantly happy look, but I'd hit my limit for surprises.

"You ready, Archie?" Mrs. Schultz called.

Archie clumsily made his way from the stockroom at the rear of the shop, the wide bottom half of the bright yellow cheese-wedge costume he wore catching on the swinging door. His long limbs were swathed in tight yellow nylon and a round hole was cut to fit his freckled face, a chunk of his wayward hair poking through.

"Whaddya think?" He gingerly made his way around the display tables.

Luckily Mrs. Schultz offered an explanation, as I was too stunned to respond.

"You've been talking about how we need a way for the shop to get some attention, and I'm pretty handy making costumes from all the theater I've done . . ."

"I can go down to the park and hand out the cheese-hunt flyers. We won't need a table for that," Archie offered. "It might make people remember us and get them to choose us for a Sonoma's Choice award."

The fact that they cared as much about Curds & Whey as I did pushed a lump into my throat that, if I spoke, would make my lips tremble and my words shaky.

"You can bring a sample tray," Mrs. Schultz timidly suggested after I still hadn't said anything.

"You two are brilliant. I love it," I managed to say without blubbering. "Archie, you don't mind?"

"It was his idea," Mrs. Schultz said.

"I was my high school's sports mascot," he told me.

"He was up for whatever costume I made for Curds and Whey, as long as we didn't go the Little Bo-Peep route."

"I'm all for a good costume, to a point."

I laughed. "You're giving our Monster Cheddar Wheel a run for its money—this should get us some attention. Since nothing's going on here at the shop, let's all go."

We left a note on the door that we were at the park and we'd return in an hour, and brought the flyers and two cheese trays. We happily left the police and the ugliness of the crime temporarily behind. We walked up the block, garnering quite a bit of attention. We took a left onto Main Street, past the town library and the post office on our right, followed by Ron's Service Station—

where you could pick up an old-fashioned curvy glass bottle of Coca-Cola for a dollar while getting your car fueled, washed, and serviced. On our left, the town hall and the church were separated by a parking lot, their two properties taking up the entire block. Behind them was the town park.

The park was casual, no fancy arched entrance or fencing, just a beautiful sprawling lawn edged in wildflowers. Yarrow Glen clung to its farming roots, so nothing was as chichi as the neighboring vineyard towns.

Tables and a few pop-up canopies were clustered in one area. Crates of produce were stacked in front of the table for Lou's Market, and the bookshop was offering some of their best sellers alongside vegan desserts from their café. From what I'd been told, this lunchtime open market on Thursday afternoons was like a dress rehearsal for the weekly farmer's market that kicked off on Memorial Day weekend and lasted into the fall. Although this spring market was only for a couple of hours midweek, it got people outside after the winter rains to picnic, browse, and remind them to shop local. It also gave some crafters an opportunity to sell their wares.

The warm sunny day brought many residents to the park. The three of us tag-teamed handing out cheese samples and flyers. I was hopeful we were making headway in boosting Curds & Whey's profile within the community.

Snippets of conversation wafted past me as we walked through the market, only drawing my attention when I heard Guy Lippinger's name. Then came other words I couldn't ignore, like *dead*, *murdered*, and *cheese shop*.

It looked like I wasn't going to be able to keep what happened under wraps. I had to face it—the newspaper story hadn't even come out yet and already people knew.

Well, if everyone was going to be talking about it, I might as well use it to my advantage.

I cocked my ear to hear one of the buzz words again. It was only a few moments before I caught a conversation coming from two women browsing the consignment-shop table of handmade jewelry and summer scarves. They looked to be in their forties. The one with long, blonde hair draped in front of one shoulder seemed to be dressed for work with a full face of makeup. She was nibbling on the last of a sandwich, probably on her lunch break. The other woman was in a T-shirt, yoga pants, and sneakers, but was also perfectly coiffed.

"Mrs. Schultz, how about we take a look at those scarves?" I said.

"You know I love my scarves, but during work hours?" she replied.

I leaned in and whispered, "I want to listen in on what they're saying over there. I think they're talking about the murder."

Mrs. Schultz instantly went into Miss Marple mode. She tucked the flyers she was holding under my cheese plate so I could grasp them, then removed her Curds & Whey apron. "You can offer me some cheese while I *look at the scarves*." She used her fingers to make air quotes.

"Good idea."

She sauntered over to the table first to play her part and I followed. I held out the cheese tray for her and she pretended to decide which one she wanted. Neither of us said a word so we could listen in.

The woman outfitted in athletic wear was talking. "Paul said he always saw him at The Cellar. Didn't you, Paul?" She addressed the paunchy man I hadn't noticed who was standing behind her. I assumed it was her husband. He'd been occupying himself on his cell phone and only looked up after she insistently tapped him on the arm with the back of her hand. "Didn't you always say you saw Guy Lippinger at The Cellar? He hung out there a lot even though he never talked to anybody. Isn't that what you said, Paul?"

"Except for Massey. I saw them drinking together enough times," Paul the husband said casually. "That guy's too nice for his own good."

Roman? I felt my face warm at the mention of his name. Maybe it was another man whose last name was Massey.

"I know Roman," the blonde friend said. "You're right, he's friends with everybody. And cute. If I wasn't married . . ."

My slim hopes were dashed. It was Roman.

"Paul tried to warn him. Didn't you, Paul?" the wife said.

"He never seemed concerned. He said Guy was just interested in the meadery. I told him not to trust him. Guy had it in for this town. But . . ." He shrugged. "He doesn't have the history with Guy's family that most of us in town do."

A woman excused herself and pushed between us to check out the scarves. Paul, his wife, and her friend moved away from the table. We shuffled toward them, Mrs. Schultz still in her paused position of choosing a cheese cube.

"Maybe Roman was smart to befriend him. Guy actually gave his meadery a good review," the blonde friend was saying.

"Lippinger wasn't nice to any business in this town without some kind of payback," Paul the husband replied.

"You think Roman might've bribed him to write that review? That doesn't seem like him."

"Nah. Massey's a good guy, maybe just a little naive."

"We think there had to have been something behind it, though," the yoga wife said. "Maybe not a bribe, but some kind of quid pro quo. Paul was afraid Roman had made a deal with the devil. Weren't you, Paul?"

Paul had returned to focusing on his phone.

"Whatever it was, Roman doesn't have to worry about it now," the friend muttered.

The friends walked off with the wife directing Paul to follow them to the table of Himalayan salt lamps.

A man came over and asked for a cheese sample. I held the tray out to him without conversing. My head was too filled with what I'd just heard about Roman. Had he made some kind of deal with Guy—one that he regretted?

The man happily left with a sample. Mrs. Schultz untucked her apron from under her arm and put it back on as Archie lumbered over to us.

"My plate's clean of cheese. I think this is working out great," he said.

I wished I could share his enthusiasm. Besides the new suspicions about Roman, it was hard to tell how much Curds & Whey was attached to all the talk of Guy's murder.

An insistent yipping drew my attention to a tri-colored Chihuahua pulling his owner forward by his leash until he was close enough to properly bark at Archie's cheese costume.

"Mom, what are you doing here?" Archie said to the woman holding the leash.

I might've recognized her as Archie's mother given her tall, lanky frame and her abundance of freckles.

He spoke to the dog. "What are you barking at? It's me." Archie, unable to kneel down in his costume, stretched his arms out, but the Chihuahua was not convinced. "Batman, it's me!"

I could see where the dog got its name—he had a mask of black fur over his brown and white snout, and oversized perky ears. His mother scooped up the dog, allowing Archie to pet him and calm him down. In no time, Batman was licking Archie's nose.

I introduced myself and Mrs. Schultz to Archie's mother.

"Archie's really helping us out today. In fact, he's become indispensable to me. He has a wonderful work ethic and a real curiosity about cheese, and he's great with customers," I gushed honestly.

Wearing a silly cheese costume didn't bother Archie, yet he shuffled in embarrassment at my praise.

"He's a hard worker. He really wants to impress you," his mother said.

"Mo-om."

Batman saved Archie further embarrassment when he almost snagged the cheese samples off my tray. I pulled it away just in time. "That was close. He almost got some of the black truffle cheddar. It's not black; it's this pretty white one. It gets its name from the Italian black truffles infused in it, and there's also a sprinkling of white truffle oil. Mellow and wonderful. It's not for dogs, but would you like to try some?" I asked her.

"I'm lactose intolerant, unfortunately, but it sounds delicious. Archie used to bring home truffle fries all the time when he was a dishwasher at the restaurant. They were a family favorite."

"Welp, looks like we better get back to work," Archie said deliberately. It was obvious he didn't want us to hear any more stories from home.

"Okay, okay." She got the point. "I just wanted to make

sure you were all right. I stopped by Curds and Whey before coming here. I got concerned when I saw the shop closed and the police out front, until I read the note on the door."

"We're fine," Archie insisted. "I know you're here because of what happened last night. You don't have to check up on me."

Her smile and her shoulders both drooped as she fessed up. "How can I not be worried? I heard the man was murdered right near Curds and Whey."

My instinct to defend my shop was overshadowed by her concern for her son.

"The detective came by this morning, if that makes you feel better. They're doing everything they can," I assured her.

Archie looked relieved when I didn't mention they'd questioned him.

"Do they have any idea who did it? Is there a murderer running loose in Yarrow Glen?" she asked.

"It's probably someone who knows him," Archie said. "They're looking into that. Everything's fine, mom, I promise."

She sighed. "Come home right after work today, okay?"

"We'll look out for Archie, as well," Mrs. Schultz assured her.

Her smile returned as we said our polite goodbyes. Archie gave Batman one last rub on the head before his mom and dog left.

"I've *got* to save my money and move out," he said, shaking his oversized triangular head. He traded his empty cheese tray for some flyers and ambled over to a group just entering the park.

"It's hard to cut the apron strings," Mrs. Schultz said

after he walked away. "My daughter's older than you and I still worry about her."

"I didn't know you had a daughter."

"She lives out of state. They're still our babies, no matter how old or how far away." Mrs. Schultz held up the flyers. "Not too many more to go. I think we'll have a really good turnout."

"Let's hope we can persuade them to think about cheese instead of murder."

CHAPTER 12

As we resumed handing out flyers and cheese samples throughout the outdoor market, conversations about Guy Lippinger continued to catch my ear.

"It was smart of his wife to spend all her time in Catalina."

"Why murder him? His liver would've given out soon enough."

"Maybe not. I heard the other night was his first night back at The Cellar in months."

A flirtatious "How you doin'?" cut in like an overly loud TV ad interrupting a show.

I turned around to see Richie Muscles (as I'd nicknamed him), the tow truck driver from yesterday morning. He was holding a beautifully handcrafted wood wine rack.

"Remember me? Richie?" he said, now standing a little too close for comfort.

I took a step back. "Sure I do."

"Not easy to forget me, is it?"

I chuckled to myself. He had an abundance of muscles *and* confidence. "Is that teak?" I pointed to the wine rack.

"Yeah. Baz custom made it for me."

"Baz made that?"

Richie stuck a thumb out, pointing behind him. Over his shoulder, I saw Baz sitting behind one of the market tables.

I parted ways with Richie, who seemed surprised that I'd leave his company so soon. Mrs. Schultz and I hurried over to see Baz's creations. He had two tables overflowing with beautiful handcrafted woodworking: more wine racks, keepsake boxes, napkin holders, clever birdhouses, and even a chessboard with all the pieces whittled to perfection.

"Hey, Mrs. Schultz. Hey, Willa," he greeted us.

"You made all of this?" I lifted the lid of a heart-shaped ring box carved from walnut. "They're gorgeous."

"It's a hobby of mine."

"Some hobby." I was more than impressed.

"I do recall you were a star in shop class," Mrs. Schultz remarked. "But I had no idea you'd honed your skills to this level. You're very talented, Basil."

"Basil?" I felt like I'd been slipped a little gift of insider info.

Baz's face reddened. "Mrs. Schultz, nobody calls me that but you and my mother."

"You know I'm a little more formal than most."

"My mom's British," Baz explained to me. "I've always hated the name, that's why I shortened it. You can probably relate, right?"

"Are you saying I should be embarrassed by my name?"

"Oh, n-n-no. I just mean Willa must be short for a name you don't like, right? Like, uh, Wilhemina?"

I enjoyed watching Baz stutter and backtrack. "Nope, it's just Willa. I was named for my father, William. My parents didn't think they'd get lucky enough to have a second child."

"Oh, sorry. No offense."

I laughed. "None taken."

"Basil is a very distinguished name. Like the great actor Basil Rathbone." Mrs. Schultz tried to remedy his embarrassment.

"That's right—he portrayed one of the first Sherlock Holmes. Fits perfectly," I said.

Baz seemed to cheer up slightly. "How do you two know each other?"

"She's working at Curds and Whey now," I said.

"Good for you, Mrs. Schultz."

Since the browsers at Baz's table had wandered off, I asked quietly, "Did you find out any information this morning?"

"Well, uh . . ." He side-eyed Mrs. Schultz.

"It's okay. She knows we're trying to solve the case."

"I thought I'd left drama behind when I retired. Who knew?" Mrs. Schultz said.

"I did find out which nail salon the business card came from," Baz declared.

"How?" I placed my cheese tray and the empty one underneath it on a free corner of his table to rest my arms.

"Nail salon?" Mrs. Schultz also gave him her full attention.

I quickly explained to her about the possible clue of the business card.

Baz continued, "There's only a couple in town and I found out Detective Heath was at A Perfect Ten over on Laurel Ave."

"Did he find out if anybody who goes there has a connection to Guy?" I said.

"The only thing I know is that he seized their appointment book."

I looked at my own short, clean, non-polished nails and was glad for once that I routinely neglected them. "Thank goodness I'm not one to get my nails done. They won't find my name in there. But now we'll have no idea whose business card that was. I suppose it's more important that Detective Heath knows who it is. But I sure wish there was a way for us to find out too."

Mrs. Schultz sighed purposefully and splayed her fingers in front of her. "It just so happens my nails could use some repair. Since we're out of the shop anyway, do you mind if I take my lunch break?"

"Mrs. Schultz . . ." Her idea was a good one, but I wasn't too sure I was comfortable with it.

"How do you plan to find out anything? You can't go in and ask," Baz said.

"I'm not going to ask about it. I won't have to."

"Then how are you going to find out?" I myself was curious.

"If the police were in that nail salon this morning, it'll be the topic of conversation for the rest of the day. I'm quite adept at listening in. I'm over sixty, which makes me invisible to most younger people. They assume I'm not paying attention. Miss Marple used her advanced age to her advantage on many occasions."

"Because Agatha Christie wrote it that way," I reminded Mrs. Schultz.

"Because it's a universal truth."

"As long as you're not going to put yourself in danger," I said.

"The most dangerous thing that could happen would be letting a manicurist under the age of thirty choose the color again. I once let one talk me into trying Island

Coral, which turned out to be fluorescent orange. *That* was a mistake. I'll let you know what I find out when I get back." Mrs. Schultz twiddled her fingers to wave good-bye and left.

Baz and I looked at each other, not sure if we should be excited or apprehensive.

"You think it's a good idea to include her in on this?" Baz asked me.

"And Archie? I don't know. I hope I haven't made a mistake, but it didn't feel right to keep it from them. We worked together to get the shop ready for weeks before it opened. I know them better than anyone in Yarrow Glen."

"You're the one with everything on the line, so it's up to you."

"I trust her and Archie. They had my back when Detective Heath questioned them."

Baz sighed, knowing he had no choice but to go along with it.

"I should probably stick by Archie to finish handing out my samples. He's the one drawing the attention. You want some before I leave?" I offered him a piece of the sharp Gouda. He wrinkled his nose at the rustic scent. "Don't be afraid of cheese, Baz. It's Gouda for you." I laughed at my own pun.

"I prefer the classics. Don't you have any cheddar?"

I plucked out two pieces of a sharp aged Irish cheddar. The lush pastures of Ireland where the cattle grazed resulted in the classic rich yellow color I knew Baz would be comfortable with.

"Here you go."

He popped both squares into his mouth.

"How can you appreciate it when you eat them in one bite?" I said.

"It's cheddar. I should be melting it on a fried bologna

sandwich." He swirled his tongue around his mouth. "That one might've been too fancy for bologna, but it was good. Maybe if I had it with a Merlot."

"You'd drink wine with a fried bologna and cheese sandwich?"

"Of course. I'm not a heathen."

I shook my head and chuckled.

"So what are we doing next?" he asked.

"I texted Roman earlier. I'm meeting with him tonight."

"After hours?"

"Yeah, at his meadery."

"What time? I'll go with you."

"What excuse would I have for you to be there?"

"Then tell him to meet at your shop. I can pretend I'm fixing something."

"Baz." I wanted to tell him what I'd overheard about Roman, but I could tell his protective nature was gearing into overdrive, and I didn't like to be bubble wrapped. "I'll be fine."

"Didn't you say you think one of these people is a murderer?"

"I get your point, but there'd be no reason for him to hurt me. I'll make sure to let him know that I told a few people I'd be meeting him. Would that make you feel better, *Dad*?"

"Be sure you're home before curfew," he said, going along with the joke. Then he turned serious. "I mean it, Willa. Be careful."

CHAPTER 13

I was rapidly coming to realize Mrs. Schultz had a wide array of experiences under her belt, and drinking mead was one of them. Unfortunately, the salon gossip had provided nothing of note, but her distinct tastebuds helped greatly for choosing pairing samples. I was confident the cheeses she helped me select would include ones that might pair well with Roman's mead.

My confidence did not extend to my look that evening, however. I had never been able to replicate the sassy hairstyle I'd left the salon with when I'd gotten it cut six weeks ago. Ruffling my bangs only made me look like I'd just awoken from a nap. I freshened my makeup, reminding myself as I passed over the eyeliner that this wasn't a date. This was strictly a business collaboration and a way to get more information about Roman, Vivian, and Guy. I didn't need another man to derail my plans. I learned my lesson years ago.

I thought I'd met the perfect guy in college. He, my best friend, and I called ourselves "the three musketeers." When I returned from my semester in France with my newfound idea of opening a cheese shop, they were just as excited as I was. We spent much of our time making plans for the shop. We'd decided to do it together—they would run the financial side of it and I would concentrate on the cheese. When my boyfriend proposed after our senior year, it seemed everything was falling into place. But first, in order to get my cheesemonger certification, I needed four thousand hours of work experience, which meant I had to do more than make cheese at my parents' dairy farm in Eugene. So I worked in various cheese shops and creameries along the West Coast, while popping back home as often as I could. I'd gotten about a year of experience under my belt when he broke off our engagement with the excuse that he didn't bargain for a long-distance relationship. Afterward, I found out the real reason—he and our third musketeer had fallen in love. They even used my returned engagement ring as a down payment to open a little chocolate shop right in Eugene. Basically, my heartbreak funded their dream. Not to mention, they forever ruined chocolate for me—talk about adding insult to injury. Thank goodness I always preferred savory to sweet. After that, I was hopelessly devoted, like Sandy from *Grease*, but only to cheese.

Still, the fluttering in my stomach would not go away. I went into the living room and modeled my jeans and light sweater for my fish.

"What do you think, Loretta? Does it say *cute* without looking like I'm trying to be cute?"

Loretta bobbed behind her SpongeBob pineapple house, apparently unimpressed.

"Tough crowd. Not everyone can look as fabulous as you, you know."

I took my impressive cheese plate and one of my cheese-hunt flyers across the street to Golden Glen Meadery. I was relieved to see one of the staff still there sweeping the floor when I arrived just past closing time.

Roman and I wouldn't be alone. The guy hustled over to unlock the door and let me in.

"Thanks." I peered at his name tag, which read Chet.

Roman must've told him to expect me—Chet said he'd go get him before I even explained why I was there. He disappeared through a sliding barnlike door in the back while I waited in the shop.

I'd stopped by briefly only once before, but now that Roman was becoming more than an acquaintance, I admired his shop with new eyes. The beamed ceilings were painted gray and the floor was poured concrete, but the exposed brick between the horizontally stacked shelves of mead warmed the room. Whereas Curds & Whey tapped all of a patron's senses, this starker palate allowed for the mead to be the star of the shop. Sleek, long-necked bottles contained a spectrum of crisp golden hues from clear morning sunshine to a deep brandy brown. I looked closer at the Golden Glen labels—blackcurrant, pear nectar, dry honey, rosemary. I wasn't sure what I'd expected, but I found myself pleasantly surprised, nonetheless.

"Willa."

I looked up from surveying the various flavors to see Roman greet me as Chet slid the door closed to the room behind them. I admonished my stomach for doing somersaults when I saw that grin of his that crept up to his eyes.

"It's great to see you again," he said.

"I was admiring your place. Sorry I haven't come by more often."

"No worries. I know how crazy it is when you first open a business. It hasn't been that long ago for me." Then he turned to Chet, who'd followed him in. "You all set?"

"Just have to scoop this up, then I'm outta here." Chet reached for the broom and dustpan.

So Roman and I were going to be alone after all. *Nothing to worry about, Willa.*

"Have a good night, then," Roman said to Chet, before giving his full attention to me.

He guided me through the rest of his shop. Besides mead, the front of the shop displayed shelves of fun accessories like horn-shaped cups and drinking tankards. The back wall was dedicated to a small selection of wines, which only got a cursory mention.

I read the label to the only brand they carried. "Enora's. This is the local brand that Vivian was raving about, isn't it? Do you have a good deal with them? I've been debating about adding wine to my shop. I feel like I'm supposed to know more about wine, and I don't. I just want to concentrate on cheese."

"Don't bother. There are plenty of wineries around. I only carry wine to lure the customers who are looking for it, but I always pitch my mead to them. Most people just aren't familiar with it. My preference would be to phase out the wine. That's not what I'm about. Now, are you ready for the pièce de résistance?" He slid open the barn door. "The tasting room."

I walked through the doorway into a cozy, softly lit room, very different than the industrial feel of the shop. A horseshoe of round, high-top cocktail tables hugged the walls, partially framing a grouping of comfortable-looking worn leather chairs in the center. However, the focal point of the room was the handcrafted black walnut bar lined with stools for eight. On the olive wall behind the bar hung a large painting of Roman's Golden Glen label. His mead was simply showcased on a single glass shelf beneath it.

"This is really nice," I said, absorbing the comfortable, masculine feel of the room. Transom windows along the outer wall added natural light, even now as the daylight was waning.

"Thanks. I know it's smaller than most, but I prefer talking to people in a more intimate setting." He took my cheese plate to the bar and swiveled one of the stools for me to take a seat.

"There may be some cheese that pairs better back at the shop, but this will get us started," I said.

"So should this." From beneath the bar, Roman produced a bottle with a clear, straw-colored hue. "I'll start you with my original dry mead before we venture into the fruits and botanicals."

I was excited to try it. "Was this a hobby or did you always intend for it to be a business?"

"I always wanted to create something of my own. I wasn't sure if this was it, but it became a passion pretty quickly." He filled two stemmed glasses a quarter each and swirled the mead in them before sliding one in front of me. "This was the recipe I played around with for two years."

I swirled it in the glass as he had, but a little too vigorously, as it came perilously close to spilling over the rim. I stopped trying to act like I knew what I was doing. "So is it a wine or a beer?"

"Something in between. Wine is made from grapes and most beer from barley. Mead's base is honey."

He held the glass up to his nose and I followed suit. It had some oaky undertones, which surprised me. The honey base fooled me into thinking it would smell sweet.

"Here's to mixing business with pleasure." He tipped his glass, clinking it softly with mine.

Oh, boy. Luckily I had a drink in my hand, because suddenly I needed one. I had to remind myself to focus on the *business* part.

I took my first sip of mead. It had the lightness of a white wine with a flavor that matched its woodsy aroma. I knew just the cheese for it—the buttery, semi-soft Tomme-style French cheese from the Savoie region wouldn't overwhelm the lingering honey taste the mead left on my tongue.

He took the proffered cheese and tried it. "You're right. That's nice." He washed it down with more mead. "I'm glad you came tonight. I think we have a lot in common."

"Oh? Like what?"

He leaned in. "Chemistry, for one."

Vivian had given some warnings that Roman was a player, but his laid-back style made me think he'd move a little slower.

"Don't you think that's a little presumptuous?" I said.

"I was talking about the cheese and mead—they're both chemistry in action."

I studied the mead in my glass until my embarrassment subsided.

"Like you and I," he followed up.

So I wasn't totally off base. "You and me."

"Are you correcting my grammar or agreeing with me?"

I gave a little shrug. He didn't deserve to know.

Undeterred, he said, "You know, we also share a mythological Greek god. Aristaeus."

"The god of cheesemaking." Of course I knew of him.

"And of honey-mead, among other things."

"That's right. I'd forgotten."

"Then you agree we have a lot in common?"

I had no snappy comeback. He was right, but I wasn't going to give him the satisfaction of agreeing. I did find myself wanting to know more. "What made you think to come to Yarrow Glen, in the middle of wine country, to sell mead?"

"That's exactly the reason, because it's wine country. I wanted to stand out from the crowd." He explained no further.

"And you like it here? You've been here how long?"

"Coming up on four years."

"Vivian seemed to imply that you've made a lot of . . . friends."

"I'm a friendly guy."

"So I've heard."

"Vivian likes busting my chops. I wouldn't mind finding someone I can have more of a relationship with. Someone who understands the demands of owning your own business, someone I have things in common with . . ."

If he was causing sparks before, they were downright short-circuiting now.

He offered me more mead and I accepted, if only to keep myself from having to respond. I diverted the conversation back to my cheese. We successfully paired five more before I realized I was having a good time and was neglecting to do reconnaissance, but it was Roman who brought up the murder.

"I saw the police by your shop most of the day. How are you doing? I assume they questioned you?" he said.

"I found his body."

"Oh, Willa. Are you all right?" His hand went to mine.

I nodded and slipped my hand out from underneath his. I gulped one of the glasses of mead and kept my fingers around the stem so there'd be no more hand touching.

"I can't believe he was killed," he said.

"After we just saw him too. You knew him, didn't you?"

"Yes. From Detective Heath's line of questioning, the police seem to think what happened last night at your shop has something to do with his murder."

"I know."

"Does it worry you?"

"Well, he says they're 'gathering information,' but it feels like he's only gathering it on me. I'm not sure why he doesn't seem to be looking into others."

"Like who?"

Oops. "Like his wife." *Good save, Willa.*

"Guy mentioned once that they were separated. Maybe she lives far away and has an alibi."

"I heard Catalina, which could explain why she doesn't seem to be the police's number one suspect."

"Maybe."

"Do you know why he wanted to move back? No one in town seems to have anything nice to say about him," I said.

"He wasn't as bad of a guy as everyone made him out to be."

"Were you close friends?"

"Just friendly. But I think I knew him a little better than most people around here. Nobody else gave him much of a chance."

"So you were just friendly acquaintances then? Nothing more than that?"

"What are you getting at?"

"I'm just curious about him," I backpedaled.

"I don't know much more about him. He kept to himself." Roman finished off his glass.

"What do you think made Guy give you a good review?"

Roman seemed taken aback. "Excuse me?"

"I don't mean it wasn't deserved. It's obvious you have a great place here and your mead's excellent. But you have to admit, he didn't give any other place a shot."

The truth of what I was saying seemed to relax his hackles. "I have no idea, but I'm not the only one. He spared the bakery too."

"Why is that, do you think?"

Roman shrugged. "I don't know and I don't particularly care. Vivian kept that bakery afloat as a promise to her sister. Maybe he has a heart, after all. Or maybe the bakery's been around long enough where it wouldn't have mattered. He never tried to touch The Cellar either. Both places are fixtures around here. Whatever the reason, I'm glad he didn't mess with it."

"Hope told me about her mom and Vivian. That's so sad. Do you know what Vivian did for a living before she came to Yarrow Glen to help her sister?"

"She told me once she had a retail job and was putting herself through college, so she was used to hard work. She said seeing her sister in such a bad way was much harder than learning to bake bread and run the bakery. But trying to raise a teenager who'd just lost her mother was the hardest part. Vivian's a saint if you ask me."

I thought of how Hope complained about her aunt Vivian quite a bit. "Hope doesn't seem very grateful, considering what Vivian's done for her."

"Have you ever met a grateful teenager?"

I laughed. "She's almost twenty-one, but I get your point. I sure did a lot of grumbling on the farm."

"Tell me more about growing up on your farm."

It seemed a simple request, but there was no talking about my life on the farm without also talking about my brother. I realized with all the sampling I'd done, I was feeling a little buzzed, which always heightened my emotions. I didn't want to end the evening crying into my beer, as it were.

"Another time," I said. "I'm more interested in you."

"Oh, you are?"

That came out more flirtatious than I intended.

"Uh . . . where did you grow up?" I tried to sound as professional as possible.

"Not too far from here."

He leaned in with his forearms on the bar, seemingly challenging me to ask him questions he'd vaguely answer. It was odd that he'd be pretty effusive about Guy Lippinger and Vivian but not about himself.

"Did you know anybody in town before you moved here?"

"Nope," he replied.

"So you don't know what secret Guy was planning to tell everyone last night?"

Roman's flirtatious energy shifted, and he backed off the bar. "I didn't know what he was talking about. I wouldn't put any significance in it. He obviously had been drinking. He was probably just trying to rile up Derrick."

"They definitely seemed like enemies. Were you here at the meadery when the murder happened?"

"You're starting to sound like the police."

Yup, his energy had definitely shifted. I let out a nervous laugh.

"No, I uh . . ."

"It's fine. I was in my apartment upstairs."

So no alibi. My lousy streak with men continues—the first charming, successful, handsome guy who seems to like me might be a murderer. Terrific.

He went on. "I came down when I heard the police cars. They wouldn't let any of us on your side of the block. I wish I'd seen you. I would've found a way across the street."

Our eyes met. This time it didn't seem like he was trying to be charming. He sounded sincere, which really conflicted with the whole issue of him being one of my murder suspects. It took me several long moments to break my gaze from his.

"Which one's your favorite?" He turned to the mead.

It was a close call, but I liked the cinnamon that created a tickle of spice on my tongue. I wanted to remember the flavor so I could go back to the shop and find a cheese that was a better pairing for it. I was already considering a creamy Muenster.

He poured two full glasses of the cinnamon mead and slid one in front of me.

"For pleasure, not business," he said, holding up his glass in mock cheers and taking a long draught. "Take your drink and come with me," he said suddenly.

He pulled out a ring of keys from under the bar and unlocked a closed door near the corner I had assumed was a closet. My relaxed state vanished.

"Come on," he said, tipping his head toward the room.

CHAPTER 14

I convinced myself I was being silly to worry and hesitantly followed Roman into the unknown room as directed. Five stairs down brought me into a space lit by fluorescent overhead lights. The vaulted ceilings of the shop and tasting room didn't extend to this cellar-like space where Roman took long strides ahead of me. Footed stainless steel tanks that looked like enormous hot-water heaters stood in two rows of six. Over to the side was an oversized sink with some hoses around it. I quickly noted the lack of windows.

Feathery shivers tickled my neck. I'd poo-pooed Baz's attempts to accompany me tonight, so I had no right to be scared now. I reminded myself of what I'd told Baz—there was no reason Roman would hurt me . . . even if he was a murderer. Why didn't that sound as convincing now as it did this afternoon?

"What is this?" I asked.

"It's where I make the mead. The tour I give starts over here." He disappeared behind the tanks.

This time, I didn't follow. I kept one eye on the door we came through.

"I don't need the tour today, thanks," I said to the tank. I almost took another gulp of the mead he'd poured for me and realized I didn't need that either.

Roman popped back around the tank, looking confused, but I wanted nothing more than to get back to the door that could be locked and was too far away for my comfort. The heck with awkwardness, I made a beeline for the door.

"Willa." Roman trotted after me.

By the time I got to the tasting room, my hands were shaking. I put the glass of mead down and thought of Mrs. Schultz's deep breaths. The low moans might even come in handy if I needed to scare him away.

"Willa, are you okay?"

"I'm sorry, I . . . I was a little claustrophobic in there." That was my tactful way of saying I didn't like the possibility of being locked in a room with a possible murderer.

"Oh, hey, I'm sorry. Can I get you some water or something?"

The look of concern in his eyes made me second-guess my feelings. Now that I was out of the confined space, the fear I'd felt dissipated. In fact, I almost felt silly, but I reminded myself that he was on my short list of suspects.

"I think I'd better go."

"Sure, of course."

Before I took another step, I distinctly heard a loud buzzing noise that sounded like it came from the front room of the meadery. Roman must've heard it too—he looked toward the doorway and cocked an ear. The way his eyebrows furrowed, it wasn't a noise he expected.

"What was that?" I said.

"I don't know. Unless Chet forgot to lock the door . . ."

A thump was followed by a clank, definitely coming from the shop. Roman put his forefinger to his lips to hush me.

Here I'd been afraid of Roman, when all this time the killer might've been trying to get him too.

He grabbed an unopened mead by the neck of the bottle, testing the weight of it in his hand.

"Wait here," he whispered.

Did he think I'd never seen a horror movie? Nothing good comes of *waiting here*. I followed him out of the tasting room, snatching my phone from my purse, ready with an itchy trigger finger to press Emergency Call. Step for step, I crept right behind him. I checked over my shoulder just as he stopped, and slammed into his back.

"How did you get in here?" Roman said to the intruder.

I peeked around him, holding my phone out like a taser. I didn't know what I thought I was going to do— blind him on flashlight mode?

There was no need.

"Baz?" My tense shoulders eased when I saw him, bent over and retrieving a pair of pliers he'd apparently dropped on the floor.

"I could've sworn you left earlier," Roman said to him.

Baz straightened. "I left to get another tool. Chet saw me come back. Sorry, I thought you knew."

"No problem."

"The hand dryer in the bathroom's all fixed."

The buzzing noise. What were the chances Roman had a faulty hand dryer so close to closing time on the evening I was coming here? The fact that Baz purposely didn't make eye contact with me told me the answer.

"It was lucky Willa and I were doing a tasting and you didn't get locked in," Roman said.

"Yeah, lucky," I repeated.

"We're going to have to figure out a new system between the two of us," I said, as Baz and I walked across the street and down the alley to our apartments.

"Like agreeing to talk to suspects together, so I don't have to hide in a bathroom for over an hour?"

"For someone who couldn't believe anybody you know is a murderer, you're awfully suspicious. I'm thirty-three years old, Baz. I've been on my own for a long time. I can handle myself."

"Have you ever dealt with a killer before?"

"All right, you got me there." Was I going to admit to Baz that I'd been frightened in Roman's mead-making room? Not a chance. But I probably ought to admit it to myself. "We'll figure out a better system, so both of us stay safe, okay? But just to be clear, I'm not a damsel in distress."

"Point taken."

"You want some cheese?" I still had plenty from the plate I'd brought to Roman's.

"Is there cheddar in there?"

"If we're going to be friends, you have to expand your cheese repertoire."

"I need some real food, anyway. I couldn't pack a sandwich for my bathroom stakeout."

"Stakeout? Are you sure you never took drama class from Mrs. Schultz? You can be a little melodramatic."

He gave me the side-eye.

I softened. "But . . . since you were there to protect me, let me make you something to eat."

At my apartment, I went through my pantry to see what I could whip up with the sparse ingredients I had. Loretta and I watched an awful lot of *Chopped*, so I was pretty good at making something out of a hodgepodge of ingredients.

"Do you mind feeding Loretta?" I asked.

Baz looked on the floor around him, presumably for a pet to feed. "Who's Loretta?"

"My fish there next to the chair. She's got a view of the mountains on one side and can watch TV from the other. Her food is right there. Don't give her too much."

Baz crouched down to get a good look at my betta fish. "I hate to tell you this, but she's probably not a Loretta."

"What do you mean? I named her myself. Look at her—she's fabulous. She's totally giving Loretta vibes."

"Only male betta fish are that colorful. Females tend to be more muted, like female birds."

"What? Well, that might explain Loretta's love for Ted Allen."

Baz gave me a confused look, but I ignored it and went back to pulling things out of my fridge and cupboards. Twenty minutes later, I served up a faux croque monsieur.

"It's a fancy grilled ham and cheese," I said.

The outside was broiled after being coated with the same cheese mixture I'd slathered on the inside with the ham and Dijon mustard: Gruyère mixed with a spot of heavy cream to substitute for the more labor-intensive béchamel sauce. I hid some Emmental in there too—a buttery Swiss that melts well and pairs nicely with the nutty Gruyère.

"The cheese is on the outside too? That's my kind of sandwich." Baz took a generous bite. I tentatively waited for his reaction, since it didn't contain his beloved cheddar. He gave me a thumbs-up as he chewed.

"See? You have a more sophisticated palate than you realize." His approval was more satisfying than the sandwich itself. I loved converting timid cheese eaters.

We sat catty-corner from each other on stools at the kitchen island enjoying our simple French-inspired sandwiches. I hadn't realized how hungry I was until I started eating and how much the mead had started to go to my head. Once I'd finished half the sandwich, I was feeling more like myself.

"So was it worth it? What information did you get tonight?" Baz asked between bites.

"Not much. The reason nobody's seen Guy's wife around town like you said is because, according to Roman, they were separated. So she might not be anywhere near Yarrow Glen, which would explain why the police don't seem to be homing in on her."

"Makes sense . . . unless it was a hit job."

"A hit job with my cheese knife?"

"Forgot about that."

I wished I could. "I couldn't get a lot out of Roman. He defended Guy, but didn't tell me much about him. He was pretty quiet about himself too. I got the feeling he was hiding something. What do you know about him?"

"Not that much. We've had a drink or two together at The Cellar, but nothing was said worth remembering."

"Did you ever see Roman there with Guy Lippinger?" I wanted confirmation of what I'd overheard at the park.

"Not that I ever saw, but I didn't hang out there that much. I can buy a six-pack at the liquor store for practically the same price as having a draught there." Baz ate a quarter of his sandwich in one bite. I was glad I thought to make him two. "I worked on his tasting room last year, so I spent some time with him then while we picked out the finishes. Come to think of it, he never really told me too much about his past. He talked a lot about the meadery, but not how he got here. I didn't think anything of it, 'cause he's not a big talker anyways. I probably did most of the talking."

I'd already experienced that with Baz. "Yeah, he's got that laid-back vibe—the strong, silent type," I agreed.

"The women sure seem to like it."

I felt my face warm and turned away to sip my water, but not before catching a smirk on Baz's face.

"He always seemed like a good guy, though. He's certainly good for his word. He kept his promise to give me the job," Baz said, finishing his second sandwich.

"What do you mean?"

"One night at The Cellar, we got to talking about our jobs. I prefer being a handyman, like I told you, but sometimes I need a bigger paycheck, so I take on larger projects every so often. He really wanted to turn the back room of his meadery into a tasting room. He said it would make all the difference for his business, but he couldn't afford to do it. He said he couldn't get a big enough loan to turn both the shop and the back room into what he wanted, so he only did the shop. Then like four months later, he asked me to do the tasting room. Paid cash."

"You didn't think that was odd that he suddenly had the money?"

"What did I care? It was good money and he was easy to work with."

I knew better than most that the first couple of years of opening a new shop, you're lucky to tread water.

Making enough of a profit to have that much cash on hand would be tough to come by . . . unless someone rich leant it to you.

"What if Guy Lippinger leant him the money?" I said, impulsively.

"Why would he do that?"

I told Baz what I'd overheard at the park.

"So what if he did?" Baz said. "Nothing wrong with that."

"On the face of it, no. But what if Guy demanded to be paid back with a really high interest rate and Roman couldn't pay anymore? That could be motive to kill him."

Baz considered this. "I don't know. Roman seems smarter than that."

"Sometimes you do stupid things when you want something bad enough. You just told me he said it would make all the difference for his business. Maybe he overestimated how well the meadery would do with a tasting room and he thought he could pay it back. He wouldn't be the first. Plenty of people have gotten into trouble with loan sharks before. It's likely Guy's parents taught him a thing or two about taking advantage of people."

"We need proof. So how do we find out?" Baz said, still sounding unconvinced.

"I don't know. That's not the kind of information we'd have access to. I tried to ask him in a roundabout way, but he got a little offended, so I had to back off."

"I'm not so sure about this theory. I feel like we're throwing darts in a windstorm."

"So then let's make a list of what we know so far." I grabbed a pen and my neglected grocery list. I turned the paper over to the blank side. "I think it's safe to assume Guy's wife hasn't been around in some time."

"Which means the nail salon business card might be

a clue. If it's not the wife's, it could be the killer's. Did Mrs. Schultz come up with anything after she went to the salon this afternoon?"

"She was right when she said everyone there would be talking about Detective Heath's visit. She found out that Guy's wife, when she did live here, never went there. They implied Mrs. Lippinger wouldn't have thought it was up to her standards, since they don't serve champagne. He didn't ask about anybody else specifically. Unless we want to add half the women of Yarrow Glen to the suspect list, I don't think that clue is the best place to start. We'll have to leave that up to the police and stick with our suspect list for now."

"All right. So Derrick's the only one with an alibi?"

"It looks like it. Vivian left Hope's within the time frame he was killed."

"That leaves Hope alone that night too," Baz reminded me.

"True. And we only have Roman's word for it that he was in his apartment. Birdie's coming tomorrow to give a talk about goat farming and making goat cheese, so I'll talk to her then. Do you know her? She told me she grew up here, but then moved away."

"I don't think I know her."

"She was the one last night with the ponytail and the T-shirt, jeans, and crocs."

"I remember seeing her, but I didn't recognize her. What's her last name?"

I thought about it. "Isn't that terrible? I don't remember it, but it's on her invoices. Let me grab my computer."

I retrieved my laptop from my bedroom and brought up my invoices. I read it aloud. "'Smiling Goats Farm. Ronald Dellacourt.' That's her husband. Here it is: 'Birdie Ormond.' She must use her maiden name."

"Doesn't ring a bell," Baz said.

"That's not surprising. She's older than you. In fact, I think she's probably around Vivian and Guy's age, so she may have known him growing up. Hey, did you ever talk to your sibs about Guy?"

"Yeah, he was in a higher grade than them. They didn't remember anything more than we already know. Sorry."

"Too bad."

I thought about Birdie some more. I felt a connection to her because we were both farm girls who had a thing for cheese. I'd done some research on her farm—they'd only started making goat cheese seven years ago. Their use of minimal ingredients was what drew me to their cheese. However, I didn't know much about her personal life.

"Should we google Birdie?" I'd already closed out my business page and was typing in her name when I asked. An article appeared about dairy farms where Smiling Goats was mentioned. Anything beyond that were articles on *Bye Bye Birdie*. "Not much about her," I said, disappointed.

"Unless Birdie's not her real name."

I deleted her first name and added "farm" to her last. Maybe that would produce something.

"There's another article on farming." Baz pointed to it.

I clicked on it, but it said it was an archived article and couldn't be viewed without a subscription.

"It couldn't be her, anyway. It's from too long ago." I returned to the online list. "Here's another old one, but she wouldn't have been more than a child."

I clicked on it and this time, the article on dairy farmers appeared. Baz and I silently read through it. He must've gotten to her name at the same time I did, as we both audibly inhaled simultaneously.

"Glenda and Dale Ormond and their daughter, Birdie . . ." Baz and I looked at each other. "So her parents had a dairy farm when she was a kid. Do you think they were a casualty of the Lippingers' land sale?"

This time I added "Lippinger" to "Ormond Farm" and hit Search.

Bingo! It was another archived newspaper article, this time from twenty years ago. I clicked on it. The headline read: Land Sale Dismantles Fifteen Farms.

My breathing hastened, as if reading fast was a physical activity. The article featured three families who had to sell their animals and equipment because they'd been leasing the land on which they were farming. My finger traced the article as we both read silently and quickly. One of the families was—

"Glenda and Dale Ormond," I read aloud.

"Birdie's parents," Baz said.

"I was right. They had to sell the family farm. Birdie would've been in her early twenties. What happened to her parents, I wonder?"

"It says they were selling their cows and equipment."

"So they didn't move the farm, they lost it." I almost fell off my stool when I leaned back, allowing the weight of this information to settle on me. "This is big."

"But she's had twenty years to get revenge. Why would she do it now?"

"Good question. Maybe something triggered her, like one of her parents could've died recently. If they never recovered from the loss of their farm, maybe they ended up penniless. She could've been holding in her resentment this whole time and now he's back in town . . ."

"It's possible."

I could tell Baz wasn't convinced.

"There's only one way to find out," I said.

"Which is what?"

"I might have to come right out and ask her."

Baz nodded, seeming to consider my approach. "And then naturally you'll be invited to join the police force once she confesses to you."

"I get the feeling you're being sarcastic."

"Go with that feeling."

"How else am I supposed to find out?"

"I don't know, but if you tell a murderer you think they're guilty, then you're gonna be the next to go, if you know what I mean. You gotta play it cool."

"I'm not good at being cool."

I couldn't help but notice Baz didn't refute me.

"Just ease into it, that's all I'm saying," he advised.

"She's going to be talking about her farm at the shop tomorrow, so I'll get Archie or Mrs. Schultz to ask a question about her farming background. Hopefully she'll expand on the topic and talk about her parents."

"That could work. It still seems like a very old score to be settling now."

"It's the only motive we have so far with Derrick out of contention."

"You're right. It's something, at least."

We chatted a little more and then my yawning ended the visit.

After Baz left, I got ready for bed. I had to move my laptop to get under my bed covers. It had been a very long day, but I still found myself propping the pillows behind me. It was the first time I was out of my shop before ten o'clock, but that didn't mean I couldn't still obsessively make graphs and charts of the daily sales, checking and rechecking my inventory and orders.

My mind went back to what we'd found out about Birdie. I wondered if she could really be the one who killed Guy. I opened my laptop but I didn't go to my spreadsheets. Instead I typed in Roman Massey's name and clicked the Search button.

Several articles on him came up, one from *All Things Sonoma*. I read that one first. Derrick was right—Guy gave Roman's Golden Glen Meadery a stellar review just after his tasting room opened. He was loquacious in his praise. My theory had to be right. Why else would he be championing Roman's place and yet be so hard on Apricot Grille and the two restaurants before it? He was more than willing to trash Curds & Whey too. I recalled the look on Roman's face when Derrick mentioned the good review. At the time, I chalked it up to Roman not wanting to throw it in Derrick's face, but now I wondered . . . was it more than humility?

I scanned the other results with Roman's name. I clicked on an article written at the time he opened, also effusive with praise. From what I'd seen of Roman's shop, the praise was well deserved. I continued reading.

Roman Massey's delve into mead making may seem an unusual path for the thirty-year-old, since wine making is in his genes. A grandson of the founder of Enora's Winery, Massey is. . . .

Enora's was the label on all the wine in Roman's shop. Why didn't he tell me his family owned it?

I typed in "Enora's Winery" and went to their website. It said the third generation of Masseys were now involved in running it. I read the half dozen articles that mentioned his family's winery, named after his grandmother. Nothing about them stood out, except for the fact that he kept it hidden from me. How many other secrets was Roman keeping?

CHAPTER 15

I was at Lou's Market almost as soon as it opened the following morning, buying the fresh ingredients for my goat cheese smorgasbord to showcase Birdie's chèvre. Thankfully, there was no longer any sign that a murder had taken place in the alley—the police had finally skedaddled.

Walking back to my shop, I noticed the vending box on the sidewalk was full of this morning's newspapers. Normally, the highlights of the *Glen Gazette* were the sections touting local events, town meetings, and used items for sale, but Guy Lippinger's murder headlined today's issue. I had the urge to take all of them and throw them in the dumpster. It wouldn't be any use, anyway. If I'd gleaned anything about this town, it was that word of mouth carried news around even faster than a free newspaper. I took one, anxious to read it as I juggled the grocery bags while I unlocked the front door and made my way inside Curds & Whey.

I left the lights off in the front of the shop and the Closed sign on the door, as we wouldn't be open for another forty-five minutes.

I absently placed the grocery bags on the counter in

the shop's kitchenette, still staring at the headline, almost afraid to read on. I decided I wouldn't—not now, anyway. I didn't want today to be tainted with whatever the newspaper said about me or my shop in relation to the murder.

I purposely folded it and went through the back stockroom to my office to stash it until later. But when it unfurled on my desk, my resolve crumbled. I plunked in my chair and read it.

The background it gave on Guy Lippinger coincided with everything I'd been told about him. Nothing new there. Detective Heath must've not been very forthcoming in his statement—the paper had few details about the murder. Unfortunately, what they did have included me and my shop. It didn't implicate me—it only stated the facts that I found his body in the alley—but being associated with the murder in any way wasn't a good look for Curds & Whey.

I took some deep breaths, but in the cramped, windowless office, it did no good. I knew I shouldn't have read it right now.

Get your head in the game, Willa.

Mrs. Schultz would be here any minute to help me start prepping the goat cheese hors d'oeuvres for Birdie's talk. We had a lot to do before we opened.

I ditched the paper and returned to the shop's kitchenette, still chastising myself for reading it. I flipped on the back lights, but stopped short at the island right in front of me.

A large knife was plunged into a wheel of Manchego, the handle of the long blade sticking out of the top.

Was that there when I came in?

Goose bumps broke out on the back of my neck and I rubbed them away.

"Mrs. Schultz?" I called. No answer.

From where I stood, I quickly scanned the store. I'd left the door unlocked knowing she would be in shortly, but the door was still closed and no one else was here. I checked the knife drawer of the kitchenette. The large one was missing.

The sound of the front door opening spun me around. Without thinking, I pulled the knife out of the cheese and held it in both hands before me like a sword.

"Good morning," Mrs. Schultz called in a singsong voice from the front of the shop.

I let out a breath and shakily put my weapon down. "Good morning." I returned her greeting, masking my anxiousness.

Mrs. Schultz breezed in wearing one of her A-line dresses, this one patterned with bright red poppies that matched yesterday's manicure.

She took a clean apron from the cupboard and set down a small paper bag on the counter. "I brought some herbs from my window garden in case you wanted to use any today."

"That's nice of you. Thanks." I couldn't quite concentrate on the food prep yet. "Mrs. Schultz, did you leave this cheese wheel here when we closed last night?" Normally the island was wiped and cleared of everything after closing.

"What is that, Manchego? I didn't have to restock that, so I don't think so." She began pulling the food out of the grocery bags.

"Do you think Archie might have?"

"I don't know. Is something wrong?"

That was the question, wasn't it? I didn't know what to make of it. Was it a threat? A prank? Or perhaps it was merely an oversight from yesterday. But the knife . . . I suddenly realized what I'd done. If it was some kind of a threat, it was too late to call it to Detective Heath's attention—I'd disturbed the evidence. I decided not to dampen Mrs. Schultz's enthusiasm. There was nothing to be done about it. "No, everything's fine."

We began prepping the appetizers, and soon the morning felt normal again and my mind was filled with nothing but goat cheese recipes. We used the market's local produce, our high-quality jarred ingredients, and Vivian's crispy breads, which Archie later delivered to us. Bitter endive leaves were stuffed with Birdie's rosemary goat cheese and topped with sweet, earthy chopped beets and crunchy walnuts for a bright, flavorful bite. We garnished the plate with Mrs. Schultz's fresh rosemary sprigs. I'd specially requested flat bread that I topped with dollops of fig jam, goat cheese, thinly sliced prosciutto, and the caramelized onions Mrs. Schultz babied in the pan for close to an hour. I cut the pears I bought into quarter-inch-thick slices to ready them to bake in the oven while Birdie was giving her talk.

I'd heavily advertised the event, and shortly before it started I had Archie ushering in window shoppers from the sidewalk. It was standing room only, as nearly two dozen customers congregated at the back of Curds & Whey. If anyone had read this morning's paper, it didn't appear to be keeping them away. As the crowd for Birdie's talk grew, I felt a little guilty for planning to interrogate her. She was a hard worker, passionate about her farm and her cheese, and she'd agreed to give a talk to my customers about all of it. Still, I knew I'd have to find a way to mention it at some point, but I'd leave that for later.

In the meantime, I was thrilled with the turnout. Especially after the appalling sales the previous day, I was giddy to see my shop filled with interested customers putting their noses to wrapped cheeses, and eager to answer their cheese-related questions so they'd be sure to take home a wonderfully unexpected flavor. Our glass jar next to the Monster Cheddar Wheel—as we'd dubbed it—was starting to fill with guesses of its weight. Mrs. Schultz was helping customers choose the best crackers or bruschetta to accompany their cheese selections, and Archie was busy at the register and getting quite good at conversing about the cheese samples, convincing customers to be adventurous. I didn't expect to be mentoring someone so soon after opening my own shop, but I was grateful to have my small crew be as avid as I was in spreading the love of cheese.

I almost didn't recognize Birdie when she arrived. Her straight brown hair was out of its elastic band and fell to the spaghetti straps of her rainbow-striped sundress. I think I even detected a hint of pink lipstick. My gaze went to her hands to see if a manicure was evident, but she had sensible short nails, like any farmer.

We exchanged pleasantrics, but she still seemed as reticent as the other night. It made me a little nervous about how her presentation would go, but I needn't have worried. Once she began, she became animated talking about her goat farm and the process of turning their milk into cheese.

I stuck the sliced pears in the oven when the question-and-answer session began. My ears perked up when someone asked what Birdie's childhood was like.

"I grew up on my parents' dairy farm right here in Yarrow Glen. We didn't make the cheese on our farm, but we sold our milk to local cheesemakers. It's where I fell in love with farming," she said.

So far, what she said coincided with what I'd read last night.

"When my husband and I decided to get back into farming, we returned to my hometown. We realized cows were a bigger commitment than we could handle, so we turned to goats."

I looked for Archie. Earlier in the day, we discussed the information I needed to get from Birdie about her parents. He agreed to ask the question if an opportune time arose, and now was that time. I found him stationed by the farm table we'd pushed to the side so he could help serve customers the goat cheese appetizers I'd put out. It didn't appear he was making a move to ask the question. I coughed, hoping to catch his attention. It didn't work. The last thing I wanted to do was stage an all-out coughing fit with all the food nearby. I tried waving at him, but it was only when my oven timer dinged that he noticed me.

Unfortunately, I'd also told him to wrap up the talk when the timer went off, and since there were no more questions, he did just that. He thanked Birdie and invited everyone to try some more of the goat cheese creations, including my baked pears, fresh out of the oven. I'd have to snag some time alone with Birdie and talk to her myself. I finished off the pears with slices of rosemary goat cheese, stuck pecans in the cheese, and then drizzled them with honey. When they cooled a bit, I cut the slices in half so they'd be closer to bite-sized. Once the customers were happily munching our delectable treats, I was able to pull Birdie aside.

"That was a great talk. You're a natural," I said to her.

"Thanks. I hope I didn't bore anybody. Sometimes I forget that not everybody loves farming as much as I do."

"They did today—you made it very interesting and accessible. It's nice to meet another farm girl."

"There's nothing like it, is there?"

"My brother used to say the same thing. I wasn't quite as enamored with it." Here was my opportunity to steer the conversation to the topic of our parents. "My parents still work their farm."

"Mine had to give it up a long time ago."

"It's not an easy business. Was it a tough transition?"

"We thought it would be, but it ended up being the best thing for them. They were always just scraping by. When we moved away from Yarrow Glen, my dad got his first nine-to-five job and discovered he loved not getting up at five a.m." Birdie smiled. "I was the only one who missed farming. My parents are happily retired now, something that would've never happened had the farm worked out. Sometimes we don't recognize life's blessings when they come. I try to remember that."

Unless Birdie was a terrific liar, my motive for her killing Guy just went down the drain. There seemed to be no hard feelings there. Maybe she knew something that would help me find another suspect with a motive. I dove right in.

"Have the police spoken to you about Guy Lippinger?"

Her smile faded. "They came to the farm yesterday. I can't believe he's gone." Her gaze dropped and she hugged herself as if suddenly chilled.

"Oh, I'm sorry. Did you know him?"

"We were close in high school. We both eventually moved away, so we hadn't kept in touch, but still . . . It's horrible how he died." She wiped a tear I didn't see from her cheek.

"I'm sorry."

Birdie was the first person who seemed truly affected by Guy's death and it gave me pause. I didn't have the appetite to ask her more questions. In fact, I had the sudden desire to change the subject, so I handed her one of our flyers for the cheese hunt.

"We're having another event tomorrow. It should be fun. I hope you'll consider coming. We've been advertising it on the cheese trail website. I think the tourists would love to meet one of our local suppliers. You don't have to do anything in an official capacity, but it'll be a chance to talk up Smiling Goats cheese."

She glanced at the flyer. "Sure. Maybe some customers will want to plan a farm tour. Truth be told, I didn't mind having a change from my routine today. I'd better head out now, though, if I'm going to play hooky from the farm again tomorrow afternoon."

"Thanks again for the great presentation. I'll see you tomorrow, I hope."

"See you then."

She zigzagged through the crowd on her way out.

Archie came up to me. "I forgot my cue, didn't I? Sorry."

"No worries. I spoke with her."

"And?"

"I don't think she's the one. She seemed pretty upset about Guy's death, so I didn't want to ask her anything else about him right now. All she said was they were friends in high school. It's frustrating only getting bits and pieces of information about him. Vivian didn't know him and Roman didn't say much. You said Derrick talked about the lawsuit when you worked at the restaurant. Did anybody else there know Guy Lippinger and put in their two cents? Was it something people at work talked about?"

"There was a lot of gossip about it, but the lawsuit didn't go on for long. Guy settled it pretty fast. Everyone was surprised."

"Why would Guy be so quick to settle the lawsuit? His family must have big-time attorneys. It would surprise me that they'd be scared of Derrick."

Archie shrugged. "I don't know the details. I just remember thinking Derrick winning the lawsuit would make him a nicer person, but it didn't."

"Derrick said Guy's family owns *All Things Sonoma* magazine. Maybe they pressured him into settling."

"I don't know. Sorry I'm not much help."

Archie and I didn't have a chance to discuss it any further. I had a shop full of goat-cheese-eating customers whom I wanted to turn into cheese-buying customers. We had to strike while their palate was hot, so to speak.

Eventually the mass of customers trickled into a steady hum for the remainder of the afternoon. I used one of the quieter moments to get the shelves back in order. This was usually a therapeutic task for me, but this time the displays seemed clunky and disorganized, much like my thoughts. If only I knew what my next move should be. I thought any information I gathered would lead me to another possible clue, but I seemed to be in a maze of dead ends.

Maybe Derrick wasn't the culprit, but out of all my suspects, he seemed like he'd have the most information about Guy. How could I get Derrick to talk to me? I thought back on my cheesemaking class. He finally opened up when I complimented his restaurant. He liked the opportunity to brag a little. What if I gave him the chance to boast about how he bested Guy Lippinger in a lawsuit?

I stepped back to see the Dry Jack cheese balanced with the Cotija cheese, just as they might be in a splendid Mexican bean dish. My harmonious cheese display told me this was the right approach. It was time to talk to Derrick.

CHAPTER 16

Later that evening, after closing the shop and taking a quick shower, I walked up the block with confidence to speak with Derrick. The party lights draped along the canopy of Apricot Grille's inviting side patio caught my eye before I crossed at the corner of Pleasant and Main. Tall patio heaters glowed among tables lively with customers.

The full patio should've clued me in, even before I stepped inside and encountered the wall of waiting customers, that I'd inadvertently come during the Friday dinner rush. I approached the hostess station. Surprisingly, the commotion of the vestibule didn't extend into the restaurant. The uncluttered interior with shiny tables and the occasional private, semicircular booths left a soothing impression, as did the cool blue color scheme amidst the dark wood tones. A soft glow cascaded from the tiny lights entwined in large bamboo orbs hung from the ceiling. A bar ran along the left side of the dining room.

I scolded myself for not having visited most of my neighbors' businesses sooner. If I hadn't been so overwhelmed with getting my shop open, I would've personally delivered my cheesemaking-class invitations instead of sending e-vites. No doubt I worked too much if investigating a murder was the only reason I ventured away from my own shop.

The hostess standing behind a podium greeted me with a smile that didn't reach her eyes. Her angular features were highlighted by her glossy hair severely pulled back and fastened at the nape of her neck into a ponytail. I looked past her as I scanned the restaurant for Derrick.

"Do you have a reservation?" she asked.

"I'm not here to dine. I came to speak with Derrick, the manager."

"Is there a problem?"

"No problem. It's of a personal nature."

Her plastered-on smile dropped. She looked me up and down. "He's busy right now."

"I'll wait. Could you let him know I'm here? I'll only take a few minutes of his time."

Again, she looked me up and down without pretense, which made me assess myself, as well. My short denim jacket over jeans and a Daughtry T-shirt was probably not the proper attire for the only upscale restaurant in Yarrow Glen.

"What's your name?" she demanded.

"I'm Willa from the cheese shop. Here, you can give this to him too." I reached into the small purse at my hip and pulled out one of the cheese-hunt flyers I'd brought along as a conversation warm-up. Although now it seemed unlikely I'd have time to beat around the bush.

"As you can see, I'm busy too," she said.

"Is he in the kitchen? I can—" I indicated I could find him myself.

"No, it's fine. I'll see to it."

She snapped up my flyer and strode with purpose in

very high heels through the dining room. I marveled at how she got through a shift in them. My feet ached by the end of the day in my Keds. She stopped just short of the server station where I saw Derrick directing a bus-boy to a dirty table. She approached him and I watched their interaction. He looked my way too briefly, leaving me with my hand in the air, mid-wave. Uh-oh. By the change in their body language, it looked like I'd caused a problem. I didn't mean to get her into any trouble. I should've remembered Derrick's temper.

I crossed the invisible barrier and walked to where they were fervently speaking to each other in the back corner.

"There's nothing going on. She owns a shop down the street," I heard him say before he noticed I was behind him.

Awkward!

"I was just . . . uh . . ." Here I was going to come to her rescue, but it looked like Derrick was the one who needed rescuing.

"Willa, I'm too busy for this," he said.

"I think you should take care of your *personal* busi-ness," the hostess said to him, before stomping away.

"I didn't mean to cause you problems," I said.

He scowled at me—or maybe that was just his resting expression I was coming to realize—and walked away without another word. I'd come this far, no sense in stop-ping now. I followed him through the swinging door into the kitchen.

In contrast to the dining room's steady murmur of voices, the kitchen was a busy train station, roaring with noise. Plates clanked, servers danced around each other, and cooks yelled out prepared orders. Derrick pulled an order slip from the warming shelf and began to place Instagram-worthy plates of fish and pasta onto a serving tray.

I caught Derrick's eye, but he didn't pause. "Now's not a good time, whatever it is," he said.

I spoke loudly over the din. "I see that. Can you stop by tomorrow? We need to talk. It's about Guy Lippinger's murder."

This made him stop and take notice, but I quickly realized it wasn't because of me. Standing directly behind me was Detective Heath.

CHAPTER 17

At five foot two, I'd never wanted to make myself smaller for any occasion—until now when I wanted to shrink behind the galley and away from Detective Heath. Was it possible he hadn't heard me?

I worked my face into what I hoped was an innocent expression and used the counter of food for inspiration. "Detective. Are you here for the truffle fries too? Archie told me they were out of this world, so I had to come and get some to take home."

I gave Derrick a pleading look. For some reason, he took pity on me and slipped into the kitchen's galley.

"Is that so?" Detective Heath said.

Maybe I'd put too much stock in his poker face—it was obvious he didn't believe me for a second.

"I'd hate for your dinner to get cold," I said. *In other words, Vamoose!*

"I was just at the bar for a drink."

I scolded myself for not having seen him. I was too intent on getting to Derrick.

Momentarily, Derrick handed me a closed paperboard container, like a taller version of a Chinese food takeout box. It was warm in my grasp.

"Truffle fries," he said. "On the house. You can go now."

"Okey dokie. Thanks. Nice to see you again, Detective." *Not.*

I scooted out of the kitchen and through the restaurant, past the unfriendly hostess who squinted her eyes at me accusingly, and outside to a chilly evening. *Well, that was a bust.*

I stood in front of the restaurant, slowly settling into my defeat. However, I'd inadvertently planted myself in the flow of traffic. I apologized to a family for blocking the door and scooted out of the way onto the sidewalk. Looking up the street, The Inn at Yarrow Glen caught my eye, its wooden sign jutting out from the porch steps that abutted the sidewalk.

When I discovered Yarrow Glen more than a decade ago, I had been following the California cheese trail in search of shops that wanted to mentor a wannabe cheesemonger. Any directions I needed around town mentioned the historic inn, a well-known marker. I'd even stopped in to check it out and ended up resting in the lobby with free tea and shortbread cookies.

Why hadn't I thought to go there earlier? Its bar, The Cellar, was the last place Guy Lippinger was seen alive. According to Detective Heath, he left there last night around nine and likely stumbled the two blocks back to his car. Was he too drunk to know the danger he was in? Or had he met up with his would-be attacker beforehand?

I'd been so intent on asking questions of my suspects, I didn't think to see who else Guy might've spoken with that night. I could follow his footsteps back to my building or follow them to The Cellar. It was time to take a new approach.

I walked past the restaurant's parking lot and another two shops up the block to reach the inn, which had a barrier of evergreens on either side. A driveway ran along the left that led to their parking lot beyond an enclosed courtyard in the rear. Much like Yarrow Glen's residents, there was nothing fussy about the turn-of-the-century inn. It had nine rooms and a second-floor balcony that wrapped around the entire white, boxy structure. This was where Guy Lippinger spent his last hours alive.

I sidestepped another patron going in. He held the door open for me and I accepted. The petite clerk at the reception desk who'd been browsing a newspaper popped to attention as we entered. The man who'd held the door for me veered through a hallway to the left, leaving the lobby devoid of people besides myself and the young front desk clerk.

The space which served as the lobby was modest, but everything one might expect from an old inn. It looked fresher than my vague memory of it from years ago. A compact sitting area with matching wing chairs and a sofa was anchored by a dark print rug over a highly polished wood floor. A bowl of perfectly placed green apples sat untouched in the center of the coffee table. An arched fireplace with a simple white mantel flanked by sconces completed the cozy space.

I passed a spindle staircase as I stepped up to the reception desk in the rear of the room. The eager clerk, her blunt-cut black hair as neat as her tightly tucked plum blouse, awaited me with a smile.

"Welcome to The Inn at Yarrow Glen," she said as I approached. She pushed aside the newspaper she'd been reading. "I'm Constance. I'll be here all evening for anything you need."

"Hi. I'm not a guest here, but I heard there was a bar?"

"Yes. Down that hall and you'll see a red door on your right." She pointed to the hallway the man had taken.

"Thank you." I was about to go straight to The Cellar, but while I was here, I decided to do some marketing. I plopped the truffle fries on the reception desk and pulled out another cheese-hunt flyer from my purse. *Always be prepared.* "I'm Willa Bauer. I own the Curds and Whey cheese shop down the street and we're having a little event tomorrow if any of your guests are looking for something to do."

"You're the cheese lady?" Her eyes widened as if my head had sprouted string cheese.

"Uh, yes." I smoothed my hair, suddenly feeling self-conscious. She said nothing else, so I returned to the flyer she'd accepted but hadn't looked at. "So, can you keep the flyer somewhere visible for guests? Just for tomorrow?"

She finally noticed it in her hands. "Oh. Sure." She placed it to the side of her next to the *Glen Gazette* she'd been reading. Her glance landed on the newspaper, then slowly returned to me.

Now I understood. "I suppose you've read about the horrible murder that happened next to my shop."

She leaned forward. "It says you found the body." Whatever apprehension she had was quickly overtaken by morbid curiosity. "The Stewarts said they were so glad they didn't go to your cheese class that night. Oh, no offense."

I'd invited the couple who owned the inn to Thursday night's cheesemaking class, but they hadn't been able to make it.

"None taken. I understand." They were already associated with the place where he was last seen alive. I could understand why they'd be relieved not to be connected to where he was also discovered murdered.

"It's just so weird. Nothing like this ever happens here. Especially to someone you know," she said.

"You knew Guy Lippinger?"

"Not exactly, but I saw him here that night. I remembered him because he came in twice that day and he wasn't pleasant either time, I can tell you that."

His first visit to The Cellar that evening must've been before he came to my shop, based on what I saw . . . and smelled. "Did you see him when he left the second time?"

"I sure did. He was loud about it because Del cut him off. I called him an Uber but he walked off down the street before it got here. There's only so much I can do."

"Who's Del?"

"Our bartender. He used to not be allowed to throw him out, so he said it felt good."

"What do you mean he wasn't allowed to?"

She hesitated for the merest of moments for propriety's sake, then jumped right in. "The Stewarts bought the inn from the previous owners like three years ago. It was about the same time the restaurant down the street opened before it became Apricot Grille. Do you know where I'm talking about?"

"I do."

"Well, Guy did such a hatchet job on them, the poor restaurant didn't stand a chance. So you can imagine how nervous the Stewarts were that he'd come after us next."

As a business owner, I was well aware that new owners were especially vulnerable to bad reviews.

"He never did," Constance continued. "The locals have

been coming to The Cellar forever, so he probably knew it wouldn't make much difference what he said about it. But the inn could've been crushed by bad reviews."

So that's why the bartender wasn't allowed to kick him out. "What changed?"

"I don't know the details. Del refuses to tell me for some reason, but they told that manager from the new restaurant, and they don't even really know him."

"They told Derrick?"

"Is that his name?"

"From Apricot Grille?"

"Yeah. They didn't want another restaurant going bust because of Guy Lippinger."

"You don't know *anything* about what they told him?"

She bit her lip as if physically trying to keep herself from saying more. I waited in hopes that any willpower she was mustering would dissipate.

"All I can say is, they learned something about Guy they kept in their back pockets if he ever tried to go after the inn."

"A secret about him?"

She shrugged. "Must've been."

"Have any of you told this to the police?"

"Nooo." She shook her head vehemently. "The Stewarts don't want the inn associated with Guy Lippinger any more than it already is. They insist it's got nothing to do with the murder. We had to talk to that detective, which I didn't mind, because he's pretty hot for an older guy, but he only asked about the facts of the night of the murder."

I was in no position to argue the point, but secrets tended to be a good motive for murder. It was a theme that kept popping up, the first time from Guy himself that night.

"The Stewarts won't even let me do extra press," she continued, pouting her lips. "I've been kind of in demand, seeing as how I might've been the last person to see him alive. Except for the killer, of course." She looked past me. "Speak of the devil."

The killer? I turned to see who she was talking about.

CHAPTER 18

Walking in was Detective Heath. *Huckleberry.*

"It was nice meeting you," I said to Constance hurriedly, grabbing my truffle fries. I wanted to leave before she got the chance to spill the beans to Detective Heath that she'd been talking to me about the murder. But when I turned, he was directly in my path. I couldn't glide by with a quick wave.

"Hello, Detective," Constance called in a flirty voice.

"Hello, Ms. Yi," Detective Heath replied. Then he looked at me. "We meet again."

I suddenly felt like a teenager who'd been caught out past curfew. This was ridiculous. I was allowed to go anywhere I wanted. Still, I found myself explaining my actions. "I was looking for the way to the bar."

"Mind if I join you?"

Like I had a choice. "Of course not." I gave a short wave to Constance, who replied with a double thumbs-up, presumably for getting a drink with the hot police detective. If only she knew.

I found the red door down a short hall as Constance had directed me earlier. As soon as we opened it, the tranquility the inn's lobby had exuded turned on its heel.

Country music commingled with overlapping conversations, all of it becoming louder as we descended the steps.

The Cellar looked like an English pub plopped into a medieval dungeon. Wrought-iron ring chandeliers hung from the ceiling, the candle-like bulbs playing up the castle elements of the stone walls and floor. The room seemed to hold as many tables and chairs as would fit, leaving only narrow pathways to get to and from the bar. The back of the room beyond the long bar had been cleared for the acoustic band. The half dozen couples dancing in the small space in front of them didn't seem to mind occasionally bumping into one another. The crowd had a slow, unbothered vibe, much like the California country ballad the band was playing.

Several oak-lined arched nooks broke up the long wall, each with just enough space for booths for two to be tucked into. As we approached one of the nooks, a couple was just getting up to leave, so we snagged the table.

I was glad the nook had muffled the music a bit. "This is an interesting space down here. You don't usually see lower levels in California," I said.

"I heard it was originally built as a wine cellar."

"I can picture it. It's very different from Apricot Grille's bar. I see why they can co-exist in such a small town."

A server stopped at our table and cleared off the used glasses while she asked for our drink order. I ordered a white Burgundy off the cuff. I hadn't expected to be drinking tonight. I looked longingly at the bar, certain the man behind it must be Del. I wouldn't be talking to him tonight thanks to Heath babysitting me. The server left, weaving her way between tables to return to the bar.

"I know what you're thinking," Heath said, looking over at the bar, as well.

"Oh?"

"This was the last place he was seen alive, so it was one of the first places we checked out."

"Who?" I played innocent.

Heath ignored my pretense at obliviousness. "Anything you might want to know, we've already discovered."

"Maybe I just wanted a drink."

"And truffle fries?"

"Yes, and truffle fries." I opened the forgotten container. A hint of the earthy aroma escaped.

"Do you usually bring your own food when you go out to a bar?"

I shrugged. "I'm not as particular about my drinks as I am about my snacks." I pulled out a fry, delicately covered in parmesan, and made a point of eating it. It had gone room temperature, but it was still surprisingly delicious. "Mmm, these *are* good." I tipped the box toward Heath, but he declined my offer.

"It's dangerous for you to go around town asking questions," he said.

I was about to toss a quick retort at him, but the knife I found mysteriously stabbed in my cheese this morning still stuck in my mind. I briefly considered telling him about it, but there'd be nothing he could do about it now except be more overbearing. Instead, I tried getting him to open up.

"How about if I just ask you instead? It'll save us both some time. Anything you'd like to share?"

He scanned the tables around us, then leaned across ours closer to me. "This morning . . ."

"Yes?" I leaned in, too, not wanting to miss a word.

"A car sped through the school zone."

I sat back in frustration. "I meant anything important."

"Going slow through a school zone *is* important," he said, earnestly.

I rolled my eyes. "I mean about the case." I stared at him, willing a proper reply.

"Ohhh, about the case." He nodded, then broke the exaggerated pretense with a full-on grin.

It changed his face entirely, like a mask blew off and I suddenly became acutely aware that he was a person, separate from being a detective. A dangerously handsome person.

The server returned with our drinks, breaking the moment, thank goodness. I didn't know what to make of this new sensation. I shouldn't be tingly about a guy whose first name I didn't even know.

"A white Burgundy for you and a cranberry seltzer for the detective," she said as she set down the drinks. She smiled at Heath before walking off.

I grabbed my drink and took much more than a sip. I focused on my fries, afraid to look at him again and see more than the frustrating detective. "This wine actually goes really well with soggy truffle fries."

"Willa."

I dared to look at him again. Yup. Now I saw what Constance saw, except he wasn't an older guy to me. Not more than a few years, anyway. I wanted to down the rest of my wine, but refrained.

"You're going to have to trust me," he continued.

I wanted to trust him, but I also wanted to eat cheese seven hours a day—not everything I wanted to do was always a good idea. Case in point, I gulped some more wine.

"So tell me about yourself then," I finally said. "I'd like to know a little bit about the guy I'm supposed to trust."

"You want my résumé."

"Not exactly, but you know everything about me and I know nothing about you."

He didn't respond right away.

"Unless you'd rather talk about the case . . ." I happily offered.

That smile made a brief appearance again. "What do you want to know?"

Are you single?

I swatted away the unbidden thought.

"Do they make you wear that suit?" I said, instead. Although surrounded by wineries and vineyards, the majority of Yarrow Glen's residents were middle-class blue-collar workers or farmers and ranchers. Even the posh vineyard crowd didn't regularly wear suits. For men, dressed up was wearing a polo shirt with their jeans. "You don't exactly blend in."

"I'm not undercover. I don't mind standing out."

He certainly stood out in more ways than one.

I forced my thoughts to return to neutral conversation. "You said you're new to town too? Sorry, I was a little freaked out when I first asked you, so I don't remember your answer."

"I moved here around the new year. I worked on the San Francisco police force."

"That must be quite a change. What made you leave the city?"

He hesitated before saying too casually, "I needed a change of scenery."

I didn't press the issue, although I could sense there was more to his decision. When people would ask why I left Oregon, my stock answer was to become a cheese-monger. It wasn't a lie, but it wasn't the whole truth either.

I put my wine glass to my lips one last time and emptied it. Heath hadn't touched his cranberry seltzer. "Do you usually come to a bar to not drink?" If he was going to point out the bad excuse I used for coming to The Cellar, two could play that game.

A grin lit up his face again. Unlike Roman's, which always came on slowly, Heath's appeared without warning, catching me off guard each time.

"Maybe I just came for the music," he countered.

"Okay, then, let's dance." *Uh-oh. Tipsy Willa was taking charge.*

It was probably only due to his desire not to be one-upped, but to my surprise, he slid out of the booth and waited for me to do the same.

As soon as we snaked into the cramped area they'd parceled out for dancing, we were pushed closer together by the rhythmic crush of couples. A hint of his cologne made its way to my senses as his arm wrapped my waist and we linked hands. My body felt zapped by pins of electricity. I snuck a look at him, but once our eyes locked, I didn't look away. Neither did he.

This was a bad idea.

CHAPTER 19

Heath's hand slipped out of mine as soon as the song ended.

"We should get some air," he said.

He threw some cash on the table as we made our way upstairs and outside to the inn's porch. Heath stood with his hands on his hips, his suit jacket flared behind him, facing away from me. I waited for him to say something, but he only shook his head at nothing and looked down at his shoes. I caught a glimpse of his strong features in the glow of the porch light. His mouth was set in a grim line. It wasn't the expression I was expecting.

"Are you mad about something?"

He finally looked at me. "No. I just need you to promise me you'll stop nosing around."

"I don't know if I can promise you that. Not until my name's cleared."

"I'll have a harder time doing that if I have to keep track of you."

"Who asked you to keep track of me?" *Is that why he danced with me?* I stormed off the porch and down the sidewalk toward my apartment.

"Willa!" he called after me.

I could hear his footsteps behind me, but I kept walking until the traffic light on Main Street stopped me. If there hadn't been a police detective following me, I would've jaywalked through it, but all I could do was cross Pleasant Ave and wait for the pedestrian signal.

He caught up with me. "Willa, I didn't mean it like that."

I lasered in on the red hand illuminated in the cross-walk signal, willing it to change.

"This is a conflict of interest," he continued.

"Because you still suspect me?"

As soon as I took my eyes off of it, the signal began to beep its assent to walk.

"Because you're a part of an active investigation," he said, keeping up with my hurried steps.

"I understand perfectly, Detective Heath. Don't worry about it." I power walked the remaining block in silence, but his long strides easily kept up with me. "I'm going straight home to my apartment. I promise. You don't have to follow me."

"It's dark. I want to make sure you get home safely."

"I can take care of myself."

Chin up to prove it, I rounded the corner to the alley that ran along the side of my shop. I was stopped short by a cloud of dread that seized my chest like an invisible gas. The harsh building lights directed at the pavement only cut two circles in the darkness. This was where I'd found Guy Lippinger dead two days prior. The shadow of the scene crossed my mind whenever I had to pass it, but this was the first time I'd been out here this time of night since it happened. It was impossible for all my senses not to hit Replay.

"I'll walk you to your door," he said.

Even though I wanted nothing more than to get through

the alley with him by my side, my bruised ego wouldn't let me. "There's no need. It's just an alley." Then much to my own annoyance, I looked to him for reassurance.

"It's understandable to be spooked returning to the crime scene. You don't have to prove to me how strong you are." He reached out his hand for mine. The streetlight glinted off the band on the ring finger of his left hand.

Now I understood. Why didn't I think to look before? Why did he dance with me?

"Go home to your wife, Heath." My anger overrode my fear and propelled me down the alley briskly. When I got to the bottom of my apartment stairs, the motion detector my dad had insisted on installing blinked on, providing a ray of light leading up the steps. Maybe dads did know best.

I trotted up the steps to the deck and was inside my apartment in no time, locking the door behind me. What a night. And what a jerk!

I had to shake off these bad vibes. Tomorrow was the cheese hunt at Curds & Whey. It was imperative that it go off without a hitch, so I had to get some sleep. I went through the motions of my bedtime routine, but I knew sleep wasn't going to come. I couldn't get Heath out of my head.

And he wanted me to trust him? Ha!

Now I really had to solve this thing on my own. I took my pillow into the living room to get cozy on the love seat, turned on the TV, and carried Loretta's fishbowl to the wide bench I used as a coffee table.

"I don't care what Baz says, Loretta, I still think you're a girl, 'cause boys stink."

My stomach grumbled audibly during *Chopped*, which reminded me those tepid truffle fries weren't much of a dinner. Watching the Food Network broke the resolution I'd made eight minutes prior to stop late-night snacking. I deserved some comfort food tonight. I stopped fighting my hunger and went to scour the kitchen cupboards. I came up with an onion and a leftover baguette from today's goat cheese feast. Luckily I had pantry staples. With beef broth and sherry, I was able to whip up some French onion soup. What better food to be eaten alone? There was no delicate way to enjoy the long, salty strings of Swiss and provolone melted atop the slightly submerged sliced baguette. With only Loretta to judge me, I pulled and slurped with abandon until my soup crock was empty. Now I could try to sleep.

Switching off the corner lamp blanketed the living room in darkness, except for the faint glow of the measly parking-strip light. As I reached for my pillow on the love seat, a bright white spotlight reflected on the wall, making me jump like a skittish cat. It took me a second to realize it was the motion detector light that automatically clicks on when someone reaches my stairs. That hardly made me feel better. It meant someone was out there.

I dropped to all fours and crawled over to the window, peeking over the sill. The deck was vacant. Maybe the light had scared away whoever it was. This time I kneeled and plastered my cheek against the glass in order to see to the bottom of the stairs. There was someone there, and I recognized him immediately. It was Heath, sitting on a lower step. What was he doing here?

The light clicked off again. I slipped to the floor and sat with my back against the wall waiting for the spotlight to invade the room again, but it didn't. Was he just going to sit there all night? Was he here because he wanted to protect me or because he suspected me?

CHAPTER 20

Detective Heath was gone by morning. Any thoughts of him went out the front door with me, as I had a big day at the shop. Within a few hours of opening, a lively cheese hunt was in full swing. Advertising it on the cheese trail website seemed to have worked—customers who found Yarrow Glen and Curds & Whey for the first time arrived in waves.

Even customers who looked wary at first to participate ended up getting into the spirit of it, cheering along with us each time someone brought the correct cheese to the counter. People loved learning a fun fact while finding the corresponding cheese. For once, everyone else was as excited about cheese as I was. Even our grand opening hadn't felt this lively.

Vivian scurried up to the register holding a wedge of Parmigiano-Reggiano aloft in one hand and a clue in the other, like a contestant from *The Price Is Right* getting called to 'Come on down!' She handed me her clue. "Am I right?"

This cheese is made in only three Italian provinces and has a hard, pale golden rind and a straw-colored interior.

"That's correct," I announced, tapping the metal bell several times. The clanging was followed by a collective "Woo-hoo!" from the customers. Leave it to Mrs. Schultz to amplify the drama of the hunt by bringing in one of those reception-desk service bells. "You get fifteen percent off your purchase. Would you like to get this cheese or another kind?"

"I might as well try this one. I've never had it fresh, only the kind in that green canister."

"Then be ready for your tastebuds to be awakened. This is a very different product than what's in the container on the grocery store shelves. In Italy, to be called Parmesan by law it must have only three ingredients and it has to be produced within twenty hours from cow to cheese from the Parma/Reggio region of Italy."

"I had no idea. I'm excited to try it."

I gave the wedge to Mrs. Schultz to ring up Vivian's purchase. "Thanks for coming, by the way."

"Of course. What fun! Besides, you've brought me quite a few customers since your shop has been open. They keep telling me they sampled my bread here. I'm starting to think I should leave my bread at every shop."

"Like a trail of crumbs leading to your bakery."

"That's it!" Her laughter bubbled over and carried through the shop.

I tried to reconcile yesterday's fleeting suspicions of Vivian with the friendly woman I was beginning to get to know and really like. I wanted to think that maybe I'd gotten it wrong, and the person who murdered Guy wasn't one of my newfound friends.Unfortunately, the fact that the murder weapon could only have been taken from someone in class that night prevailed over wishful thinking.

Out of the corner of my eye I saw Birdie arrive. She

was welcomed by Archie, who was standing near the door to apprise customers of the cheese hunt rules.

"Oh look, Birdie made it," I said.

Mrs. Schultz and Vivian both noted her arrival.

"Your baguettes and flatbread worked perfectly with her goat cheese yesterday. I think she said she wanted to get some bread from you today." I stepped out from behind the counter so Vivian and I could say hello to Birdie.

Vivian didn't take my lead. Her ebullience vanished. "Hope wants to come by, so I need to get back to the bakery and take over for her. Thanks for the cheese." She took the Parmigiano-Reggiano and scurried out of the store, not even looking up to wave to Birdie on her way out.

"That was odd," Mrs. Schultz noted.

I agreed. "Did you get the feeling she didn't want to see Birdie? They seemed fine together at my class the other night. I wonder what that's about."

I went over to see Birdie on my own. I mentioned that she'd just missed Vivian to gauge her reaction, but all she said was she'd stop by her bakery later. If Vivian had a problem with Birdie, it didn't appear Birdie was aware of it.

A trio of friends who were up from San Francisco correctly guessed the Smiling Goats chèvre. They were excited to be introduced to the woman who made it.

I left Birdie regaling the customers with anecdotes about her goats and the cheesemaking process, and returned to help Mrs. Schultz with the next group of customers who were at the register. I was happy to see the jar for the Monster Cheddar Wheel guesses was filled with slips of paper and business cards.

"It seems like most of our customers have been from

out of town. What do you think, Mrs. Schultz? Have you seen anyone you know today?"

"Some. But you're right. From the conversations I'm hearing, most seem to be tourists."

"I'm glad the advertising worked, but I'm a little disappointed we're not getting more locals." Archie dressed as our mascot the other day must've not worked as well as I'd hoped. I wondered if the buzz about the murder was affecting business. I recalled Constance's initial uneasy reaction to meeting me. Tourists were great for business, but we wouldn't do well if we didn't get a foothold within the community.

"There's a local." Mrs. Schultz pointed out Roman, who was partaking in the free sample platter in the kitchenette.

I hadn't noticed him come in. The three women from San Francisco seemed to be checking him out, and I felt an unwanted pang of jealousy. I had mixed emotions about him, although apparently my subconscious was still attracted to him. Normally, I'd give him the cold shoulder, but under the circumstances I had to talk to him and find out why he had lied to me. I left my post to meet him.

"Thanks for coming," I said to him, trying to sound as neutral as possible.

"I wouldn't miss it. Sorry I couldn't get away sooner. Looks like your shop's doing well," he said, without looking at anyone but me.

I ripped my gaze from his and admonished my lack of self-control. I immediately reverted to my safe zone: cheese talk. "Yeah, everybody's having a great time. Most of the customers are using their discount to buy the cheese they found in the cheese hunt, which I'm happy about. I love when I can get people to buy types they might not ordinarily try."

"It's a clever game. Maybe I should try to be a little more creative with my marketing."

"I bet you know quite a bit about marketing, growing up in a wine-making family and all."

There, I said it.

He dropped his head, knowing he was busted.

"Why did you lie to me about it?" I said. "I directly asked you about the brand when I saw it in your store and you didn't say a peep about it being your family's wine."

"Listen, Willa—"

He stopped mid-sentence as soon as we both saw Detective Heath enter the shop. How did Heath know whenever I was about to get information? I noticed Birdie's attention was also fixed on him. Did she look nervous too?

He walked straight to me and Roman, and we greeted each other politely, if not awkwardly.

I kept my voice lowered. "This isn't the best time for more questions. As you can see, it's pretty busy."

Heath addressed Roman. "They told me at the meadery I could find you here."

"What can I do for you, Detective?" Roman said, seemingly unruffled.

"We should step outside."

I was relieved they wouldn't be talking about murder in my shop full of customers, but I was dying to go with them to find out what Heath wanted with Roman. They'd already questioned him once. Was he now their prime suspect? I wondered if my theory about his connection to Guy was right. Maybe I wasn't the only one Roman had lied to.

I felt like I should say something comforting to Roman as they left without another word, but I didn't know if he deserved to be comforted. My gaze briefly met Birdie's as we watched them leave together.

I waited another couple of minutes and then went to the open front door to see if I could eavesdrop. They'd walked across the street and were talking on the sidewalk in front of Roman's meadery.

Hope came bouncing up the sidewalk and brushed past me through the doorway. Archie's face lit up. I stepped the rest of the way outside to get some air.

I was relieved Roman wasn't being arrested and then mad at myself for being relieved. Didn't I want this murder to be solved? I was frustrated that the probable suspects were people I liked. Here I was mad at Roman for not being truthful with me and yet how truthful was I being with him? With any of them, for that matter? Vivian and Birdie had both been supportive of my shop already, and even Derrick tried to be a good sport by coming to my cheesemaking class. And my loyal employee Archie was head over heels for Hope, who was also on my suspect list.

I once again considered that maybe it wasn't one of them. Maybe somehow someone else had gotten their hands on my gift basket cheese knife and used it to kill Guy.

I went back inside still curious as to what Detective Heath wanted with Roman. Would Roman even tell me now that I'd called him out on lying to me earlier?

I tried to put it out of my mind and enjoy the success of the day. Birdie left a short while later just ahead of the crowd, and Hope left a smiling Archie.

While there was a lull, I did a quick inventory to make sure our remaining clues still had some corresponding cheese on the shelves. I was reaching an upper shelf when I heard a voice I thought I recognized.

"Is this something I need to be a part of?" It was Derrick speaking to no one in particular. To my surprise, he was standing in my shop holding up the flyer I'd given to him the night before.

Archie scurried away from him and was suddenly intent on straightening the front window display. He was probably paranoid about Derrick finding out that he'd snitched on him.

Ignoring Archie, Derrick walked over to me.

"It's something fun that I hoped you and your customers would share in if you were so inclined," I said.

"It's not the only reason you came by last night." He stared down at me waiting for me to respond. He was tall, like Detective Heath, and similarly felt no need to fill a silence. But unlike Heath, he had an underlying anxious energy about him that belied his lack of conversation. I sensed his impatience as he waited.

There was no making small talk with Derrick. "I wanted to talk to you about Guy."

"I already talked to the police. I went straight to the restaurant as soon as I left here that night. We had a big party that stayed past closing, so I was there well after eleven."

Defensive seemed to be Derrick's go-to mode.

"I wasn't asking about your alibi. I wanted to know more about Guy. You knew that he gave Roman's meadery a good review. Do you know anything about their relationship?"

"I only knew about the review because we prepped for the lawsuit."

"Why did he settle your lawsuit so quickly?"

"Because he was wrong."

"Come on, Derrick. He had a sudden change of heart?"

"The restaurant didn't deserve the review he gave it. You saw how busy we were last night. It's like that every night. No customer complaints."

"You don't have to convince me that he gave you a bad review for no reason. I personally saw how unreasonable he was. I want to know what you know about him. When you and your attorney were digging up stuff, did you find out anything else about him? What about old lawsuits that his parents may have been involved in?"

I still couldn't shake the coincidence that Birdie's family was thrown off their land because of Guy's family. She insisted her parents were fine with it, but if there was some kind of proof that they weren't fine with it—maybe a lawsuit—that motive could still be plausible.

"There was nothing that was relevant to me."

Derrick wasn't going to tell me anything he knew. I bet he didn't share his toys as a child either. I guess everybody couldn't be as loose-lipped as Constance. That reminded me of what she said about a secret involving Guy that the inn's owners shared with Derrick.

"Could it have anything to do with Guy's secret that the Stewarts shared with you?"

"How do you know about that? Did they tell you too? That information saved me, but that doesn't mean Guy wasn't wrong about the restaurant."

"Of course not. Listen, we're on the same side here. I didn't hear the details from them, only that they had something on him. Come on, Derrick. Tell me what you know about Guy."

His jaw muscles worked overtime. If he was internally wrestling with a decision to tell me something, I had to get him to do it.

"I swear, anything you tell me will stay between me and you," I promised.

Time slowed while I waited for him to say something. I seriously considered biting off a piece of cheese from one of the wedges on the table to pacify myself.

He scanned the room once more and then leaned in to speak. "Besides the fact that he was wrong and defamatory, he also had a secret that he didn't want known at any cost."

"Which was . . . ?"

"He was having an affair."

"An affair?" I wasn't sure what I expected to hear, but it wasn't that.

"It apparently started before he separated and he was desperate that his wife not find out. There was a lot of money at stake in the divorce. When I confronted him about the affair, he folded like a pup tent. He settled the lawsuit and wrote a retraction."

"I see. If his wife found out, she'd be able to get a lot more in the divorce."

"The amount he gave me to keep it quiet was a good deal for him in comparison. I mostly wanted the retraction."

"So who was it? Who was he having the affair with?"

Derrick shrugged and shook his head.

"You don't know or you're not saying?"

"It's not for me to say."

"What do you mean? She could be the one who killed him. Or his wife could've found out. This is important information. Did you tell the police?"

"No. And you swore it was between me and you."

"That was before I knew it was this important."

"Willa. Don't make me go against you."

Whoa. "Is that some kind of threat?"

"What happened here on Guy's last night looks bad for you. The police asked me about you. I said as little as possible, but I could change my mind."

"Why would you even say that? Why would you *do* that? You can't lie about it—there were four other people here that night."

"I could tell the police what happened in a way to make them wonder further about you. I didn't like Guy, and frankly, he probably got what he deserved. I don't care if anybody ever gets caught for the crime."

"Then why would you threaten to point the finger at me?"

"If it comes out that Guy dropped his lawsuit because I threatened to expose his affair, then my credibility goes out the window. Besides, in legal terms, that's called blackmail and I don't need to be in hot water with the police. Is this what I get for trying to help you out?"

"Okay, okay. Calm down. I won't tell the police. But I do think you should reconsider and tell them yourself."

"No chance."

Archie was handing clues to the latest stream of customers. I suddenly had no desire to spend any more time with Derrick.

"Thanks for the information," I said abruptly, and walked away, still feeling the sting from his sudden turn against me. I immersed myself in helping my customers and when I looked up again, he was gone.

By the time I locked the door after the last customer, I was wiped. It was a banner Saturday. Mrs. Schultz cashed out the register and Archie helped me get the shop back in order. Normally I'd go through the sales and inventory, but neither Archie nor Mrs. Schultz took their proper breaks today. I wanted to help them with restocking and cleaning so they could get home. Archie began sweeping, and Mrs. Schultz checked the cheese for remaining stickers and ditched the extra clues strewn here and there. I went to clean the kitchenette that we'd used for a second sampling station. As tired as I was, I was still on a bit of a high about the great day. *"Do good work and good things will come."* My parents sure knew what they were talking about.

I cleared one last platter from the island that was now devoid of all but a lonely square of cheese. When I picked up the plate, I found a piece of paper underneath. It was one of my flyers, turned upside down. On it, in block letters, was written: STOP SNOOPING OR YOU'LL BE NEXT.

CHAPTER 21

Detective Heath was in my shop for the second time that day, but this time I was glad to see him. I handed over the threatening note. He put latex gloves on before taking it by the corner and slipping it into a plastic bag. Oops. I guess I shouldn't have handled it . . . or passed it around to Archie and Mrs. Schultz.

I walked him through my day, hardly able to remember any of it now. He questioned Archie and Mrs. Schultz about seeing anybody near the platter the note was hiding under. Unfortunately, everybody had been near the platter—it had free food on it. Once he was done questioning them, I sent them home. It had been a long day for them too.

"We'll try to get prints off it, but I wouldn't hold out too much hope that we'll get anything conclusive," he told me when we were alone.

"What about handwriting samples? I know it's in block letters, but maybe there'd be enough of a similarity if you got the five suspects to write these words down?"

"The five suspects?"

"Come on, Heath. Detective," I corrected myself. "The

knife was missing from my gift basket. I made those baskets after we closed that day. That means someone who was here that night took it and used it to kill Guy. Personally, I don't want it to be any of them. I like them all. Well, except for Derrick, but he's got an alibi. Can't you make them copy the note to see whose handwriting it looks like?"

"I can't force private citizens who haven't been arrested to do anything."

"Okay, then, can't you *ask* them to?"

"I'm more curious about the contents of the note. Why would whoever wrote it ask you to stop snooping?"

"Because they're afraid of getting caught, obviously."

Heath kept his eyes on mine, but this time he was completely in detective mode. Here came the *I told you so*.

"I saw what you were trying to do last night at Apricot Grille and The Cellar. What other snooping have you been doing, Willa?"

"Nothing." Why was my voice suddenly so high? I cleared my throat. "Not much. I've asked a few questions."

"Such as . . . ?"

"I wanted to know more about Guy. And I asked if they'd seen or heard anything that night. I went about it carefully. It wasn't like I came out and asked them if they had an alibi. I wasn't *that* obvious." I rolled my eyes and my gaze landed on the note in the clear plastic. To his credit, Heath didn't point out that, apparently, I *was* that obvious. I shoved the memory aside of Roman's comment that I'd sounded like the police. "Okay, so maybe I wasn't as clever as I thought. I didn't get around to asking Birdie, but Vivian and Hope don't have alibis. Neither does Roman. Is that what you were questioning him about earlier?"

"No. You can't eliminate or include suspects solely based on alibis, anyway. There's a lot more involved to an investigation than assumptions and hearsay. You have to put all the pieces of evidence together, and that's not going to happen by asking them obvious questions and putting yourself at risk." Detective Heath softened. "Did any of them have the opportunity to put this note here today?"

"They were all here at some point in the day. Any one of them could've done it." The weight of the threatening note crashed down on me. "I hate this. I hate not being honest with them. I hate not knowing if they want to be friends with me or kill me." A fat tear spilled over without warning. I swiped it away, hoping Heath didn't notice.

He put a hand on my shoulder. *Oh no, he noticed.*

"Willa, I'm sorry this happened. You have to trust me."

"You keep saying that, but how can I trust you when you think I did it? I saw you come back to my apartment last night. Are you trying to find something against me? Is that why you came to The Cellar with me—were you hoping I'd trip up and say something incriminating?"

"I know you've been asking questions. This was exactly the kind of the thing I was trying to avoid by keeping a closer eye on you."

"Oh." I swallowed hard. He wasn't suspecting me, he was trying to protect me. I wrestled with whether to tell him that someone had tried to scare me off yesterday by leaving that large knife in one of my cheese wheels while I was alone in the shop. I'd almost convinced myself there was some other explanation, but after this, I couldn't pretend anymore.

Before I could muster up the courage to tell him, he said, "I don't mean to scare you more, but you see now how dangerous it can be to get entangled in this. It was just a warning note—it could've been worse."

Another lecture. I decided to keep the other threat to myself. I'd been scolded enough. But if he was this worried about me, it must mean he didn't consider me a suspect anymore. The note had frightened me, but feeling Heath's protectiveness and knowing he didn't believe I killed Guy blanketed me in relief.

"So will you check their handwriting? See if any of them match the note?" I asked.

"Sure."

I smiled. Maybe I *could* trust him to solve this murder soon.

"Do you have a piece of paper?" he asked, as he slipped his pen from the inside pocket of his suit jacket.

I grabbed one of the spare flyers from the counter. "Will this do?"

"Perfect." He flipped it over to the plain side and placed it on the sampling counter next to the threatening note. He handed me his pen. "If you don't mind being the first . . ."

"What?"

"I have to be thorough, make sure you didn't plant the note to throw suspicion off yourself."

"Are you serious?"

His face told me he was.

CHAPTER 22

I angrily complied with Detective Heath. Since there was nothing more to discuss after that, I was happy to see him leave. I didn't follow him to the door.

"Don't you think you should lock it behind me?"

"Since you think I wrote the note myself, I have nothing to worry about, do I?"

His hand slipped off the doorknob and he walked back to me. "I have to do my job. That doesn't mean I don't believe you might be in danger. I want you to stay safe. How many times do I have to say it?"

I didn't know what to believe. It wasn't until he was back at the front door and waiting for me that I gave in and locked it behind him.

A rap on the door window a few moments later made me practically jump out of my Keds. I turned around to see it was Archie. I unlocked the door again. He was followed by Mrs. Schultz and Baz.

"What are you guys doing here?"

"I saw them hanging around on the corner," Baz said. "They told me what happened."

"We didn't feel comfortable leaving you here by yourself after what was written on that note," Mrs. Schultz said.

"You three are the best," I said.

I didn't know who to hug first, so we ended up in a group hug.

"What did Detective Heath have to say about the note?" Mrs. Schultz asked.

"He seemed more concerned about what I might have done to warrant such a threat."

"At least he knows you're not a suspect now," Archie said.

"Don't be so sure, Archie. He thinks it's possible I wrote the note to throw suspicion off myself."

"What?" they shouted in unison.

"That's preposterous," Mrs. Schultz said.

"I'm not sure that's what he really believes, but the fact that I'm still in his mix of suspects means he's not any closer to finding who killed Guy than we are."

"You obviously hit a nerve with someone," Baz said. "Are you going to leave the investigation up to Detective Heath now?"

That was the question I'd been asking myself since I'd found the note. There was only one answer.

I looked around the shop while my memory flipped through a catalogue of the tastiest melting cheeses. I knew just where I kept them. I grabbed my three choices and snatched a couple of spare baguettes from yesterday, and brought them to the kitchenette. I unlocked the cabinet under the counter and took out a bottle of dry white wine I was storing for future classes.

"What are you doing?" Baz asked. He, Archie, and Mrs. Schultz followed me to the rear of the shop.

"I'm making fondue. The three of us didn't get a proper lunch break today and I, for one, can't think clearly on a cheese-less stomach."

"Well, all right!" Archie cheered.

In no time, the Gruyère, fontina, and Gouda cheeses melted into a decadent gooey base in which to dip Vivian's tangy sourdough baguette, which I cut into substantial cubes. It was the best use for day-old bread, as it wouldn't fall apart once it was slathered in cheese fondue.

The four of us dunked our skewers in the indulgent sauce without any attempt at being delicate. Cheese was my fuel, and in melted form, it became high-octane. I could feel my brain clearing and my body recharging. It seemed to lift everyone else's spirits, as well. I told them what Derrick had said about the affair and we batted around theories.

"You never answered my question," Baz said after downing a quick four pieces of bread dripping with the rich cheese trio. "Are you going to stop trying to find out who killed Guy?"

"You can't give up," Archie said.

"Archie, we don't want Willa to be in danger," Mrs. Schultz said.

"I didn't say that."

"It's okay, Archie. I feel the same way. I'm not giving up. I need to go about it a little more carefully, that's all. I wish I knew which direction to go in. The answers I'm getting aren't eliminating anybody."

Mrs. Schultz's fondue method was to dab the bread on the surface of the cheese three times until it was partially coated. She was dab, dab, dabbing another piece when she asked, "Do you still think what happened here after your class Wednesday night was the reason Guy was killed?"

"It has to be because he was going to reveal that secret."

"Too bad he didn't get it out." Archie went for the full dunk, until the bread was no longer recognizable.

"Do you remember if Guy was looking at anyone in particular when he said he knew someone's secret?" Baz said.

"What did Guy say that night exactly? Who looked the most nervous?" Mrs. Schultz wanted to know.

"I don't remember. If I had known he was going to be killed for saying what he did, I would've paid closer attention."

Mrs. Schultz abandoned her skewer, her hazel eyes alight with an idea. "Why don't we do a reenactment of that night? Maybe it'll trigger a memory you've forgotten. Something could come to light."

"I suppose." I wasn't very optimistic.

"Archie, you'll play Derrick. Baz, you'll play Roman until you come in as yourself," Mrs. Schultz directed.

"This is very meta," Baz said.

"I'll play Birdie and Vivian. Willa, you play Guy."

"Who plays Willa?" Archie asked.

"I guess she can play both parts."

"How will we know when she's being Guy or when she's being Willa?" Baz asked.

"Maybe we need some costumes," Archie suggested.

I interjected, "I was pretty useless as myself the first time. I mostly followed him around anyway. I'll just be Guy."

"Good idea. It's more important what Guy did and how the others reacted." Mrs. Schultz went into full director mode. "Let's take it from when Guy was pounding on your door. Where was everyone standing, Willa?"

I thought back. "Everyone was standing exactly where we are around the island when I went to see who was at the door."

"So now she's Willa again?" Archie asked.

Mrs. Schultz tried to keep her cool. "Oh for heaven's sake, let's just begin after he enters the shop."

"Okay then, you guys are here in the kitchenette and I'm up front." I moved to the front of the shop and went straight for the wedges on the center table. "He's making comments about the cheese and ruining my displays." I moved to the second display table, but left my displays alone. I didn't need to be a method actor.

"Are we still back here?" Baz called from the kitchenette.

"I think so," I said. "I was focused on what Guy was doing. I had no idea who he was. Oh, wait, Derrick told me who he was, so Derrick came up here."

I pointed to where Derrick had been standing. Archie moved from the kitchenette to the other side of the table to take his spot.

"And then the others followed just a little behind him." Mrs. Schultz and Baz moved closer to us.

"Let's see, Guy moved over here . . ." I went over to the refrigerated case and grabbed a log of cheese from it. "He said, 'I don't like where you get your cheese from,' or something like that."

"He said it when he was holding that one?" Baz said.

"I'm not sure which one he was holding exactly. He reached into here is all I know." I looked at the log in my hand. It was a Smiling Goats chèvre. "This case has Birdie's cheese."

"So he could've had something against Birdie," Baz said. "You've suspected Birdie before."

"She said her family was fine being kicked off their land and having to leave their farm, but I don't know if I buy that. I think there could be bad blood between them."

"What happened next?" Mrs. Schultz said.

Now that I realized she might be onto something, I was a little more enthused than when we'd started. "Okay, so now he started saying he didn't like the company I kept. No, wait. This is when Hope came in."

"Where did she end up?"

"She didn't come in any farther than the sampling counter." *Where the gift baskets were.*

"Willa?" Baz snapped me out of my thoughts. "What happened then?"

"Uh, she and Vivian got into a disagreement, then I went back to begging Guy to come back. That's when he said he had a secret to tell. He was looking at all of them, except for Hope, since she was behind us."

"And what are we doing at this point?" Mrs. Schultz asked.

I thought back on how they had reacted. "They were quiet, all except for Derrick. He challenged him about something." I tried to recall what it was. "I don't remember what."

"Did anybody look scared?" Archie asked.

"Not that I can think of. I was still trying to convince Guy to give me a second chance, so I wasn't paying too much attention to anybody else."

"Is that when Baz came in?" Mrs. Schultz asked.

"Am I myself now?" Baz said, ready to barrel through the door again like he did that night.

"No," I said. "Roman was here."

"Where?" Baz asked.

"Here, he moved up next to Guy." I motioned Baz to stand next to me. "He told him he had too much to drink and tried to get him to leave."

"So Roman kept Guy from revealing his secret?" Baz said.

"I wouldn't say that."

"You just said he interrupted him."

"You're right. I guess I didn't think about it like that. He was trying to calm him down, but he and Derrick were pretty insistent on ushering him out. At the time, I just thought they were being chivalrous."

Archie came and stood on the other side of me, still playing Derrick's role.

"So it was Derrick and Roman who wanted him to leave most of all?" Mrs. Schultz said.

I thought about it again. "That's right."

"Then it must be Derrick or Roman," Archie said eagerly. "But Derrick has an alibi." His enthusiasm quickly deflated.

"Detective Heath said it wasn't smart to entirely count on alibis. But if we can't build on what we know, what have we got?" I said.

"Don't forget about Birdie," Baz said. "You suspected her before and Guy was probably holding her cheese when he said he didn't like where you got your cheese from."

"Birdie could have a motive for killing him because of her parents' farm, but Guy talked about secrets. What secret could he have on her? Why would she suddenly decide that night to take my cheese knife and kill him?"

"Maybe it had to do with Guy's own secret—the affair," Mrs. Schultz said. "Could he have been having an affair with Birdie?"

"Birdie said she knew him in high school. You hear about people rekindling their high school romances all the time," I said. "Mrs. Schultz, do you recall Guy and Birdie dating in high school?"

"I stayed out of *that* kind of drama," she said.

"What about Vivian?" Baz suggested. "Her bakery is one of the few he left alone. Maybe that's the reason—because *she* was the one he was having an affair with."

I hadn't considered Vivian, but now that he said it, I could see the possibility. She was kind of like the sexy-librarian-in-glasses stereotype—under her bandana and apron was a vivacious woman. As far as I knew, she wasn't romantically linked to anybody else.

"There's just one problem with that scenario," Mrs. Schultz said. "Guy paid off Derrick to *keep* his secret. He even wrote a retraction."

"You're right, Mrs. Schultz. It doesn't make sense that he'd be the one to tell that secret now," I agreed.

"Unless they broke up," Archie chimed in. "Then all bets are off. After I broke up with a girl in high school, she said pretty nasty things about me."

"There's a fine line between love and hate," Baz agreed.

"Good point, Archie. They could've had a falling out since the time he paid off Derrick." I thought about it some more. "But the article I read yesterday in the *Glen Gazette* referred to his 'estranged wife,' which means the divorce hasn't gone through. Revealing the affair would still hurt him financially."

"Okay then, what about Hope? She was here too," Baz said. "Could she and Guy have been . . ."

"No way. I would know it," Archie insisted. "We talk all the time. Willa said Guy wasn't even looking at her when he was talking about secrets. Right, Willa?"

"That's right. I think if something was going on with them, she'd have been uncomfortable suddenly seeing him in my shop. She only seemed concerned to talk to Vivian." For Archie's sake, I hung onto anything that might clear her as a suspect. I didn't mention her proximity to the gift basket cheese knives.

"Sorry, Arch," Baz said. "Older rich guy, younger woman—I thought maybe . . ."

"Not Hope." Archie crossed his arms. "Her mom left her the bakery in her will when she turns twenty-one, so it'll be hers this summer. She doesn't need anybody's money. She wouldn't do that, anyway."

"Sorry, dude. I didn't mean any offense. I was just throwing it out there."

Archie's stiffened posture relaxed at Baz's apology and they fist-bumped each other in forgiveness.

Mrs. Schultz counted on her fingers. "If Guy had no connection to Hope and it's not about his affair and we're still counting out Derrick because of his alibi, who does that leave?"

We all looked at one another, knowing the answer even before Baz said it.

"Roman."

I hated this conclusion. Roman, the one who lied to me about who his family was. The one who might've made some deal with Guy that he couldn't follow through on. The one Detective Heath interviewed a second time earlier today. The one who made sure Guy didn't reveal his secret that night.

I tried to separate the facts from my gut feeling that he was innocent. Could I trust my instincts, or was it because I liked him that I believed he didn't do it?

"Gosh, I hate to think it," Mrs. Schultz said.

"Me too," Baz agreed, looking glum. "He's always been a nice guy."

"I'd much rather it be Derrick," Archie said. "I would've put my money on him."

"I could see Derrick writing that note. He didn't have

any trouble threatening me earlier when he didn't want me telling Detective Heath about Guy's affair." It still chilled me to think about it.

"Maybe it could still be him, then?" Archie said, sounding hopeful.

"I suppose it's possible. We can't rule out anybody for certain yet. This reenactment made me remember more than I thought, but we're still left with unanswered questions."

"Like what was going on with Vivian earlier today?" Mrs. Schultz brought up.

"She definitely seemed to be avoiding Birdie. She got along perfectly well with her during my cheese-making class, so I don't understand it. It could be nothing. She said she had to get back to the bakery because Hope wanted to come to the shop to participate in the cheese hunt."

"She was rushing back for Hope?" Archie seemed surprised.

"That's what she said. Why?"

"When Hope wants something, her aunt usually does the opposite. That's what Hope says, anyway. Like when Hope wants an extra day off, Vivian makes sure there's something special to do at the bakery, so that Hope isn't able to take off that day. Hope says her aunt always wants to be in control of everything."

From my conversation with Hope, it seemed she didn't understand all the responsibilities of owning a bakery, so I took what Archie said with a grain of salt.

"I did some work there last fall for a few weeks when they had a roof leak, ripping up and laying new floors and fixing some of the walls," Baz said. "I hate to talk about my clients, but from what I saw, Vivian was pretty tough on her. There were a few times Hope pitched in to put up wallboard in her apartment. She was surprisingly handy and wanted to do it, but Vivian only wanted her to work in the bakery, even if there weren't any customers."

"Vivian still treats her like she's got to tell her everything. Hope should have more say," Archie said.

I didn't want to tell Archie that Hope should feel lucky Vivian's watching out for her and their business, especially if Hope was going to be taking over the bakery soon. It was something Hope would have to realize for herself. I chalked up Vivian's behavior toward Hope to tough love. She did come to the cheese hunt after Vivian returned to the bakery, so I didn't think Vivian lied about her reason for leaving. I still thought it would be worth asking her about her reluctance to see Birdie.

"Archie, tomorrow morning, why don't you let me pick up the bread?" I said.

"So you're not giving up?" Archie replied, knowing perfectly well why I wanted to go to the bakery.

"Not a chance."

Since it was dark out, Baz offered to stick Mrs. Schultz's bike and Archie's skateboard in the back of his pickup truck and drive them home. I finished up the dishes and went upstairs to my apartment.

I had to admit, I wasn't feeling as brave as I let on. On such a busy day as we had, I'd normally be so desperate for my bed, I'd brush my teeth, skip my nighttime beauty routine, and conk out immediately. But not tonight. I padded into the living room with my favorite pillow and moved Loretta's fishbowl onto my makeshift coffee table. I scrunched up on the love seat next to it with Grandma's throw blanket over me. I was going to turn on one of my favorite old black-and-white movies, like *Rebecca* or maybe a classic Hitchcock. However, *Chopped* was already queued up and I'd woken Loretta, so I started an old Tournament of Champions series of episodes. Besides, I didn't need to see handsome men in suits and be reminded of Detective Heath.

"You've got good taste, Loretta. Ted Allen is sweet. Look how sad he always looks when he has to chop a contestant. I wonder if it haunts him. He must hear himself say that in his sleep: 'You are chopped.' I bet he feels bad. I wonder if Heath feels bad when he's 'just doing his job.'"

I fell asleep on the love seat and dreamt I was just about to kiss Roman when Heath stood between us and told him he was chopped.

CHAPTER 23

I awoke sometime in the night with a charley horse and hobbled to my bed just to toss and turn fitfully for the remaining few hours of sleep. I realized as soon as my alarm blared that I'd forgotten to reset it to an hour later for Sunday store hours, but there was no going back to sleep. I remembered I volunteered to get the day's bread before work anyway so I could talk to Vivian. I went over in my mind how I was going to bring up Birdie's name to her. I had to be a little more casual about asking questions since I'd proven to be so bad at it.

I was going through my script to Vivian in my head as I rounded the corner from my alley onto the sidewalk and practically slammed into Roman. I stumbled to avoid the crash and had to be propped up by him. When I got my footing, we were both holding onto each other. I let go as if I'd touched a scalding skillet handle just out of the oven.

"Sorry," he said, letting go, as well.

"No, it was my fault. I wasn't paying attention."

"I was coming to see you. We didn't get a chance to talk yesterday." He gestured for us to sit on the sidewalk bench in front of my shop. After the verdict we'd come to last night, I felt rigid with apprehension.

"I guess I should've brought you a coffee or some kind of peace offering," he said.

"The truth will suffice."

"Touché. I'll get right to it, then. So you found out my family owns Enora vineyards, named after my grandmother. I grew up learning about wines and I worked at the vineyard all my life. I know I should be grateful to be born into a successful family business, but I wanted to create something of my own. When I got into mead making, I found my passion."

"Why keep it a secret?"

"I've tried to do other things in the past, other endeavors I guess you'd say, but I was always judged by who my family is. People either thought I'd been handed everything so I couldn't possibly be a hard worker, or they thought I should be a lot further along than I was. When I came to Yarrow Glen to open my meadery, I made a decision that I wanted to be solely judged on my character and my business. It's as simple as that, but I understand that you feel misled, and I'm sorry."

Great. Now I couldn't be mad at him. Breaking away from your family was something I could relate to and something Baz was doing too. And darn it, I admired them both for it.

"I get it." Now I was the one feeling guilty. "You have every right to keep your private life private."

"Thanks for understanding. As a mea culpa, ask me anything. I'll be up front with you."

He deserved to be let off the hook for keeping this secret, but I needed some answers about another. "If you insist. . . . What did Detective Heath want to talk to you about yesterday?"

He hesitated and I got the feeling he was sorry for giving me carte blanche. "He wanted to know more about Guy."

"What does he think you know?"

Roman shifted on the bench. "They were looking into his bank accounts. He'd been taking large sums of cash out periodically and they wanted to know if I knew where it went."

"Why would they think you would know what Guy Lippinger spent his money on?"

He shrugged. "Beats me."

"Well, *do* you know?"

"I have no idea. Why would I?"

"The police must think you might know or else they wouldn't have asked."

"I'm assuming they asked everybody who knew him. If you've got something to say to me, Willa, just say it. You think I'm guilty of something just because I was nice to the guy?"

"Of course not." *Not when you put it that way.* "Aren't you nervous the police might suspect you? They suspect me, too, if that's any consolation."

"It's not. I don't want either of us to be in this bind."

"If only we had alibis like Derrick."

"I do."

"You have an alibi? But you told me you were alone in your apartment."

"I said I was in my apartment. I didn't say I was alone."

I could feel the heat spreading up my neck and blooming on my cheeks. "I see."

"It's not anything serious."

"You don't have to explain anything to me, Roman."

"She's an old friend—"

"Honestly, you don't need to explain. I shouldn't have

assumed." For the first time, I didn't want to hear any details about that night. "I have to get my bread from Vivian before I open my shop." I popped up from the bench, but he caught me by my hand.

"Hey, you said you wanted me to be honest."

"You're right. Absolutely. Thank you for your honesty." I tried to leave him with a smile, but my emotions wouldn't cooperate. I pulled my hand out of his and walked down the sidewalk toward Rise and Shine without looking back. I couldn't decide if I was more disappointed with him or with myself. Vivian had warned me. A lot of good it did me to keep him at arm's length. Knowing he was with someone else stung just as much as if I'd admitted to myself that I was starting to have feelings for him.

I berated myself all the way to the bakery, so that when I stepped inside, I didn't remember having walked there. The aroma of warm bread and sugar snapped me out of my daze. The same cashier who wasn't Hope was behind the counter helping the half dozen customers on her own. The kitchen door swung open and Vivian came bustling through with a tray of bread.

"Willa, I'm glad you're here," she said, as she tipped the tray toward a wide basket and slid the bread into it.

Crud. Roman threw me so off course, I forgot what I'd rehearsed. I hurriedly collected my thoughts.

"Hi, Vivian. I'm picking up the bread today instead of Archie."

"Have you spoken with Archie this morning?" she asked, adjusting her royal blue bandana that held her red hair back and her bangs in place.

"Not yet. Why?"

Vivian called me over to the side counter, where we each leaned across it to speak in private. "Hope didn't come in this morning. I thought maybe Archie would know where she is."

"Have you heard from her?"

"I've been calling and texting. She texted me back once, short and icy. She gets like this with me sometimes, but I usually know what it's about. This time I'm in the dark."

"I'll ask Archie when I see him."

"Thanks."

Before she walked away, I asked, "Did Birdie come by yesterday?"

"No, why?"

"She's going to be setting up some farm tours and she loved the bread I had for my tastings. She said she wanted to talk to you about ordering some."

"Ah." Vivian nodded and said nothing further.

So I wasn't imagining her odd response to Birdie yesterday. I wasn't sure how else to approach it, so I decided to take Roman's cue and go with honesty. "Can I say something, Vivian?"

"Sure."

"It seemed like you were trying to avoid Birdie yesterday. You guys seemed friendly enough at the cheese-making class, so it was sort of odd to me."

Vivian was suddenly focused on brushing the flour off her apron. After a few moments, she said, "I'm feeling a little uncomfortable around her, because I'm not sure what to do. Maybe it's a good thing you brought it up. I need someone to talk to about it."

"You can talk to me."

"I'm not friends with Birdie, but I know she's well respected in town. I wouldn't want to do anything to hurt her."

"What do you mean?"

She looked behind her and for a moment I thought she was going to say she had to get back to work while my curiosity was at its zenith.

"I saw her arguing with Guy Lippinger," she finally blurted out.

There was no hiding my surprise. "The night he was killed?"

"No, a few days before that. I mind my own business, so I put it out of my head, but now that he's been murdered, I've been wrestling with my conscience. I didn't tell Detective Heath about it, but maybe I should have. It could be nothing, but . . ."

"It could be something," I finished.

She nodded.

"Did you pick up on what they were arguing about?"

"Not in actual words, but their body language said it was personal. Intimate, even."

Intimate. "I think you should tell the police. If it's nothing, they'll get it sorted out."

"All right. I'll go this afternoon. Right now, I'm one person short and Jasmine hasn't been working for us for that long."

"Are you going to be able to manage?"

"You know my motto: 'Take one problem at a time.' Right now we're okay."

"I'll talk to Archie and let you know about Hope."

"Thanks. She tends to be a drama queen, but she usually warns me what the drama's about, at least."

I left Vivian's with my day's bread: two loaves of molasses enriched pumpernickel. I crossed the street and saw Baz coming out of the bookshop café with an extra-large, fancy iced-coffee drink. He spotted me and waited for me to catch up.

"Having a little coffee with your morning whipped cream?" I teased him.

"Until they put caffeine in milkshakes, bottoms up." He made a show of taking a huge sip from the straw, cheeks sucked in.

"I'm glad I caught you before work," I said.

"I only have one job later today. I try to take it easy on Sundays."

"In that case, walk with me. I've got loads to tell you."

The high-pitched trill of a bell turned our attention to the street. It was Mrs. Schultz, skirt tucked between her bottom and her bicycle seat, pedaling past us to Curds & Whey. We met her at the door as I fumbled to unlock it with the bundle of bread in my arms. Once inside, I filled them both in on what Vivian had said about Birdie.

"So maybe Birdie was the one having an affair with Guy," Baz said.

"At the least, she lied to me about not having kept in touch with him. *Something* was going on," I said.

They followed me to the kitchenette where I sliced one of the rich brown pumpernickel loaves and then cut it into single-bite servings. I planned on highlighting our Danish, German, and Swiss Tilsit cheese, a bolder counterpart to Havarti. Tilsit cheese was made by accident when the Dutch, settling in East Prussia, were trying to recreate their beloved Gouda. The caves of that area where it was aging were damp and infected it with unintended molds, yeasts, and bacteria, which created a new cheese they named after the town. For sampling, it needed an equally bold bread like the tangy, deep-flavored pumpernickel.

"Maybe we were wrong about Roman," Mrs. Schultz said.

"I have some news about that too." I told them why Detective Heath had questioned Roman a second time.

"Any guesses as to what the cash was for?" Baz asked.

"I was thinking, you know how Guy settled Derrick's lawsuit?"

"Yeah," they said in unison.

"What if Derrick got greedy? Maybe he thought that if Guy was willing to settle a lawsuit because of the affair, he could be blackmailed for more."

"Maybe everyone's been putting too much stock in Derrick's alibi." Baz sucked up the last of his sugary coffee drink.

"Oh no." Mrs. Schultz nervously began rubbing the tassels of her summer scarf between her fingers like worry beads.

"What's the matter?" I asked.

"Now I'm worried about Archie," she said.

"What do you mean? Where is he, anyway?" It wasn't like him to be late for work.

"He texted me this morning just in case he ended up running a few minutes late. He said he was going to Apricot Grille to talk to his friends who work there. He wanted to see if they'd heard any gossip about Derrick."

"I don't like that," I said. "If Derrick's a killer, I don't want Archie over there asking about him. We promised his mother we'd watch out for him. Mrs. Schultz, do you mind working solo for a bit?"

"Of course not."

"Come on, Baz. Let's go find Archie."

CHAPTER 24

❦

I was too worried to even walk the long block to Apricot Grille. We hopped in Baz's pickup truck instead. I kept my eyes focused on the sidewalks for Archie in hopes he was already en route to Curds & Whey. He wouldn't be hard to spot, as most of the shops were just opening and the sidewalks were still sleepy. When we stopped at the red light at the corner of Pleasant and Main—the only traffic light in Yarrow Glen—I almost hopped out of the car. I could see Apricot Grille on the opposite corner, its modern black and gray exterior setting it apart from most of the older downtown buildings. They served Sunday brunch, so the covered patio along Main was starting to fill up once again.

My phone dinged and I immediately checked my texts in case it was Archie or Mrs. Schultz.

"Is it Archie?" Baz asked.

"No, it's Vivian. She hasn't seen Hope since last night and she's asking again if I've talked to Archie about it."

"Hope's missing?"

"Not missing. They've texted, but I guess they're in some kind of tiff."

"She's sure nothing has happened to her? There *is* a

murderer loose in town. Anyone can send a text from Hope's phone."

"I never thought of that."

"Maybe Vivian's starting to think that too. She doesn't seem the type to admit if she's worried. She's a tough cookie." Baz snorted at his pun.

"You're probably right. I'll let her know that as soon as we find Archie at the restaurant, I'll ask him about Hope."

The light turned green and Baz's truck jumped through Main Street with a clear shot to Apricot Grille.

"Park in the back of the lot," I directed Baz. "If Archie came to talk to his friends, he probably went in through the alley to the service entrance."

We hopped out of Baz's pickup and saw Birdie walking from the back alley of the restaurant to her car. I waved and called to her. I was itching to ask her about her argument with Guy, but now wasn't the time. I was more concerned about Archie at the moment. She nodded when she saw me and we met up. Baz hung behind.

"You're a regular in town these days," I said to her.

"No kidding. This was an emergency run to drop off more cheese. Derrick miscalculated how much cheese they'd need to make those goat cheese balls he's adding to the menu.

"That's great that he's using your cheese for it."

"Thanks to you introducing us in your class."

"Glad I could make the connection for you. Listen, did you happen to see Archie while you were inside?"

"The kid who works in your store?"

"Yes. You remember him?"

"Sure, but I didn't see him inside. Sorry."

"That's okay."

"I gotta run. It was nice seeing you again!"

She walked off to her car, leaving me with my questions. Baz caught up with me.

"Where is he?" I asked, getting more worried by the minute.

"Maybe Birdie just didn't see him. She doesn't really know him."

"Could be. I hate to go inside. The last thing Derrick wants to see is me in his kitchen again. And if the hostess from two nights ago is working again, I won't get past her either."

"If Archie's trying to stay under the radar when he talks to his friends, you'd be giving him away. Why don't I go in?"

Just then we saw one of the kitchen staff in an apron exit the rear service door and walk our way. He lit a cigarette and disappeared into the eight-foot-high wooden dumpster enclosure. Baz and I followed. As we walked around to the opposite side so we could enter, I was surprised to see the wide gate crack open and Archie emerge with another aproned staff member, this one close to Archie's age. He was just as surprised to see us.

"Am I that late for work?" Archie grabbed his phone from his board shorts' pocket to check the time.

"No, you're fine. We were just concerned."

"Remember, you promised," the guy who'd exited said to him.

"I got you," Archie replied.

They fist-bumped and the guy walked back down the alley and into the restaurant.

"What was that about?" I said.

Archie looked back at the enclosure where the other employee had gone and tipped his head toward the parking lot, directing us away from the dumpster enclosure.

"I don't want anybody to overhear," he said when we were far enough away. "Derrick's alibi is fake. He left the restaurant for at least twenty minutes that night."

"You're sure?"

"He told the hostess that he had to go and pick up something they ran out of. He wanted her to cover for him just in case anyone noticed him gone, because he didn't want anyone knowing he hadn't ordered enough. Then when the police came around after Guy was murdered, he told her to keep it secret."

"Why did she? Was she afraid for her job?"

"They're in a relationship. I guess something happened the other night, though. She was mad at him and it came out when she was complaining to my friend Lester about him."

"That was who you were just talking to?"

Archie nodded.

"We have to tell the police," Baz said.

"We can't. I promised Lester I wouldn't tell," Archie said, his forehead creasing with worry.

"*We* didn't promise him," Baz said.

"He said he'd just deny it. He's afraid for his job. He's got a new baby." Archie looked at us, his brown eyes pleading.

Drats. "Maybe we can get the hostess to tell the police."

"They're back together as of last night, so she threatened Lester not to tell."

We stood in the parking lot, stumped. Archie's phone pinged. He glanced at it.

"It's just Hope," he said.

"Hope! I almost forgot. Does she say where she is? Vivian's been looking for her all morning," I told him.

"What do you mean? She hasn't been at the bakery?"

"No. Vivian's getting worried about her, and frankly, so are we."

Archie read the text. "It just says she wants to talk."

"Text her back. Find out what's going on."

Archie's thumbs moved at lightning speed across his phone. We all stared at it, waiting. It pinged again. "She wants me to meet her at the park. She didn't say what's going on. I'll tell her I can meet at two o'clock when I get my break."

"You don't have to wait that long. Go back and help Mrs. Schultz at the shop now and as soon as I get back, you can go meet her. Tell her it won't be long."

"You sure?"

"Yes. You've gone above and beyond your duties today."

"Okay, thanks. What are you going to do about Derrick? You can't tell him or the police what you know."

"We won't tell them. I promise."

Archie nodded. He retrieved his skateboard that was propped against the dumpster enclosure and rode out of the parking lot toward Curds & Whey.

"You're really not going to tell Detective Heath about this?" Baz said, looking skeptical.

"I don't want to be responsible for someone losing their job. If they're going to deny it, it won't do much good anyway, and Heath will just lecture me about butting into the investigation again."

"We can't just sit on this."

"I don't plan to. We'll have to find another way."

We were about to retreat to Baz's truck when we heard the bang of the service door again. This time it was Derrick exiting out the back of the restaurant. He strode straight to the dumpster. Baz and I hurried to hide behind the enclosure where we heard Derrick's raised voice yelling about dishes piling up. I peeked around to see the chastised dishwasher who'd taken a smoke break hustle back to the restaurant, passing the hostess from the other night who was coming to join Derrick. Baz and I each put an ear to the wood, but we couldn't hear any conversation.

I came out of our hiding spot and waved on Baz to follow me around to the front of the enclosure where the wide gate was unlatched. We still couldn't hear anything.

My impatience won out. I motioned to Baz that I was going in. I opened the gate just enough to allow room for me to slip inside. I instantly regretted it.

CHAPTER 25

The hostess, her back against the side of the enclosure, was locking lips with our suspect. They immediately sensed my presence in the tight space and parted.

"What are *you* doing here again?" she said. "Derrick?" She looked at him accusingly for an answer.

He raised his hands in innocence.

Her mouth tightened, her lipstick now slightly smudged from the make-out session. She stepped past me and forcefully pushed open the gate, knocking it into Baz on the other side. With no apology, she marched around him and back to the restaurant, her high heels clicking with each rapid step on the uneven pavement. Baz joined me in the enclosure.

"So what *are* you doing here?" Derrick said, plucking an electronic cigarette out of his pocket.

"I could ask the same of you," I replied. A large dumpster sat in the center of the enclosure with barely enough room to squeeze around it if you had to. The front area where we were standing was maybe six feet deep from dumpster to door. The stench of garbage that seeped from the lidded dumpster wasn't horrendous, but it certainly wouldn't be my first choice for a romantic tryst. "You guys . . . hang out here?"

"I don't like our customers who are coming or leaving the restaurant to see my employees smoking. You didn't answer my question. Why are you stalking me?"

As I coaxed my nerve to confront him, my stomach did somersaults. Was it because I was scared or because of all the cheese I'd been stress eating lately? I was glad Baz was with me.

"I think you know why we're here," Baz said.

He ignored Baz and said to me, "I figured you wouldn't give up."

"So you're admitting you wrote the threatening note?" I said, finding my voice.

"What threatening note? I shouldn't have even told you about Guy's affair. I had a feeling you wouldn't leave it alone."

"Were you blackmailing him?" I asked.

Derrick laughed, one of those forced ones when something's particularly unfunny.

"You think I'd be working sixty-hour weeks if I was blackmailing him? Besides, he settled the lawsuit. I didn't even take advantage of that, although I probably could've. I just wanted my good name back."

"Does your good name include lying?" Baz barreled in, as he tended to do.

"Is this some kind of small-town shakedown? You've got nothing on me." He stepped around us to leave.

"Someone saw you that night," I bluffed.

He froze, his hand on the gate, then slowly turned back around. If death rays could've shot from his eyes, they would have. "What do you mean?"

Baz kept it cool. "You weren't here the whole night Guy was murdered."

"Who told you that?"

"It doesn't matter. You were seen near his car at the time the police say he died." I upped the ante.

Derrick brought his e-cigarette to his lips. He took his time puffing on it. "I was afraid of that. I thought she'd keep quiet, though."

"Yeah, well. You might as well come clean," Baz coaxed.

"I was gone fifteen minutes, twenty tops. We had a big party come in at nine o'clock. I had messed up the fresh produce order and we ran out of a bunch of vegetables that were used to make our specials. With Guy's stupid review fresh in everyone's mind, the last thing I wanted to do was admit we couldn't complete their orders, even to my staff. So I contacted Lou from the market and asked him for a favor."

"So you *were* there during the time he was killed."

"Why do you think I didn't mention it to the police? I didn't think she would tell anybody either. She was the one in the car with him. It looks even worse for her than it does for me."

"Who?" It just came out. I couldn't help it. I'd thought he'd been talking about his hostess girlfriend, but now I realized there was another *her* he was referring to.

His brows furrowed. "Wait, was this some kind of trick? You were baiting me and I fell for it? What, and you think I'm going to confess to the police on just your word? I don't think so."

"Not exactly. You know you work with people who will corroborate that you left the restaurant that night.

Especially if one particular person stays angry . . ." I felt no loyalty to the jealous hostess.

His long exhale was made visible by the e-cigarette vapor. "I should've known."

"So tell us. Who did you see in Guy's car?"

"I'm not telling you anything. You'll turn it around on me," Derrick said.

"We'll go to the police, then," I countered.

"Stay out of it. I'll go to the police. She's got more to worry about than I do. They'll find her fingerprints or hair or something in the car."

"How can we be sure you'll tell them?"

"How fast does word travel around this town?"

"We'll know in a couple of hours," Baz answered for my benefit.

"All right, then," I conceded. "But if you don't go, we will."

"I'll go." He stared me down as he said it.

There'd be no befriending Derrick after this. The line in the sand was drawn.

I was happy to leave the smelly, confined space of the enclosure to return to Baz's truck. I hopped into the passenger side, all the while wondering if it was a mistake to trust Derrick.

Baz raised his hand, palm out, high in the air. "Don't leave me hanging."

I high-fived him.

"You think Lou would've told the police Derrick was at his market around the time Guy was killed," I said.

"Not if he didn't know Derrick was a suspect."

Mrs. Schultz had said it before—people in this town

aren't going to volunteer information that would rat out their neighbors.

"Who do you think was in Guy's car? Birdie? I guess we'll have to wait to see who gets arrested," Baz said.

"Yeah, my guess is Birdie too. Vivian saw them arguing. Guy made that comment about her cheese. She was probably the one having an affair with him, but she broke it off, and he threatened to tell. She could lose her goat farm if her husband divorced her. It seems kind of obvious now when you put everything together." The thought of Birdie being the murderer didn't make me feel so triumphant.

"What's the matter? You solved the case. That's what you wanted."

"I know, but it's hard to be happy about Birdie getting arrested. I liked her."

"She took your knife and killed a man, and she was ready to let you take the blame for it. I wouldn't feel so bummed if I were you. Come on." He stuck his hand up again. "Give me another one."

I begrudgingly high-fived him again.

Baz drove the long block back to Curds & Whey and dropped me off before leaving for his handyman appointment.

Mrs. Schultz and Archie were handling the fairly quiet morning at the shop like pros. I filled them in on what happened with Derrick, then Archie took off to meet Hope.

"I guess that's that, then," Mrs. Schultz said when we were alone. "It's a relief for us, isn't it?"

"Yes, it's a relief." I repeated in my head Baz's wise words, but I still couldn't shake feeling bad about Birdie.

"It doesn't erase what happened, though, does it?" Mrs. Schultz said, sensing my glumness. "I was going through my school memorabilia to see if there was anything from Guy's senior class year that I could share with his parents in their condolence card. I came across his last poetry journal. He must've neglected to pick it up before he graduated."

"Will you be sending it to them?"

"Yes. There's a haiku he'd written they may want to include in the service. 'In this cage alone / You can enter for a time / But must fly away.' Isn't that something?" she said. "He was probably writing about a lost crush, rather than life and death, but it seems to fit now."

"That was very thoughtful of you to go through the trouble, Mrs. Schultz."

"A parent should never have to bury their child, no matter how old."

"Indeed." I ruminated in my own thoughts. The haiku repeated in my head.

> *In this cage alone*
> *You can enter for a time*
> *But must fly away.*

But must fly away. Was he writing about Birdie?

Archie returned less than an hour later, quiet and introspective, traits I'd not seen much from our Tigger-like Archie. We took care of the remaining customers in the shop before we spoke.

"What's wrong, Archie? Is Hope okay?" I asked.

"Not really." He ran his hand through his mop of hair. "She found out last night that Guy Lippinger is her father."

CHAPTER 26

My head rocked back on my neck as if I'd been sucker punched. "What?"

"How can that be?" Mrs. Schultz looked just as stunned as I felt.

"Crazy, right?" Archie said.

"Poor Hope." Silence overtook us as we tried absorbing this bombshell. "How did she find out? Did Vivian tell her?" I asked.

"She found her mother's diary. She hasn't talked to anyone about it yet, except me."

"Did she tell you anything else about it?"

"The diary said her mom met Guy at a party when he was going to college at Stanford."

"I wonder if that's when she got pregnant."

"No, he broke it off when he graduated. She followed him here, but he'd gone to Europe."

"So she was in love with him," Mrs. Schultz remarked.

"Sounds like it. She stuck around and ended up apprenticing under the owners who wanted to sell the bakery. By the time Guy came back from Europe, she had bought it and was here to stay."

"They must've been together again if she eventually had his baby." Mrs. Schultz and I were across the sampling counter, listening raptly to Archie.

"Just once more. After that, he told her he was in love with someone else and didn't want to be with her."

"What a snake," Mrs. Schultz spat. "Did she ever tell him the baby was his?"

"Yup. His parents gave her some money upfront and had her sign papers she didn't understand. They told her if she told anyone, she'd be in legal trouble."

"They can't do that!" Mrs. Schultz's slapped her palm on the counter in protest.

"It was probably a scare tactic just to keep her silent," I said. "She must've been a really strong woman to push on all by herself with a new business and a new child."

"Vivian's the same way," Mrs. Schultz commented. "She swooped in and took care of everything when her sister no longer could."

"Did Vivian know this whole time?" I asked Archie. "Is that why Hope was angry with her?"

"Hope wasn't mad at her, she just wanted time by herself and didn't want her aunt hounding her. I don't know if Vivian knew about it."

"Did Hope say how she found the diary?"

"I didn't think to ask. Her mom used to live in the apartment attached to the bakery where Hope lives now. It's where she grew up. That's why she wanted to stay there and why Vivian got another place once Hope was old enough to be on her own. Maybe it was hidden somewhere in the apartment."

"And she found it after all these years? I suppose that's possible."

"Can you imagine? That would rock your world."

"That means Guy knew Hope was his child all this time and never acknowledged her. How could you have a child and not want to get to know her?"

"That's tragic," Mrs. Schultz agreed, her exhausted fury changing to sorrow.

I could see how sad Archie was for Hope. I was too, but the timing of it seemed too coincidental to me. Did she really only just find out about him today? Finding out something like that could make you hate a man. I wasn't going to accuse Hope of anything in front of Archie.

Some new customers came into the shop, so I put aside my lingering doubts about Hope, and we went back to work. Later, I tried to take Archie's mind off it by having him help me put together a new sampler platter, but he couldn't fake his lack of enthusiasm for the task. I looked at the wall clock. It was after two.

"I think it's time for your break," I told him.

"Is it?" He was suddenly as excited as a puppy who'd just gotten a new chew toy.

"Yes. Go check on Hope."

"Thanks, Willa. You're the best. I won't be long, I promise."

He slipped off his apron, bunched it up behind the counter, and raced out of the store. Through the front window, Mrs. Schultz and I saw him hurry down the sidewalk toward the bakery.

"He really likes her," I commented.

"That's what worries me," Mrs. Schultz replied.

"You too? I didn't want to say anything while Archie was here, but do you really think Hope *just* found out that Guy is her father?"

"I wondered that myself. Do you think she found out earlier and confronted him? Maybe it went bad?"

"It's a possibility."

"If that's what happened, what would prompt her to tell people now?"

"Maybe she wants to get some money from his family? The more important question is, did she have something to do with his death?"

Mrs. Schultz and I contemplated that for a moment.

"Do you think it's safe that Archie's going to see her?" she said.

"Derrick said he was going to the police earlier, so if Hope is the woman he saw in the car with Guy that night, the police would've taken her in for questioning by now."

"I hope we're wrong, for Archie's sake."

I was afraid Mrs. Schultz's scarf wasn't going to survive her worrying fingers, so I instructed her to slice our leftover pumpernickel bread from this morning into bite-sized pieces and put out a wedge of Stilton, a blue cheese from England. I wanted the wedge left whole so its beautiful blue marbling could be admired. We'd only need to break off a small bit of it for customers to taste its intense flavor.

I needed something to busy myself with, as well, and noticed the jar was almost overflowing with guesses for the Monster Cheddar Wheel.

"Look at that! We need a bigger jar." I looked around the shop to see if we had something to replace the cookie jar that I'd rooted through my unpacked boxes to find. I'd used it over the years for a plethora of things, but never cookies, ironically enough.

I found the largest glass barrel jar we sold and transferred the strips of paper and customers' business cards to it. It reminded me that we had never discovered who the nail salon business card belonged to. Was it more likely to have been Birdie's or Hope's? I recalled Hope's long, polished nails. I worried how Archie would take the news if Hope was the one arrested.

CHAPTER 27

"Was she there?" I asked Archie as soon as he returned from break. I held my breath waiting for his reply.

"Yeah, she's holed up in her apartment. She cheered up a little after we talked again," he said with a shy grin.

Mrs. Schultz and I surreptitiously passed a glance at each other, her obvious relief mirroring my own.

"I'm sure you're making her feel much better. Did she say anything about Vivian?" I still wanted to know if Vivian had a role in any of this.

"Hope said her aunt Vivian didn't know and that she was really upset too. Vivian's being super nice to her, letting her take the rest of the day off."

"Good. I'm glad Hope's feeling a little better."

"Me too." A smile returned to Archie's face.

Coincidences do happen, I suppose. I let my suspicions about the timing of the discovery fade. Derrick said he would tell the police who was in the car with Guy that night. If it had been Hope or Vivian, the police would be there to question them. My initial hunch must've been right—it had to be Birdie.

The shop hummed with customers, and I finally started to feel optimistic. Maybe it was the shock of everything

Derrick told me this morning that had me so glum. Now that I had some time to process it all, I realized Baz was right. I'd helped to solve the case. I wouldn't be suspected any longer and Mrs. Schultz, Archie, and I would continue to make Curds & Whey thrive. I looked out the front picture window where people strolled past. Perky white and yellow daffodils opened their blooms underneath the budding crepe myrtles dotting the sidewalk. Yarrow Glen was once again the endearing town I'd fallen in love with.

Golden Glen Meadery across the street caught my eye. Roman wasn't a murderer. That thought made my heart soar, but it quickly thumped back down to reality. I'd treated him like a suspect, the very thing I was angry at Detective Heath for doing to me.

When the shop became quiet again, I decided to bring a peace offering to Roman. Which cheese best said *I'm sorry*?

"Do you two feel comfortable watching the shop again without me for a little while?"

"No problem," Mrs. Schultz said.

"Will do." Archie saluted me.

French cheese was especially close to my heart, so I headed across the street with one from the Pyrenees mountain range made from sheep's milk. I took a deep breath before opening the door to the meadery. Roman's assistant Chet was ringing up a customer at the register, so I was met with no fanfare. I saw an animated Roman showing off a bottle of his cinnamon mead, which had been my favorite, to a customer. The passion he had for his products was evident as he spoke with the man about his mead.

I kicked myself once again for accusing him of lying to me just because he didn't want to announce who his family was—he wanted to be judged for his own work and his own passion. I'd suspected him of murder just because he was nice to Guy when nobody else had been. Did the cheese I brought also say *I was an idiot*?

The customer decided on the mead. Roman noticed me then, as he carried the customer's bottles to the front counter. I flashed a smile, which wasn't reciprocated. I supposed I deserved that. I continued to stand awkwardly in the corner of the meadery with my little container of cheese, sidestepping customers. Taking his time, Roman finally sauntered over to me.

"Hey," he said.

"Hey." More awkwardness. I held out the container. "Here. It's for you."

"For another tasting?"

"As a peace offering."

He chuckled and took it. "Cheese as a peace offering?"

"Some people break bread, I share my cheese." I shrugged.

The dimple deepened in his cheek as his crooked smile widened. "Come on." He led me to the tasting room, empty of customers. "You want a glass of something?"

I sidled up to the bar once again, but declined. "I'm still working, but thanks."

He took a stool next to me this time. "You left your shop to come here?"

"Don't get all puffed up about it." I smiled to show him I was joking, but this time he returned the warmth. "I didn't want to wait any longer to apologize to you."

"About?"

He wasn't going to make this easy on me. "For being mad that you didn't tell me every single thing about yourself. It wasn't for me to say what parts of your past you should or shouldn't share with me. Or what parts of your present, for that matter." My face warmed against my will. "We're just getting to know each other and it's none of my business. I mean, you don't know everything about me either."

"I'd like to."

All my internal sensors flipped on like a switch. *How did he do that?*

"Anyway, I think I haven't been exactly myself because of what happened with Guy and not knowing . . ."

"If I killed him?"

"No. Okay, maybe. Can you forgive me?" I bared my teeth in what I hoped was a pleading smile, but probably looked more like an excited chimpanzee. Maybe he wouldn't be impressed with me, but I hoped my cheese would win him over. I opened the container and let him take a piece of the light ivory-colored cheese. "It's called Isatara. I don't offer that to just anyone." With the slightly oily texture of Gouda and a gently rich flavor, I could probably even get Baz to like it.

We tapped cheese chunks in a clumsy cheers and bit into them at the same time. My tastebuds picked up hazelnuts and olives underneath the mild sweetness.

He nodded and popped the rest of it in his mouth with an *mmm*.

"So am I forgiven?" I asked.

"I suppose." He winked at me, putting those sensors on blast again. "Can I ask you why you finally decided I didn't murder Guy?"

Gosh, why did I turn down that drink? I tried to make light of it. "It's not like I ever really suspected you."

He raised his eyebrows in skepticism.

I couldn't blame him. I was a lousy liar. "Okay, I'll fess up. It was because of Derrick. He saw Birdie in Guy's car that night. At least, I think he was talking about Birdie.

Anyway, I talked with him at the restaurant and he was going to the police with the information."

"Why didn't he tell them that in the first place?"

"It puts him at the scene of the crime. He didn't want to implicate himself, but we found out that his alibi had a hole in it—a twenty-minute one. So he was forced to be honest." I was feeling pretty chuffed recounting our investigative skills. Too bad Heath would never know we solved the case for him.

"Let me get this straight," Roman said. "You confronted Derrick that his alibi didn't hold water and he told you that it wasn't him, but that he saw someone else with Guy."

"Y-Yeah." When he said it like that, it didn't sound as plausible as when Derrick had said it.

"You don't think he was just telling you that to get himself off the hook?"

Boy, now I felt stupid. "We'd been suspecting Birdie, so when he said he saw her with Guy . . ."

"Why did you suspect Birdie?"

"Because Derrick said they were having an affair."

"*Derrick* said."

"Oh. I see your point." I'd never considered myself a gullible person, but from this perspective, it appeared I may have made a major mistake in judgment.

"Did you ask Birdie about it?" he said.

"Well, no because he never mentioned her by name, so I wasn't sure if it was her."

"You just said Derrrick told you Birdie was having an affair with Guy and that he saw them in Guy's car together that night."

Oh gosh, I really looked like a dummy now. "N-No. He didn't exactly say it was her either time. I just assumed." Hadn't Heath told me not to assume?

"So Derrick told you Guy was having an affair with a woman. Then he told you he saw a woman in the car with Guy that night. And now you think he's at the police station telling Detective Heath that he lied about his alibi and was, in fact, at the scene of the crime? But this mystery woman Guy supposedly had an affair with—who you think is Birdie—is the real killer?"

"Well, when you put it that way . . . I really fell for it, didn't I? But it all seemed to make so much sense. The owners at the inn said Guy had a secret, and well . . . I guess I jumped to conclusions."

"Did you at least go to the police and tell them about Derrick's false alibi?"

I put my head in my hands. "No. I let him do it. I didn't want Detective Heath to know I was still meddling in the investigation."

"When did you talk to Derrick?"

"This morning."

"This morning? He could be out of the country by now."

"Oh my gosh, you think? Oh, no. I better get to Detective Heath."

"I'll come with you."

CHAPTER 28

I let Mrs. Schultz and Archie know my short break would now be a long break, and Roman and I took off at a quick clip. We went left on the corner of Main and Pleasant, but I couldn't help but look over at Apricot Grille.

"Is that a police cruiser?" I said, spotting the black-and-white in the parking lot on the far side of the restaurant.

"It sure looks like one."

"What would they be doing there?"

Roman didn't answer. I felt the pull of my curiosity, but it was more important we get to the security complex to talk to Detective Heath.

We hurried past town hall, whose working clock tower rose higher than any other building downtown, even the neighboring church steeple. Most of the government offices remained in the old building, however, the police department had moved across the street to the new public safety complex, which also housed the fire department.

We hastened to the glass-walled entrance between the two departments of the security complex and into a bright, uncluttered atrium with two seating areas and waxy-leaf floor plants on either side of the sofas. We went straight to the bullet-proof partition that had Police painted at the top of it. A sober man in a security-guard uniform sat on the other side of the partition at a semi-circular reception desk. Several office doorways could be seen behind him and what looked like mailbox cubbies hung on the wall.

"Hi. I need to speak with Detective Heath," I demanded.

"Your name?" the security officer asked.

"Willa Bauer. He's not expecting me, but he knows me." His resemblance to a broader Bruce Willis made me check myself. This guy wasn't going to take any nonsense. "Could you tell him I have some important information about Guy Lippinger's murder?"

Roman and I stepped away from the partition as he made the phone call. I couldn't stop my foot from tapping, as if some snappy music was playing. But in fact, the two-story lobby echoed with silence.

I worried aloud. "He's gonna kill me. He told me to stay out of it."

"Willa." Roman grasped my arms and looked at me the way he always did, putting my anxiety to temporary rest like a hypnotist who snaps his fingers. "The police believed Derrick's alibi, so Heath at least has to give you credit for blowing a hole in it."

For someone who'd spoken with Detective Heath a few times, Roman didn't seem to know him very well. I went back to the desk just as the security guard got off the phone.

"He's occupied at the moment," he said.

"Can you tell him he really needs to hear this?" I said.

"Officer Shepherd will be by to take a statement."

Momentarily, a police officer I recognized from the crime scene appeared in the hall behind him. They nodded to each other before the door was buzzed open and the officer came out into the lobby. "Willa Bauer?"

I left the indifferent security guard to make my case to Officer Shepherd. "Yes. Can we get in to see Detective Heath?"

"Not right now. Is there a crime you need to report?"

"No. He knows the crime. We—*I* have more information about it."

"I see. I can get you a pad of paper for you to write your statement down and we'll be sure it gets to Detective Heath."

"But the person he needs to arrest might be getting away as we speak."

Roman put a hand on my arm to intervene. "Could you tell him it's urgent, Officer Shepherd?"

Officer Shepherd. Shep. I switched gears. "Officer Shepherd! We have a mutual friend. Richie Mus—" I stopped myself. Richie Muscles was the nickname I'd given Baz's brawny friend when we saw him waiting to tow Guy's car the morning after the murder. He'd mentioned his old friend, Shep, to us. I had no idea what his true last name was. "Richie. He drives a tow truck?"

"You know Richie? He's one of my best buddies."

"Yeah, he's a great guy. He suggested I ask for you here. He said you might be able to help me out." Telling a little white lie to a police officer would just have to go on the list of offenses I'd committed during this investigation. "I have to speak with Detective Heath about Guy Lippinger's murder."

"Sorry, there's nothing I can do. Detective Heath's in with the suspect they have in custody now."

"They have a suspect in custody?" I exhaled my relief. I wanted to laugh and cry at once. Instead, I socked

Roman in the arm. "You had me all worried for nothing. See? He really did tell the police." I thought about the police car at Apricot Grille. "Unless he's the one they arrested."

"I'm shocked. The whole thing sounded pretty preposterous," Roman said.

I was glad to be right for once. "I'm still going to wait for Detective Heath." I turned to Officer Shepherd. "Can you let him know I'm waiting to talk to him?"

"Suit yourself." Officer Shepherd was buzzed back through the door.

"Sorry, I guess you were right," Roman said.

"I should still tell Heath what I know. You were right about that. I need to call the shop again and let Archie know Heath's probably going to want to talk to him, too, since he was the one who found out Derrick's alibi was a lie." I noticed Roman glance at his watch. "You don't need to stick around if you don't want to. I know it's still business hours."

"I do have a group coming in for a tasting in fifteen minutes."

"Go. There's nothing for you to do here."

"Sorry I made you worry."

"I'm glad I'm here. You were right, I should've come straight to the police. Thanks for coming with me."

Roman left and I called the shop for the second time that afternoon and updated Mrs. Schultz and Archie. They assured me they could handle the shop. I called Baz and told him where I was. He said he was already on the road, having just left his appointment, and offered to come to the station, which I decided was a good idea. He'd been with me when we talked to Derrick, so they'd probably want to question him too. I waited in the atrium long enough for my nervousness about confronting Detective Heath to turn to smugness that I'd helped solve the case. Whether they'd arrested Birdie or Derrick, I still wasn't sure.

Baz came just before the security guard told us we could go in and buzzed us through. An officer I didn't recognize awaited us on the other side of the partition. He led us down a hallway and steered us into one of the stark interview rooms that held nothing more than a rectangular table and three uncomfortable-looking plastic chairs. I pulled out one of the chairs and sat.

"Both of you on that side," the officer said.

"Oops. Sorry." I trotted around to the far side of the table with Baz.

When I sat in the hard chair beside Baz, I heard the door shut—we were alone in the spartan room. The bare walls looked newly painted, but the happy yellow color didn't bring any joy to the space. Without windows, the only light came from two strips of LED lights attached to the ceiling, dispersing an unnaturally bright glow.

"This doesn't feel good," Baz said.

He was right. It sure didn't feel like we were doing them a favor. I noticed a video camera in the corner by the ceiling, its soulless black lens directed at us. "This must be where they interview people."

"Suspects, you mean."

"But we're not suspects. It's the whole point of why we're here, to wrap this up once and for all. Derrick must've told them we talked to him this morning. I bet Heath's mad about it. He's probably got a bruised ego." I didn't believe that for a second, but it made me feel guiltless to pretend I did.

Detective Heath came in and shut the door behind

him. He was dressed in his customary well-tailored attire, but the usual steady demeanor that went along with it was rocked. He promptly took a seat across from us and said, "Make it quick. What do you have to tell me?"

My smug admission went right out the window. "We're here to make sure Derrick told you what he told us today about the night of Guy's murder."

"You talked with Derrick Fitzpatrick? When?"

"This morning."

"Time?"

"Uh—" I looked to Baz and we both muttered, "Around eleven."

"Tell me everything."

We went over what happened with Derrick that morning. Detective Heath's fists clenched.

Uh-oh. "What's going on? We saw a police car at Apricot Grille. Did you arrest Derrick or Birdie?" I asked.

"Birdie came in on her own and confessed to being with Guy in his car that night," Heath said.

"So it *was* her." I still had a hard time believing it.

"She didn't confess to killing him. Just to being in the car with him. She says when she left, he was alive and well."

"Do you believe her?"

Detective Heath didn't respond.

"Is that why there's a police car at Apricot Grille? They're talking to Derrick now?" Baz asked.

"They're interviewing his staff. He's been missing since late this morning."

"He's *missing*?" Why was it suddenly so hot in here? I needed a window. "How could he be missing for that long? His restaurant staff would've noticed immediately if he wasn't there."

"He told his staff he was coming here, but he never

made it. We didn't know, because we didn't try to contact him until after Birdie came in to make her confession and told us she covered for Derrick that night. We tried Derrick's phone and his apartment and it wasn't until we went to the restaurant that we discovered how long he'd been gone. We put out an APB on him," Heath said. "So tell me again how you let him know his alibi was blown."

"Come on, give us a little credit. We were the ones who found out it was fake," Baz said.

"We knew that as soon as we talked to Lou from the market."

"So then why wasn't Derrick arrested?" I said.

"We had nothing to arrest him on. Why do you think I was at Apricot Grille Friday night? We needed more evidence than the fact that he had opportunity, and we didn't want him to know we were looking closely at him. We wanted him to feel secure in his next moves, so he wouldn't do something . . . *like this*."

I sunk down in my chair. *Oops.*

CHAPTER 29

After the grilling by Detective Heath, Baz and I sat in Baz's truck in the town hall lot. Both of us stared blankly out the windshield at the park, trying to decompress. Heath was not happy with us, to say the least. Frankly, neither was I.

"It was stupid not to go straight to the police," I admitted to Baz. "I gave Derrick the heads-up to skip town."

"Don't beat yourself up. He convinced me too. We both thought it was Birdie. And that part was true—she admitted she was with Guy that night."

Baz reached for the key in his ignition, but I put a hand on his forearm to stop him. "Look, there she is, coming from the station." Birdie was waiting to cross the street from the security complex to the town hall parking lot where we were sitting. "Stay here, I'm going to talk to her." I didn't wait for a response. I immediately got out of the truck and briskly walked toward her as she crossed to the near sidewalk.

"Birdie," I called. She stopped upon hearing her name and let me catch up to her. "Are you okay?"

Her face was splotchy and she held a wad of tissues in

one hand and her car keys in the other. "Willa. It's not a good time." She tried to hide her haggard face from me.

"We just came from the police station too. I talked to Derrick this morning. He told me he saw you with Guy that night after class."

Tears eked out the corners of her eyes. It looked like there'd been a steady stream for quite a while. "He told you too? He said he was telling the police."

"Why would he let you know that's what he was doing?"

"Because we'd agreed not to rat each other out." Birdie looked up to the sky as if asking for divine help. "I told the police everything, I might as well tell you too. Everyone's going to know eventually." She blew her nose and collected herself, but she was still shaking. "I knew Derrick saw me. I saw him too. When we heard Guy was murdered, we made a pact. Neither of us wanted anyone to know we were there right before Guy was killed. I saw Derrick hurrying to Lou's Market. He saw me getting out of Guy's car. But we're not killers. I guess he figured he owed me a heads-up."

"Why were you in Guy's car in the first place?"

More tears.

"Were you having an affair with him?" I asked gently.

She nodded and closed her eyes, but it didn't keep the tears from escaping and dribbling down her cheeks. I looked around. Luckily, no one else was on the sidewalk. I led her to the bench in front of town hall.

"I was much closer to him when we were younger than I let on to you the other day. We dated in high school and when he went away to college."

According to Archie, that was when Hope's mother met him. Guy must've still had a relationship with Birdie at home while he was dating Hope's mom in college.

She continued, "Even though we'd been together for years, his parents didn't think I was good enough for him. I guess they wanted someone more polished than a farm girl. But we were in love. He promised we'd get married after college, his parents be damned. He didn't want to rock the family boat until then, because they'd threatened not to pay for school. But when he graduated, they made some excuse and sent him away to Europe for a year. I believed it was to get him away from me. I wanted him to stay and marry me, but he wouldn't. He wouldn't defy them. Maybe they were threatening to cut him off, I don't know. I told him I didn't care about the money, but he did. He said if I stuck with him for another year until he got back from Europe, he'd be able to have a good career on his own and wouldn't need his parents' money anymore. I believed him, so I waited for him. Before he came back, his parents bought the *All Things Sonoma* magazine and bribed him with a cushy job working for it. We tried to make it work for a little while after he returned, but I knew there was no way he'd ever choose me over them. Then out of the blue, they decided to sell their land and move. So my parents had to leave their farm. There was no reason for me to stick around either. It was too painful. He ended up leaving the area eventually too."

I didn't think it was as out of the blue as Birdie contended. It would've been about the same time they found out about the pregnancy. It sounded like they didn't want to be in the same town as Guy's secret child. Birdie looked like she was in enough pain. I didn't feel the need to let her in on what Guy had been doing behind her back all those years ago. I decided to stick with the present. "Did you stay in touch? How did you both come to move back here within a few years of each other?"

"I never talked to him again until after my husband and I came back and started our goat farm. Guy told me he found out I'd moved back and he wanted a redo, he called it. He said he regretted listening to his parents and marrying the kind of woman he was 'supposed to' marry. He was my biggest heartache. I . . . I guess I just wanted to be able to go back and have the fairy tale that I thought I'd missed out on."

"But you were married."

"Yes. I learned too late that you can't go back. I was trying to wipe away the heartache of my twenty-two year-old self without considering that I'm not that girl anymore. I love my husband and our farm and our life."

"So how did it happen?"

"Guy's wife never wanted to live here. They'd already been having problems for years. So after he and I started talking again, it was the incentive he needed to separate. He wanted me to do the same, but I couldn't do it. And then eventually . . . the affair just happened."

"You didn't think anyone would find out? It's a small town."

"I know. At the time, I almost didn't care. I was living in a fantasy world. I trusted him to keep it quiet because he was afraid his divorce would turn ugly if she found out. He had almost as much to lose as I did. But he'd turned bitter since I'd known him twenty years ago. He drank too much. He wasn't the same man I remember. I wish it hadn't taken me almost a year to figure it out.

"Anyway, he told me last week that his divorce was going to be finalized soon. Instead of being happy, I panicked. I realized I didn't want to leave my husband for him. I broke it off with him a few days before he was killed."

That must've been the argument Vivian saw. "I assume he didn't take it well."

"Not at all."

"So why were you with him the night he died?"

"When I saw him drunk at your shop, I felt bad for him. But when he threatened to tell a secret, I knew he meant he was going to tell everyone about him and me. I went home, but I couldn't think. I couldn't do anything until I knew for sure he wouldn't tell. So I drove to his house, but he wasn't there. I knew he used to hang out at The Cellar, so I came back to town, but I didn't want to talk to him in public. I saw his car was still in the alley, so I waited for him. We talked. He swore that wasn't the secret he was going to tell. He said he'd never hurt me like that."

"Did you believe him?"

"I don't know. I wondered if he was just saying that so he could get me back. He was very drunk by then and I didn't see the point in talking to him anymore that night. I promised him we'd talk again soon, but it was an empty promise. But I didn't kill him. I swear I didn't. I couldn't. I didn't want to leave my life for him, but he was my first love. Now I have to go home and tell my husband." She looked at me with desperation in her swollen eyes. "Not only will he know about the affair, I may be arrested."

"Oh, Birdie." I hugged her. "I don't think they'll arrest you. Derrick's disappeared."

"What do you mean?"

"He hasn't been seen since he called you this morning. He must've left town because he's guilty."

"So I should've told the police all along that I saw him that night."

"We've all made mistakes. Just be honest now. It'll be okay."

"I'm not sure how I'm going to be honest with my husband. He didn't deserve any of this."

We hugged again and walked to our cars. I was truly shaken by the time I returned to Baz's truck. I told him Birdie's story.

"I'm not sure I feel as sorry for her as you do. She did bring this all on herself."

"Baz, a woman's first love is a powerful thing, especially if you planned your life's dreams with him. Trust me, if it didn't turn out the way you had hoped, you never quite get over it."

"Hey, guys are sensitive too. I still think about Bella a lot."

"You've never mentioned Bella. How long were you two together?"

"Thirteen years."

"Wait a second. How old are you?"

"Twenty-nine. She was my childhood dog. Man, I loved her."

I smacked Baz in the arm.

He laughed at me. "Anyway, let's leave your sympathies for Birdie out of this. She had motive and opportunity."

"I suppose you're right. And she's pretty good at lying. She lied to the police, she lied to her husband . . ."

"So why is Derrick the one running from the police?" Baz pointed out.

"That's what's even crazier. It's got to be him, right?"

"Then he's not very smart. Why didn't he just play his hand?"

"What do you mean?"

"He got Birdie to turn herself in. He found out about the affair between her and Guy from the innkeepers, so he wasn't the only one who knew about it. After he called her, why not just let her take the fall?"

"He probably wasn't quite sure what she'd tell the police. There might be something more implicating him that we haven't discovered."

Baz started up his truck and we drove down Main Street. There was still a police cruiser in Apricot Grille's parking lot. We ignored our craving to see what was happening firsthand and drove home. He parked the car next to mine behind our building.

"You going back to the shop?" he asked as we hopped out of his truck.

"Yes, but first I want to get my laptop from my apartment. I need to find out more about Derrick. Maybe he's got a cousin or a girlfriend or someone who was willing to help him go on the lam."

Baz followed me up the creaky steps to my apartment. "Aren't you in enough trouble? You really think you're going to find a fugitive if the police can't?"

"I have to try and help."

"You're like a dog with a bone."

"I'm a dog who lost the bone and it's a very important bone and I need to help everyone find it."

"Okay, you've gone over the edge with the analogy."

"We had him, Baz. Archie found out about the hole in his alibi and he admitted it to us. I should've called the police right then and he'd be in custody now."

"Heath said they didn't have any other evidence against him. They'll find him. He can't have gotten too far."

"It was hours ago. He could be in Canada by now." I could hear the shrillness of my voice.

I pulled my house key out of my pocket, but dropped it on the deck. My hands were shaking.

Baz picked it up for me, but held onto it. "Wil." He didn't continue until I looked at him. "It's gonna be okay.

The police had every opportunity to find out the same thing we did about Derrick. Birdie kept the information from them for days. This isn't our fault."

I sighed deeply. "You're right. I'm just so mad. We were so close." I turned around, wanting to scream into the treetops. The glen view to the distant mountains that surrounded it tended to give me peace and perspective, but this time it also brought to mind how many places Derrick could be hiding.

I turned back to Baz. "I still want to find out more about Derrick. Maybe there's some way I can help Detective Heath." *And save face with him.*

"No offense, but do you really think he's gonna want help from you?"

Baz was right. I felt suddenly tired from it all. I leaned back against the deck railing, allowing it to support my weight. With barely a creak, the railing gave way in an instant. My arms swung around wildly for something to grab onto, but all I found was air.

CHAPTER 30

One of my flailing arms was grabbed and I was yanked forward onto the safety of the deck. Baz now held onto both arms and pulled me into him and away from the edge. We clung to each other, not moving a muscle. He eventually loosened his grip on my arms and I released the sides of his T-shirt from my clenched fists.

"What the huckleberry?" He stared past me.

I carefully turned around and saw the back portion of my deck railing completely gone.

"Let's get off of here," I said, bolting for the stairs.

Baz was right behind me.

We stood at the bottom of the steps. I felt safe being on solid ground. We walked behind the deck by where we parked our cars. The wooden rail was in two pieces on the pavement. Just as my heart was starting to slow down, I looked up and saw my precarious balcony minus its outer railing.

Baz inspected the broken pieces on the ground.

"How did that happen?" I asked him.

"That's a good question. I didn't hear it snap or crack."

"You're right," I replied, although the four seconds

in which it happened was a blur to me, the shock and adrenaline having erased the details.

"Look." He held the rail out for me to see.

"What am I supposed to be looking at?"

"The screw holes. They're still round."

"What are you saying? Someone unscrewed the railing?"

Baz put it down and took the stairs two by two.

"What are you doing?" I didn't follow him. The feeling of almost falling over the edge was too fresh in my mind.

I saw him at the edge of my balcony, looking carefully at our connecting railings.

"Be careful," I called up unhelpfully.

My pulse slowed when he finally came back down.

"There's no sign of damage up there where the wood would've broken against the screws. The only damage seems to be when it hit the ground," he said.

"What does that mean?"

"Wil, I think someone tried to kill you."

This time we called the police right away. My stomach lurched upon seeing a patrol car in my alley again. It was only a matter of minutes until Archie came galloping toward us, worry written all over his face.

"What happened?" he asked us.

Detective Heath's unmarked car pulled in behind the patrol car.

"It's okay, Archie. I'll explain everything in a little while. I'll be back in the shop as soon as I can."

Archie reluctantly walked back down the alley to the shop. He looked over his shoulder at us several times after Detective Heath passed him, surely trying to work out what was going on.

I'd seen Heath exasperated by me before, but this topped even our earlier meeting at the station. When he was done checking out the broken railing and my balcony, he paced like a caged tiger, while a uniformed officer looked on.

Finally, Heath said to him, "Call Shepherd, and you two tape everything off, from here to the building."

"How am I supposed to get into my apartment?" I complained.

"You can't. Not today. You'll have to stay with somebody."

"What do you mean, I can't? I don't have anybody to stay with."

"You can stay with—" Baz started to volunteer but I shot him a warning look and he clammed up.

"It's safer for you to be somewhere else. Can you stay with the woman who works with you?" Detective Heath asked.

"I don't recall hiring you as my security advisor, and I'm not going to put Mrs. Schultz at risk," I replied.

"You ignored my advice at the inn. You ignored my advice yesterday after you received the threatening note. And today there was an attempt on your life. Are you going to wait until it's successful?"

"Well he's gone, isn't he?"

"Who?"

"Derrick. He must be the one who did this out of revenge."

"We don't know who did this. We don't even know for sure if he's the murderer."

"Oh, come on."

"We haven't located him yet. He could still be around

somewhere in hiding." Heath pulled me aside so we were alone and lowered his voice. "Why are you fighting me on this? I don't want you to be by yourself until Derrick is caught and we have more answers. It's for your own safety. Maybe I can pull an officer and assign one to watch you."

"Never mind. It's fine." Once I simmered down, I realized he really was trying to look out for me, but the last thing I needed was a cop watching my every move. "I'll stay with Baz. Is that all right if I stay with you?" I shouted over to Baz.

He nodded and gave us a thumbs-up.

"All set." I knew I wasn't completely fooling Heath, but there was nothing he could do about it.

"Willa!" Roman came trotting down the alley, calling my name. "What's going on? Has something else happened?"

"It was a near miss. We're okay," I told him.

The officer called for Heath and he walked off to speak with him.

"Someone tried to hurt you? When I left you at the police station, I thought this was all wrapped up," Roman said.

"Derrick's on the lam."

Roman remained silent in his surprise. He stared past the parking strip out into the woods, as if he'd spot him there, then turned back to me. He started to speak, but stopped himself.

"I know, I know. You told me so. Let's make this official—you were right," I said.

"I didn't want to be right. Are you really okay?"

Now that the veil of suspicion was lifted from Roman, I could see how much he seemed to care about me. Impulsively, I hugged him. It wasn't until I felt his arms return my embrace that I realized how much I needed it. A lot had happened in just a few short days and this near miss affected me more than I wanted to admit. We released each other and I stepped back, now a little embarrassed.

"What was that for? Don't get me wrong, I'm glad," he said, that slow smile replacing his earlier concern.

"I just appreciate you being here for me and being so understanding, no matter how I've behaved."

"Do you need a place to lay low for a little while? You can put your feet up at my place and have a mead."

"That sounds amazing, but I have to get back and help close up the shop. I've left Archie and Mrs. Schultz hanging for too long."

"Well, I'm here if you need me."

"I know you are. Thank you."

"Any time." He winked at me right before he turned and walked away, causing a full migration of butterflies in my stomach.

Another patrol car pulled into the lot and Officer Shepherd emerged, carrying that dreaded yellow crime scene tape. I needed to close up the shop, so Baz and I went to Curds & Whey.

It was only after I'd left my defiance with Heath that I started to feel shaky again about what happened. I left it to Baz to fill Archie and Mrs. Schultz in on what had transpired. Somehow, their concern for me didn't bug me the way Heath's did. Maybe because their loyalty to me was steady.

"I hope they catch him soon." Mrs. Schultz hugged me. "Thank goodness you were there, Baz. You're a hero." She hugged him next.

"Yeah, I owe you one," I said. "Or like, a million."

"It was just reflexes." He brushed off the praise.

"So you didn't mean to save me, then? It was just reflexes?"

We laughed together. We sure needed it. I locked the front door and hung the Closed sign on it. We started our closing routine and Baz took a broom to help.

"Do the police have any leads as to where Derrick might have gone?" Mrs. Schultz asked while wiping counters.

"He must be long gone by now," Archie commented.

"One of the officers told me they found his car near the bus station, so they're checking that out, but it could be a decoy. They don't know if he took off or if he went into hiding," Baz answered.

"If we knew more about him, maybe we could find someone who would give us a clue as to where he might've gone," I said. "What do you know about him, Archie? Does he have family or close friends around who might help him out?"

"The lawsuit was the only personal thing I ever knew about him and that's just because he complained to everyone about it. All I know is that he moves around a lot because of his job. Maybe if I'd hung out by the dumpsters with him on smoke breaks, I would've known more, but I don't smoke."

That reminded me of who *was* hanging out with him on his smoke break—the jealous hostess.

"I wonder if the police are still interviewing the staff at Apricot Grille or if we can sneak over there when we're done closing up."

"They're not open for dinner on Sundays," Archie said. "You'd better get there pretty soon if you want to talk to anybody."

"Let's hop to it, then," I said.

We got the store cleaned and the money counted in

record time. I left the restocking for tomorrow, since we were closed on Mondays. As they left for home, I promised Mrs. Schultz and Archie that I'd text them later with any news.

Baz and I walked the block to Apricot Grille, a route that was becoming routine.

"Do you really think we can find out something the police haven't?" Baz asked me.

"That hostess lied to the police to protect Derrick's alibi, and the other staff she told were willing to keep a secret too. There might be other things Derrick shared with some of them that they wouldn't tell the police."

"You think they'll tell us?"

I shrugged. "It's worth a shot. If I let them know he tried to kill me, they might be sympathetic." A shudder went through me. "Do you think he messed with my deck after he wrote the note last night or did he do it today after we confronted him?"

"It depends if it was to scare you or if he was out for revenge."

We crossed Main Street and checked out Apricot Grille's parking lot. There were only a handful of cars left, probably the restaurant staff, and no police car. So far, so good.

"Let's check the dumpster area. Maybe one of his smoking buddies is in there," I said to Baz.

We walked to the alley behind the building where the fenced-in dumpster was. We listened outside the closed gate for a moment. Surely, the police visit and learning that Derrick fled would be gossiped about. Maybe we could find out something without even having to ask any questions.

I cocked my ear. Nothing. I turned to Baz who shook his head too. We couldn't hear anything. Just as I opened the gate, I heard the distinct sound of the restaurant's industrial back door being pushed open.

Two guys emerged in matching white shirts, black pants, and thick rubber aprons, like I saw the dishwashers wearing when I'd been in the kitchen briefly. One of them stuck a block at the foot of the door to prop it open. They each held a bulging garbage bag that caused them to list to one side while they walked to the dumpster. We waited for them to reach us, curious looks on their faces.

"Hey, guys." I tried my best to sound friendly without crossing that fine line to stalkerish.

They said nothing, but their eyes scanned me and Baz.

"Are you guys friends with the manager, Derrick? I just have a few questions."

"Friends?" One of them guffawed. "Nobody's friends with Derrick. We tolerate him so we can keep our jobs."

"Are you with the police?" the other one asked. "We already talked with them today."

I thought hard about saying yes, but I didn't want Detective Heath adding "police impersonator" to the list of reasons I was interfering with his investigation.

"We're privately looking into his disappearance," Baz offered.

"Like private investigators? Cool."

Okay, sure.

"So, did he ever mention anyone or any place he liked to hang out where maybe he'd go to hide?"

"Nah, not to us. You could try Angela." He unlatched the gate and swung it open.

"Angela. The hostess?"

"Yeah," he said without turning around.

They both took their trash bags into the enclosed area. Baz and I followed them in. I held my finger under my nose to try to block the dumpster stench. It seemed even worse than earlier. The others must've been used to it.

"She was the only one he'd give the time of day to," he finished.

"Okay, thanks," I said.

"I don't think you'll get much from her, though. We all talked about it. Most of us don't think he killed the guy."

"Why is that?" Baz questioned.

"He's a blowhard, but the past couple of days, he's seemed kind of nervous. Angela thinks he took off because he was scared, not guilty."

Scared he'd get caught. If Baz hadn't been there to save me, Derrick would have *two* murders on his hands.

The dishwasher wielded the bag like a shot put, up and over. I had to step out of the way so as not to get clipped, but my foot caught something and I stumbled backward into the side of the enclosure.

"Sorry. You okay?" he said.

I looked down to swear at the object I'd tripped over. My mind couldn't quite make sense of what I was looking at wedged between the dumpster and the fence until I followed the object along the ground. It wasn't an object at all. It was a leg attached to the rest of Derrick's dead body.

CHAPTER 31

I sat on the curb of the parking lot, head in hands, still taking deep, cleansing breaths that weren't cleansing the image or the odors from my memory. Detective Heath's car sped to a stop in the lot, across several parking spaces. Baz was pacing in front of me, but stopped as soon as Heath got out and slammed his car door. Two more cop cars followed with their red lights on.

Heath strode toward us.

"Where?" he said.

I pointed to the dumpster enclosure, but he was looking over my head. I hadn't noticed the two guys we'd been talking to were standing behind me, also pointing.

"Nobody move. Baz, you too. Stay over there with the others and stop messing up the crime scene."

Baz loped over and sat next to me on the curb. "What's he mad at us for?"

Heath took a pair of latex gloves out of his pocket and put them on before walking into the dumpster enclosure. I hadn't stayed long enough to see how Derrick had died. I prayed it wasn't with an engraved Curds & Whey cheese board this time.

Momentarily, Heath appeared. He conversed with

one of his officers, who then directed the others to set up the perimeter. Heath returned to us, the blue gloves having been disposed of. I felt the beads of sweat dripping down the back of my neck. I couldn't blame it on the sun, which had already begun to lower behind the mountains. The thought of explaining to Heath why I was once again at the scene of a murder was the reason.

"Were all of you in there?" he asked.

We nodded.

"Ms. Bauer, this way."

Uh-oh, we were back to *Ms. Bauer*. I pushed myself up off the curb and followed him.

"Stick around. I'll talk to each of you too," he said to Baz and the others.

I looked at Baz for support, but it only increased my jitters—his leg looked to be bobbing to "Flight of the Bumblebee."

By the time we walked the few yards away from the others, I'd mentally put on my armor.

"Tell me everything." He pulled out his pen and mini notebook that I remembered from that first night I'd met him. Was that only four days ago?

I told him all the logistics from the time we arrived until I tripped over Derrick's foot and ran out of the enclosure, screaming.

He put the pad and pen away and pushed open his suit jacket to stick his hands on his hips, a posture I recognized. He was frustrated.

"Why?" he said.

"Why did I trip over him or why did I run?"

"Why did you come back here? Don't you have a shop to run?"

"Yes. And I have a life to live without being afraid that

he might come back and try to kill me a second time. I was trying to find out where he was."

"Well, congratulations. You found him, didn't you?" Heath said sarcastically.

"I did." For the first time, it occurred to me what finding Derrick dead meant. "He didn't do it, then, did he?" I looked to Heath to make some sense of it. That's where his ire was coming from. I'd sent him and his men on a wild-goose chase looking for Derrick and he wasn't the culprit at all. "Whoever killed Guy and tried to kill me is still out there and we have no idea who it is."

Heath moved back and forth like he was learning the cha-cha. I think his dueling thoughts were physically manifesting.

"I can hold you without cause for seventy-two hours and I'm tempted to do it," he said.

"You can't do that! I mean, you can, you just told me you can, but you can't."

He sighed. Obviously my level of confusing arguments were a bit of a match for his logic.

"You have to stay away, Willa. I don't know how to say it more plainly."

"But I found him for you. Now you know you should be looking for someone else."

"He would've been discovered without you here." He threw his hand up, sensing I was about to say something else. "We have a double murderer on our hands. It won't take much for someone who's killed two people to kill a third."

There was no retort for that. I agreed to stay out of it.

"With this new development, I don't know when we'll be able to process your deck," he continued, more calmly.

"Then I've got to be allowed in to get some things before I stay with Baz."

"That's not a good idea."

"I can't just slip into my apartment really quick?"

"I mean staying with Baz."

"Why? Is he not allowed to go in his apartment either? It's a different set of stairs."

Heath took some time to answer. "We're bringing him in for questioning."

"To the station? Why? He saw everything I saw."

"We inspected your deck. It looked like someone unscrewed the railing on purpose."

"That's what Baz thought too. That's why we called you." I didn't like where this conversation was heading.

"Exactly. He knows about deck construction."

"Oh, so you're bringing him in for his expertise?" Relief blew over me like a fresh breeze.

"No. His expertise gives him the ability to unfasten the railing just enough to keep it standing until you lean on it. He'll be questioned as a suspect."

"You can't be serious. But it's Baz!" I looked over at him, still sitting on the curb jiggling his leg in nervousness.

"Who you've known for . . . how many days?" Heath said, not reacting appropriately to my outrage.

"Yeah, but other people know him." As it came out of my mouth, I heard how lame it sounded. "I mean, everybody trusts him. It's got to be one of the others."

"He was in your shop the night Guy was there, wasn't he? And by your side as soon as you found the body?"

"Well, yeah, but . . ." My brain raced to grab onto something that could make sense of this. "He wasn't there when Guy threatened to tell his secret. He didn't know about any of that at the time. What's his motive?" Before he could even answer, I continued, "And what about the cash Guy kept taking out of his bank account?"

"How do you know about that?"

So Roman was telling me the truth. "You didn't question Baz about it. That has nothing to do with him, does it?"

"We don't know if or how the money is connected to Lippinger's murder."

"So you're just going to suspect everyone in town then? Baz didn't do it."

"Thanks for your input, but we still need to question him."

This was preposterous. Baz? "Can I talk to him before I go?"

"No. I'm going to let you go freely, but don't make me regret it. Just leave before I change my mind. Who are you going to stay with? I still don't want you to be alone."

"I'll call Mrs. Schultz."

He nodded, finally satisfied with something I said.

I got as far as the sidewalk, but couldn't bring myself to leave. I tried to get Baz's attention, but he was still sitting on the curb, gnawing on his cuticles. I didn't care what Heath said, I had to warn Baz. I turned and started back.

"Whoa, whoa, whoa." An officer who'd been standing guard in front of the parking lot stopped me. "Nobody goes beyond this point."

"I was just over there."

"Don't care. You still can't go beyond this point."

I did as I was told—I was in enough trouble. I started to walk away when a cruiser swung up to the curb in front of us. An officer hopped out.

"Melman, where's Detective Heath?" he directed his

question to the stubborn officer who'd been keeping me away. "I have to talk to him."

"You're going to want to wait on that. I've never seen him this mad. I'm glad to be doing guard duty for once," Officer Melman said.

"I've got something that will cheer him up. We got the subpoena for Roman Massey's accounts. We can find out now if his business partnership with Lippinger went sour. We could have ourselves a new suspect."

A business partnership? So Roman *did* make a deal with the devil.

CHAPTER 32

I walked sullenly back to my building. Roman and Baz were now their prime suspects? I didn't know what to make of any of it.

I got all the way to my deck stairs before the yellow tape reminded me I wasn't supposed to go in. I weighed my choices. I'd promised Heath I wouldn't sleep in my apartment tonight. I never said I wouldn't go in it. After all, I had a hungry, lonely fish to rescue.

I quickly ducked under the tape and ran up the stairs to my door. My heart raced being on the deck again with only flimsy police tape substituting for one of the railings. I pushed the door in as quickly as I could and locked it behind me. I changed into comfy clothes and collected a few things I'd need to sleep elsewhere, then scooped up Loretta's bowl and fish food in case I couldn't get back to my apartment until later tomorrow.

I precariously carried my bag, bed pillow, and fishbowl down to the alley and let myself in through the service door. My fingers found the light switch, and the harsh overhead fluorescents illuminated the darkness. The back area of the shop included a stockroom, a makeshift break station, and my office—a compact, windowless room I rarely used with a cluttered desk, a safe, and a comfy couch left over from my last larger apartment. I dropped my bag and pillow on the couch and continued through the swinging door to the shop. I turned on just the kitchenette lights and set the fishbowl on the long farm table. I'd have to right her tipped SpongeBob pineapple house. Poor Loretta had no idea five minutes ago that she'd be swimming in the high seas.

I found my phone in my bag. I ignored the two texts from Roman, and called Mrs. Schultz, as I'd promised Heath. Maybe I should listen to him for once.

She asked how I was doing as soon as she answered. When I assured her there were no residual effects from my earlier scare, she wanted the scoop. "Did you find out anything at the restaurant?"

"Well . . ." As I debated how much to reveal over the phone, I heard some background voices on her end. "Do you have company?" A loud whirring suddenly sounded in the phone.

"Just the girls. It's my turn to host poker night. Excuse the noise. We're making chocolate martinis."

"I'm sorry, I'll let you go then. We can talk about everything tomorrow."

"Are you sure?"

"Of course. You have a good night."

"You too. Tell Baz to keep you safe."

I tapped the phone's screen and ended the call. Maybe it was for the best. I sat, unsure of what to do next, until my gurgling stomach reminded me that I hadn't eaten in quite some time. Eating my feelings was definitely the way to go. There were plenty of good restaurants nearby to get dinner, but I wasn't in the mood to be out in public. Best to stay here and wait for Baz's interview with the police to be finished. Luckily, I had the best food at my fingertips.

I went through the store plucking ingredients from the displays to make a savory charcuterie board. I stuffed crisp green olives with a crumbly, pungent Gorgonzola that would pair well with a spicy soppressata. Tart dried apricots and a silky Gouda would make my tastebuds sing. I hoped it would drown out the chatter in my head. I sat at the farm table with Loretta and tried to nibble away at my anxiety and the case simultaneously.

Roman never told me that he owned the meadery with Guy. It was never mentioned in any of the articles I read about his meadery either. Maybe it was a secret agreement. Baz had said Roman suddenly got the money to renovate the tasting room. My hunch was right—it must've come from Guy, and Roman got in over his head. His accounts would show his losses. It's possible the cash Guy was taking out was going directly into the meadery. He might've gotten angry about not being paid back and was going to reveal his association with the meadery. That would tank Roman's business for sure.

I wished Baz was here to talk this through. The fact that Heath even mentioned him as a suspect rattled me. He was my first ally, my partner in crime.

In crime?

No, Willa. Baz did not do this.

I knew why I wouldn't even entertain the idea. From the moment we started talking between the dead vines of our decks, I felt a kinship with Baz. It was the only connection that even came close to the one I had growing up with my brother Grayson.

After my fiancé and my best friend went off to live out their own Willy Wonka dreams, I gave up the idea of becoming a cheesemonger. I returned to the farm and worked in our small creamery. The only reason I got through those initial months was because of Grayson. He was in college by then, but he had his own big plans he wanted to include me in. We talked about taking over our family's creamery and expanding it, and I'd started to think things had turned out the way they were supposed to. Maybe working side by side again with my brother was how it was always meant to be. I should've known by then that life doesn't care what plans you've made. A tragedy can slice through them whenever it pleases. The weekend before graduation, Grayson was in a car accident with his friends and died.

After that, I couldn't bring myself to stay on at the farm. Every inch of it reminded me of my brother. I left Oregon again, maybe selfishly so, and moved from town to town, putting in my hours for certification and immersing myself in cheese. Even after I passed the exam, I continued to bounce from one city to the next for years. There wasn't any place that called to me but home, and I couldn't bear to return.

Finding Yarrow Glen and meeting Baz were the first feelings of home that I'd had in ten years. Detective Heath wasn't going to make me turn my back on him.

I switched my thoughts to a suspect I'd barely considered before—Hope. We only had her word for it that she just today discovered Guy was her father. I never even got to talk to Baz about it. She was near the gift baskets where she could've taken one of the cheese knives. It was very possible that she knew who her father was. Maybe she was blackmailing him. Or maybe Vivian was. But if Guy was going to reveal that secret, it would hurt him, not them. And why would Hope or Vivian kill Derrick? Birdie was the only one with something to lose if Derrick went to the police.

My head was pounding. How could so much have happened in the last five days and I still didn't feel any closer to finding the murderer? I checked my phone, hoping to find a text from Baz even though it had been silent, but still nothing. I was afraid to text him while he was still in with Heath. I was supposed to be keeping to myself.

I went to the front door to double-check that it was locked. Seeing the meadery across the street felt different now. The lights to Roman's second-story apartment were on. I wanted to text him back, but he'd lied to me more than once. How could I be sure he'd tell me the truth now?

I cleaned up my dinner and brought Loretta's bowl into the office with me with promises to her that this would be her last move for a while. I hadn't gotten a good night's sleep in days. Heck, months. The office couch would have to do. I hoped I'd wake up tomorrow and Detective Heath would have the case solved.

When I switched off the office light, the green glow from the exit sign in the hallway barely penetrated the total blackness. My head found my pillow. I pulled one of my grandmother's afghans off the back of the couch and fell almost instantly into a deep slumber.

CHAPTER 33

I dreamt I was a contestant on a game show surrounded by a circle of audience members. The host, a big guy with large, startling white veneers, said, "Your question is . . . who murdered the magazine critic?"

All eyes were on me.

"Ummm, Hope?" I answered.

Buzzzz. A loud buzzer sounded. Wrong answer.

"Vivian?"

Buzzzz.

"Birdie?"

Buzzzz.

Oh no. I had to answer. The clock was ticking down. I just knew something bad would happen if I didn't answer correctly. "Roman? Baz?"

Buzzz. Buzzz. Buzzzz.

My eyelids sprung open. It took me a few seconds to get my bearings. I was in my office. The dream was already rapidly fading.

Buzz. Buzz. Buzz.

The service entrance door.

I threw the blanket off of me, found the light switch,

and stumbled out of the office to the side door to stop the incessant buzzing. I pushed the intercom button.

"Who is it?"

"You're there. It's us." I recognized Baz's voice.

I pushed the bar to open the steel door. The sky was overcast, but I still squinted against the daylight. My three friends stood at the door, Archie with his skateboard propped against his leg and Mrs. Schultz holding her bike by the handlebars. Now I was really confused—the shop was closed on Mondays. It was Monday, wasn't it?

"What's the matter?" I said, allowing them in. Mrs. Schultz pulled her bicycle in with her and leaned it against the wall next to Archie's skateboard. The heavy door clunked shut behind us.

"Why haven't you answered your phone since yesterday? I knocked on your door upstairs this morning, but you didn't answer that either," Baz said, more than a hint of concerned irritation in his voice.

"My phone." I patted my thighs needlessly, as if my yoga pants had sprouted pockets. I checked the office: overnight bag, Loretta, pillow. No phone. "I must've left it in the shop when I carried Loretta's bowl into the office with me."

The three of them stood in the office doorway looking skeptically at my sleeping arrangements.

"Did you stay here overnight?" Mrs. Schultz asked, as they followed me into the shop's kitchenette. Sure enough, my phone was still on the farm table.

"There it is." I reached for it. Lots of missed texts and calls from all three. "I'm sorry I worried you. I didn't mean to. I just needed a good night's sleep, I guess. You two know there's no work today, right?"

"We're here because we were worried about you," Mrs. Schultz said.

"I read in the news this morning that Derrick's dead." Archie plopped on one of the farm table's benches. "I called Mrs. Schultz and then Baz texted us that he didn't know where you were."

"He told us how you found Derrick. Why didn't you tell me on the phone last night?" This was the first time I heard Mrs. Schultz use her teacher's voice. I felt duly scolded.

"I wanted you to enjoy your evening. You've earned it. Besides, there's nothing we can do. Did the news say anything else about it? Was there an arrest made?" I asked, hopeful.

"No arrests yet," Mrs. Schultz said.

With the shock of Derrick's death, I hadn't thought to tell Heath about Hope's discovery. But now I had to broach the subject with Archie. I sat on the bench next to him. "I wonder if it's time we tell Detective Heath about Guy being Hope's father."

"Wait, what?" Baz jutted his head between us like a rooster. "Guy is Hope's father?"

"Oh yeah, sorry, I never got around to telling you. So much has been going on."

"That's kind of a big thing to forget."

"She said she just found out. That's why she was upset and was missing yesterday morning."

"Who else knew? Vivian?"

I shrugged. "She says she didn't, but if she did, she probably wouldn't admit it to Hope."

I could see he was about to fire off some more questions, so I furtively nodded toward Archie to ward Baz off. He noticed Archie looking dismal and kept any more questions he might've had to himself.

"We can talk about it later," I said. "Have you guys had breakfast yet?" It was only a little past nine. "I can make us a pot of coffee and something sweet, cheesy, and delicious. I think we deserve it." My mind flipped through the sweet cheese recipes I knew by heart. I snapped my fingers. "Cheese blintzes. Well, my scrappy version of blintzes, anyway. I have sour cream in my kitchenette fridge and . . ." I went over to the refrigerated case and pulled out some farmer's cheese and showed it off to the others like I was one of those *Price Is Right* models. A glimpse of my dream came and went in an instant, leaving me with an uneasy feeling.

"I've never heard of blintzes," Archie said, not leaving me time to mull over my feelings.

"They're basically crepes with a sweet cheese mixture. My husband's mother used to make them on occasion," Mrs. Schultz said.

"Sounds great. I'm in."

"The only problem is, I don't have crepes," I said.

"I can pop over to Lou's Market," Mrs. Schultz volunteered.

I sent her and Archie to the market with a short list. It was really an excuse to speak to Baz alone, but if we could also get some blintzes out of it, all the better.

Baz leaned back against the counter with his arms crossed while I prepared the coffee maker.

"I didn't want to say anything in front of the others. How did your interview with Heath go?"

"How do you think? Here I'm helping the guy out by showing him why the deck railing didn't break on its own. Then he turns around and thinks I did it? He's trying to chase a bee on a honey farm. He doesn't know which way to look."

"That doesn't make me feel better."

"Me neither. I told him where I was yesterday before

I met you at the police station. I've got witnesses when I got there and when I left. I hope it's good enough."

"It's going to have to be. He needs to focus on the real suspects."

Baz stuck his hands in his baggy jean pockets and became suddenly interested in his work boots. "So you're not worried it could be me?" He didn't look at me when he said it.

"Not for a minute."

"I was afraid you weren't answering my texts because you suspected me too."

"No way. I told him he was crazy."

"Thanks for having my back. You know, you're kinda like the sister I never had."

"I thought you had three sisters."

"I do. You're like the one I always wanted, but never got."

I laughed, but felt touched by the sentiment, especially because I felt the same way. "And you're kinda like the brother I used to have."

His brows knit together in question, but he didn't ask.

"I'll tell you about him someday," I promised.

Baz nodded and left it at that.

"I'm sorry I pulled you into this," I said.

"You didn't pull, I volunteered. I gotta admit, though, it kinda freaked me out being interrogated like that. I called Richie when I got home."

"Richie Muscles?"

Baz snorted in laughter. "Yeah, him. Remember he said he was friends with Officer Shepherd? So I asked him if he could find out more about Detective Heath from him. I wanted to see how worried I should be."

"Did you find out anything about him? Heath didn't

say much about himself when I talked to him at The Cellar."

"You were at The Cellar with him?"

"Briefly on Friday night. He was making sure I didn't get to talk to anybody who could help me with the case. Annoying. Not only that, but he was flirting with me and he's married! It makes me wonder how trustworthy he really is."

"Shep said he's not married."

"Why does he wear a ring then? Is he divorced and still hung up on his wife?"

"Widowed."

"What?" My righteousness was immediately squashed.

"He keeps to himself, so all they know is his wife died and that's why he left San Francisco."

"That's awful." I felt terrible for Heath. Then my words came crashing back to me, compounding my anguish. "Oh, no."

"What's the matter?"

"That night after we left The Cellar, I told him to go home to his wife. Oh boy."

"Oh huckleberry is more like it."

"If he hasn't taken off his ring, he must still be having a hard time with it. I'm going to have to find some way to apologize to him."

"I'd leave it alone if I were you. Shep told Richie he doesn't ever talk about it."

Momentarily, Archie and Mrs. Schultz returned with my missing ingredients.

"It's lucky Lou's is only a couple of doors down. It's started to rain," Mrs. Schultz said, patting her curled hair.

"We could use the rain, especially on a day we're closed and don't have to worry about it affecting sidewalk traffic."

I mixed the white, crumbly farmer's cheese with egg yolks, sugar, and vanilla to make the sweet, creamy filling for our faux blintzes. I told the others to sit and enjoy their coffee, but Archie wasn't the type to sit still. I gave him the job of stuffing and wrapping the crepes like burritos. In his hands, they were bloated, some busting at the seams like a well-worn favorite stuffed animal. They managed to hold together while I fried them in a pan coated with butter, turning the outsides a golden brown.

When we each had a plate of pregnant blintzes in front of us, we passed around blackberry sauce Mrs. Schultz was clever enough to pick up at the market, and drizzled it over the top.

The delighted faces of my friends after their first bite satisfied me as much as the blintzes themselves. I looked up to the heavens. "Thank you, Mrs. Hornstein for letting me take poetic license with your blintz recipe." I explained to the others, "She was my neighbor growing up in Oregon, rest her soul. She'd make all of this from scratch, even the cheese."

"I feel sort of guilty enjoying this," Archie said. "I can't believe Derrick's dead. I'm starting to feel bad that I didn't like him."

"Don't feel bad, Archie." Mrs. Schultz reached over and patted his hand. "I'm sure you were never unkind to him."

"He gave you reason not to like him. He gave a lot of people reasons, apparently," Baz said.

"He didn't deserve to be murdered, though," Archie said.

"Of course not," we all agreed.

"I'm still not sure why he was," I said. "Maybe that's the key to figuring this out. Maybe we should focus on Derrick."

"Didn't you say he was supposed to go to the police after you spoke with him? The killer must've known that's where he was going and wanted him stopped," Mrs. Schultz theorized.

"Birdie was the woman he saw in the car with Guy. She said he called her to warn her he was going to the police about it," Baz said. He reached for his third blintz from the platter of extras.

"Does that mean it's Birdie who killed him?" Mrs. Schultz said.

The possibility of it being Birdie had played in my head last night too. "But she turned herself in. Why would she kill Derrick if she was going to confess to the police anyway?"

"Could he have told anyone at work?" Archie asked.

"Yeah, like that hostess he was hot and heavy with?" Baz said.

"I suppose it's possible, but what motive would she have for killing him?" I said.

"I think we're out of suspects," Mrs. Schultz said.

"Maybe not." As much as I may have wanted to, I couldn't forget what that police officer said about Roman. "The police discovered that Roman and Guy were business partners."

The others froze for an instant, duly surprised.

"And Roman never told you?" Mrs. Schultz said.

"All he ever said was that he was friendly with Guy. He lied to everybody about it. It had to be why Heath asked him about all the cash Guy was taking out of his account. The police subpoenaed the meadery's financial records. They must think there's a connection."

"But what does any of that have to do with Derrick?" Archie said.

"I don't know. Maybe nothing."

We were stumped. I continued to eat the rich, sweet blintzes long after I was full. It was going to take a whole lot of cheese to push down my anxiety this time. Was it the rain or the gloomy subject matter that seemed to be darkening the room?

"Do we all agree it has to be Guy's killer who murdered Derrick too?" I said. Everyone concurred. "So then the person who killed him must've somehow known Derrick was going to the police with information."

"But how would Roman or any of them know? If we exclude Birdie and the hostess, we were the only two who knew," Baz contended.

Archie was picking at his blintzes, so I knew something was wrong. For as lean as he was, he never missed an opportunity to eat. And he hadn't said a word, another Archie anomaly.

"I'm sorry, Archie. You were the only one who really knew Derrick and we're not being very sensitive about his death," I said.

He screwed up his mouth. "It's not that. You guys weren't the only ones who knew."

"What do you mean?"

"You told us, too, remember?"

"Sure I told you and Mrs. Schultz, but . . . did you tell someone?"

Archie grimaced, as if he didn't want to open his mouth to say the words. "I told Hope that Derrick saw someone in the car with Guy that night. I wanted to make her feel better about her dad. I thought if I told her his killer was about to be caught, it would cheer her up."

That meant Hope knew Derrick was a witness. And she had been missing that whole morning . . . loosening my railing?

"But there's no way Hope killed her father and Derrick." Archie said it almost pleadingly.

The glances that went around the table didn't escape his attention.

"Do you really think it was her?" he asked us.

"I don't think so," I said to comfort him. In truth, I had no idea. "We need to find out exactly how and when she learned about Guy being her father."

"I could go talk to her again."

"That's not a good idea. She could be dange—" Baz stopped mid-sentence in an attempt to be sensitive to Archie's feelings.

"She's not going to do anything to me," Archie said.

Again, the three of us communicated with mere warning glances. I knew we were all thinking the same thing. We weren't about to take that chance. Hadn't we promised his mother we'd watch out for him?

I brought my empty plate to the kitchenette's sink to keep myself from taking the last blintz on the platter. The others followed suit.

Baz set his plate next to the sink where I was standing. "I'll go with him," he said.

"How's Archie going to explain you being there?"

He looked across the shop to the front picture window, streaked with rain.

"I replaced part of the roof when they had a leak last fall. I'll make an excuse about a missing roof shingle and needing to check the attic."

"You feel okay about that, Archie?"

"Sure. Let me see if she's home. The bakery's closed, but she always complains that Vivian makes her work Monday mornings anyway doing office work and proofing bread."

I washed plates and forks while Archie texted Hope.

"She says Vivian's letting her take it easy this morning and it's okay if I come over," Archie informed us.

"Let's head out, then," Baz said.

"You guys be careful, okay?" I unlocked the front door for them so it would be a closer walk in the steady rain. "I think I've got an umbrella in my office."

They waved off my offer and went out in the rain.

"You think Hope will tell them anything different than what she told Archie yesterday?" Mrs. Schultz said, as I locked the door behind them.

"Baz isn't wearing love goggles like Archie is. Hopefully, he'll be able to get some specifics from her and decipher the truth."

I stood with a damp dish towel in my hand. "You know, Vivian could be the key to all of this, depending on when she knew."

"She supposedly found out from Hope yesterday, right?"

"That's what they're saying. Maybe we should compare her story to Hope's to double-check."

Mrs. Schultz perked up at the suggestion.

I thought about it. "She gave Hope the day off, but she's probably still at the bakery. We could pretend we didn't know it's closed on Mondays. Mrs. Schultz, are you in dire need for some bread?"

"I don't think so—oh! Yes. Let's go and see about Vivian."

CHAPTER 34

Lou's Market was the lone shop on our block that was open on Mondays, so with the added rain, we were the only people on the sidewalk. I glanced over at the meadery where Roman's apartment windows glowed like prying eyes. Mrs. Schultz and I walked in step under the cover of a single umbrella until we reached Rise and Shine Bakery's bright blue awning.

The lights were on inside, but a Closed sign hung on the door. I stuck my nose to the glass and cupped my hands around my face to look inside. The glass display cabinets were bare. A face suddenly sprang in front of mine. Startled, I stepped back from the door. Vivian stood on the other side of it and shifted her glass cleaner and paper towels to one hand so she could unlock the door with the other.

"I saw you through the window," she said when she pulled it only slightly open. "Sorry, we're closed today. Aren't you closed on Mondays too? I thought we discussed that you didn't need any bread orders on Mondays."

"No, you're right. We *are* closed. I forgot that you were too. We had a hankering for Hope's cinnamon rolls."

"Oh. Sorry about that." Vivian stood in the doorway and didn't sidestep to invite us in. It didn't look like we were going to get past the Bake Someone Happy welcome mat.

"How is Hope feeling today?" Mrs. Schultz asked Vivian, to my surprise.

Vivian seemed slightly taken aback, as well. "So you know?"

We nodded.

"Come on in," she said, pulling the door all the way open and allowing us inside. She locked it behind us.

"Archie couldn't help but share his concern about Hope with us," I told her. "We won't discuss it with anyone else, of course."

She placed her cleaning supplies on the counter and let her stiff shoulders drop, as she leaned back against the counter to face us. "I'm glad to have someone to talk to about it. It was such a shock."

"We can only imagine," Mrs. Schultz said. "How are *you* feeling?"

"I'm still trying to wrap my head around it. And I'm worried for Hope, of course. I still can't believe Guy fathered my sister's child and she never told me. She kept it from everyone. It feels wrong to be angry with her, but I am."

"That's understandable. He could've helped her out," I said.

"My sister was too kind for her own good. I remember when she was head over heels for some college boy she'd met at a party. I didn't know then it was Guy Lippinger. She never brought him around, but she was twenty-one, old enough to do her own thing. The next thing we knew, she was moving here. What we didn't know was that it was because of him. We thought it was all about the bakery. Our parents cosigned a loan for it, which I thought was crazy. They had a lot to lose, but they were so happy when they thought she'd found her calling.

"When she told us she was pregnant, she said the father was a casual fling who'd just been visiting from Alaska and she preferred to raise the baby alone. Her journal said something different."

"Hope mentioned that she used to get letters from him."

"A friend of my sister's who lives there wrote them as a favor to her. They pretended he was a fisherman in case Hope tried to get in touch with him—there would be an excuse why he'd be hard to reach."

"So Guy was really her father?" I knew, but I wanted to hear the story from her.

"Yes. He came back from Europe and found her living here in Yarrow Glen. She'd bought the bakery and was ready to have a life with him. They had one night together, but that was all he wanted. He was in love with someone else."

I was quite certain I knew who—Birdie.

She continued, "His family scared her into taking hush money."

"She could've taken him to court," Mrs. Schultz said.

"She was probably too ashamed to go public about it. She said in her journal that she didn't want Hope to know her father didn't want her. She did it for Hope, but now it's all for nothing. I don't know how to comfort my niece. I've raised her for the past eight years, but we've always had a rough time of it. By the time we learned how to get along with each other, she was coming out of the teenage years and wanting to take over the bakery. We've been bumping heads about this place for three years now. She never wanted me to act like her mother, but I had no choice. She didn't have anybody else. I don't blame Hope for how she feels—who could live up to her mother? My sister was selfless."

"You're very selfless too, Vivian," I said.

"I wonder if I've made the wrong decision now, staying in Yarrow Glen with Hope. I promised my sister I'd keep the bakery, and Hope was adamant about wanting to follow in her mother's footsteps. Maybe if I'd sold it, Hope would've never come across her mother's journal."

"The truth has a way of coming out. Maybe in the long run it'll be for the best," Mrs. Schultz said gently.

"I hope you're right." She looked around. "I'd better finish cleaning, so I can spend some time with her. I hope she lets me comfort her. So far, she's just wanted to be left alone."

"Having someone you can count on in your life is a huge comfort, even if she doesn't say so," I said.

Vivian let us give her a hug and we left the bakery. We huddled under the umbrella as we made our way back to Curds & Whey.

We weren't waiting long inside the shop before Baz and Archie charged in the front door, dripping.

"Well?" I asked them, shoving paper towels in their hands to dry off with.

"Hope said the same thing she told me yesterday," Archie said. "If she was lying, she'd have messed up, right?"

"There was a journal," Baz said.

"Archie told us about that. Did you guys see it?"

"She showed it to me this time and the part where her

mom talked about Guy. It said she never told her sister," Archie said. "I read it right from the page."

So Vivian never knew. Archie went on to convey the same information that Vivian gave to us. Their stories matched.

"Archie, I think it's time we let Detective Heath determine if this new information has anything to do with the case. It looks like Hope's telling the truth, so she should have nothing to worry about."

Archie reluctantly nodded. "Okay."

"I'll give him a call," I volunteered. "But I don't think he'll want you to give Hope a heads-up after what happened with Derrick. You can't tell her."

"I don't feel right about it, though. She wasn't going to keep it a secret, but I don't know if she's ready to be interrogated about it."

Mrs. Schultz took over. "We understand, Archie. But this could be one of the pieces of the puzzle that could lead to who murdered her father. She'd want the killer to be caught."

"Who knows? Maybe Guy confessed to Birdie about it after all this time. That could've been the argument Vivian witnessed between Birdie and Guy. Say Birdie didn't break it off with him like she told me. Maybe she *was* going to leave her husband and then found out that Guy had lied to her about such a huge thing," I said. "This information might be the only way this case will be solved. It could give Birdie motive."

"You're right," Archie said.

He looked crestfallen, but I knew it was the only thing to do.

"I can drive you guys home again," Baz said. He'd been unusually quiet since returning from Hope's.

"I don't want to put you out," Mrs. Schultz demured.

"The rain doesn't look like it's going to let up anytime soon."

"Besides, the last place you two should be on your day off is here in the shop," I said.

Baz took his keys out of his pocket and tossed them to Archie. "My truck's behind the building. Stick your stuff in the back and you guys hop in. I'll be right there."

"Thanks," Archie said.

"You're a good man, Basil Tooney," Mrs. Schultz said.

Baz blushed. Whether it was because of the compliment or his full name, I wasn't sure.

Baz stayed quiet until they'd disappeared behind the stockroom door.

"What's up? Why have you been so quiet?" I said.

"You didn't tell me about the journal. You only said she found out Guy was her father."

"So?"

"The journal she showed us? *I* found it.

"*You* found it? When? How?"

"When we were ripping up the walls in her apartment because of the roof leak. The back of the closet had a false wall with a small storage space."

"Are you sure it's the same journal?"

"Positive."

"So Hope knew this whole time!"

"Not Hope. Vivian. It looked like something personal, so I handed it over to Vivian. She looked surprised, and even more so when she opened it."

"She must've recognized her sister's handwriting. Wait a second, didn't you do that work last fall?"

"October."

"You found it and gave it to Vivian in October?"

Baz nodded slowly. "She's known about Guy being Hope's father since last fall."

"What has she been doing with that information for the last six months?"

"That's a question for the police to ask her. You need to call Detective Heath and tell him everything."

"I will. They'll want to know about the journal directly from you."

"I'll come back after I run Archie and Mrs. Schultz home."

"Okay. I'll call Heath."

Baz nodded and left out the back.

I let this new information roll around in my head. How did it fit in with what happened here the night Guy was murdered?

Guy said he had a secret he was going to tell. That's certainly a secret, but wouldn't it hurt him as much as Vivian? Had she been blackmailing him with this information? That would explain the cash he was taking out from his bank account. If he had been giving in to her blackmail, what made him suddenly change his mind and be willing to tell their secret? Maybe it was Birdie. She said she broke it off with him just a few days before he was killed, but he was still in love with her. It could've been Birdie he most wanted to keep the secret from. If she found out he cheated on her all those years ago and fathered a child he never took responsibility for, there's no way they'd get their second chance.

It all made sense now. Vivian was the one who killed Guy. I had to call Detective Heath. I looked around for my phone—I really needed to change out of these pocketless yoga pants. I spotted it on the farm table again and walked over to retrieve it. Heath was not going to be happy with me for sending all four of us to Hope and Vivian's, but I hoped he'd feel the end justified the means. I picked up the phone to call him.

"Put down the phone."

I whipped around at the sound of Vivian's voice. My eyes immediately fell to the large knife she held out in front of her.

CHAPTER 35

I put down the phone like she said, without taking my gaze off the knife. "How did you get in here?"

"The front door was unlocked. You made it easy for me."

I forgot to lock it again after Archie and Baz returned from Hope's apartment. I was so in my own thoughts, I hadn't even heard it open. The front door seemed impossibly far away. The swinging stockroom door was closer, but she could easily eclipse my path to it. I had to stall her until Baz returned.

"Vivian, what are you doing?"

"I think you know what I'm doing. I figured you were putting the pieces together when you and Mrs. Schultz showed up at the bakery. But once I saw Archie and Baz leaving Hope's apartment, I knew you would figure it out. Did Baz remember finding the journal?"

I wanted to take the time to weigh my answer, but I was too nervous to lie. "Yes. He said he gave it to you months ago. Were you blackmailing Guy with it?"

"Very clever, Willa." She wiped her damp bangs with the back of one hand and then returned both to the blade she pointed in my direction. I had to keep her talking.

"Has Hope known all along too?" I glanced behind her at the front door to see if I was outnumbered. "Is she in on this, as well?"

"No. Don't bring Hope into this. I should've ditched that journal once I killed him, but it was my sister's. I couldn't bear to part with it."

"So then how did Hope find it without knowing you'd already seen it? That doesn't make sense."

"Are you saying I'm lying?"

"No," I answered quickly. "But you say Hope's not involved. I just want to know how she found out." *I just want you to keep talking.*

Vivian said nothing at first, then changed her mind. "I showed the journal to Guy as proof that I knew everything, but then he ransacked my condo looking to destroy it. It was dumb luck that it wasn't there—I'd forgotten to take it out of my purse. So I put it somewhere I thought he'd never look—the bakery crawlspace. But our new hire Jasmine mistook the crawlspace for the supply closet, and accidentally found where I'd hidden it. She gave it to Hope."

"Why didn't you just let everyone know he was her father? You could've made him pay back child support."

"That family is well versed in lawsuits. Besides, I wanted to abide by my sister's wishes for Hope not to know about her deadbeat father. I was trying to do what was right."

"So then why the blackmail? What if he decided just to confess to his wife?"

"It wasn't his wife he cared about. It was Birdie. . . . But then she broke it off with him. He said he wouldn't pay me anymore. That I could go ahead and tell, because he now had more on me than I had on him—six months of payments to me that Hope didn't know about. He was living up to his horrid reputation and turning the tables on me. I thought it was all talk until that night when he threatened to tell everyone that I'd been blackmailing him."

"Why didn't you just tell Hope then? Explain to her how you didn't think you two would win against his attorneys. She might've understood why you did it for her."

Vivian laughed one of those tired laughs. "You think I did it for *her*? I've been running that bakery since my sister got too sick to work. I kept my promise to her and I kept the bakery thriving. I always knew it would legally be Hope's once she turned twenty-one, but I never thought she'd want it once she found out what it really took to run a business. I figured I could keep the legalities from her until she was ready to walk away and then she'd sign it over to me. But she decided she wanted it, enough to take her mother's papers to an attorney. Once Hope realized it would fully be hers when she turned twenty-one, everything changed. She tried to run the show. And where did that leave me? The only choices I had were to work for my niece or walk away empty-handed and let her run it into the ground. Neither of those options appealed to me. If I'm going to walk away, I deserve something for my efforts."

"What about Hope? You took money from Guy that was rightfully hers."

"She's got her mother's bakery. That's all she was ever going to have anyway."

Baz, where are you?

I had to keep her talking. "And Derrick? Why did you kill him?"

"That was your fault. Jasmine told me yesterday morning that she found the journal the night before when she and Hope were closing the bakery, so I knew right then why Hope ran off. I wanted to find her before she told anyone about it. When you texted me you were going to see Archie at Apricot Grille, I went too. I knew if Baz found out about the journal, he'd put two and two together and realize I knew months ago. But I overheard something much worse when Derrick was talking to you two—he said he saw me in the car with Guy the night Guy was killed and he was going to tell the police."

"You weren't the woman he saw, it was Birdie."

"What are you talking about? I heard it when you did. Why lie to me now, Willa?"

"I'm not lying. Birdie confessed to meeting with Guy in his car earlier that night. It was Birdie Derrick was going to tell the police he saw. He even called her so she could turn herself in."

Vivian's ruthless calm exterior turned to confusion. She shook her head as if to deny what I was telling her.

"You didn't have to kill him. You didn't have to kill either of them," I said. If I thought this would make her break down in regret, I was seriously wrong.

Vivian snapped out of her confusion. She looked directly at me, her eyes squinted in anger. "You're right. I didn't have to kill Guy. But it felt good to avenge my sister. Do you know why she died? She didn't have time to go to a doctor. She wasn't feeling well for months, but she didn't want to take time from the bakery to see what was the matter. If he had been paying her child support all those years, she wouldn't have had to work so hard. She could've had health care and caught her cancer early enough to survive it. I wouldn't have had to give up my life to rescue hers and my parents' life savings. I haven't been living my life, I've been living hers. It was never my choice.

"I thought Hope's father had left her, and my sister had to make do, but that's not what happened. Even if she was too scared or ashamed to tell anyone when she was alive, she should've told me. Instead, she chose to take it to her grave and let me take on her burden. So when I finally found out, I made my choice. I love Hope, but I'm done working twelve-hour days for a girl who doesn't appreciate a thing I do. I followed my sister's wishes—I took care of her child, I didn't tell Hope that Guy was her father when I found out, and I'm handing over a successful bakery. I spent the best years of my life doing my duty and now I deserve a little reward. It's not like it's enough to buy a beach house and retire. But I can take weekends off or go on a date or get a manicure for once—things I never got to do because I was thrown into her life. I can move away from here and decide for once what I want *my* life to be."

There was no changing her mind. Where was the Vivian I knew with the great sense of humor who kidded with Roman and took such care with my bread orders? She had to be in there somewhere. "Vivian, I know you don't want to do this to me. We've gotten to be friends."

"You're right. I didn't want it to be this way."

I allowed a glimmer of hope to penetrate my adrenaline-fueled body.

"If you and Baz had fallen off your deck as I planned, this would be over," she said. "But now more people know, don't they? You had to get Archie and Mrs. Schultz involved."

An icy chill coursed through me. Was she going to go after my friends now too? "They don't know anything. I swear. Are you going to keep killing to cover your tracks? Vivian, when does it end?"

"Don't you worry about me. Remember my motto?

'Take one problem at a time.' Or maybe in this case, one killing at a time."

She started toward me, her damp shoes squeaking on the wood floor. I moved over to the kitchen island, keeping it between the two of us as we carefully circled it like a macabre dance. She stopped being deliberate, and advanced—the knife in her hand looking larger by the second. I juked left and she went left, so I went right. We stepped back and forth like mirror images, one measly kitchen island the only thing between me and Vivian's knife.

The buzzer at the back door sounded. Baz! I was on the wrong side of the island to make a run for the stockroom door.

"Baz! Help!" I yelled, but I knew he wouldn't be able to hear me. It was enough to shake Vivian from her calm menace. She gunned for me. I took off toward the front of the shop, Vivian practically at my heels. One wet shoe slipped out from under her. It was enough to get me a few steps ahead as I ran toward the front door. I heard her footsteps only a few paces behind me. All she had to do was lunge with that long blade to get me.

I reached the checkout counter, sensing she was practically on top of me. I wasn't going to make it to the door. I grabbed the Monster Cheddar Wheel with both hands, spun around, and struck her with it. It connected with the side of her head and she collapsed to the ground. The knife she'd been holding flew out of her hand and across the floor. She tried getting up, but her head lolled back to the floor.

At that moment, Baz and Detective Heath both raced in the front door at the same time and saw me standing over a prone Vivian, still gripping the Monster Cheddar Wheel.

"What happened?" Heath said, approaching with his hand on his holster.

"How did you—?" Baz began.

Breathing hard, I lowered the cheese wheel once I realized she was staying put. "With seventy-eight pounds of aged cheddar."

CHAPTER 36

Baz and I stayed out of the way while the police took photos and bagged evidence. Baz kept stealing glances at me with a weird expression on his face.

"Why do you keep looking at me like that? I'm fine," I said.

"I know you are—you clocked her with seventy-five pounds of cheese like it was nothing," he said.

"Seventy-*eight* pounds. I've picked up and carried that amount of weight before, but not like that. I credit the adrenaline."

"Still, I'm impressed, Wil. You were right—you're no damsel in distress."

"Thanks. I'm still glad you and Heath got here when you did, though."

Detective Heath had cuffed Vivian, and she was transported to the hospital under police supervision. She might've had a concussion, but she seemed alert as they took her away. I'd given Heath my statement. A few officers were finishing up, bagging her knife and my Monster Cheddar Wheel as evidence. I shouldn't have felt so sad to see it being taken away. After all, it could've been me instead being carted off in a body bag.

Heath came over and pulled me aside. "How are you doing?"

"I think I'm okay."

"It'll take a while to process all your emotions. Give yourself a few days off, at least."

"I can't. I have a shop to run. Please don't tell me you're going to have the whole store taped off. My business won't survive that."

"No, we'll be out of your hair tonight. She already started confessing in the ambulance, trying to defend what she's done."

"How did you know to come? Did Baz call you?"

"I was coming to talk to you again and I saw him running up the alley to the front door."

"My good luck, then."

"You seemed to have it pretty well handled. When you're feeling up to it tomorrow, I'd like you to come into the station and give your statement again. Ask for me."

"I will."

He started to turn, then changed his mind and seemed to be studying me. "I'm glad you're okay."

"Thanks." I opened my mouth to say more, to apologize for that comment about his wife—his *late* wife—when I heard a chorus of voices calling my name.

It was Archie, Mrs. Schultz, and Roman trying to get past the police officer at the front door. I dashed to them and we exchanged hugs.

"Roman told us he saw the police and an ambulance out front. Are you okay?" Mrs. Schultz stood in the spitting rain with the others, no longer worried about what it might be doing to her hair.

"I'm fine," I told them. Baz joined me at the door. "*We're* fine." I spoke for both of us.

"It's over," Baz said. "Willa knocked her out like a champ."

"Who?" Archie asked.

"You're going to have to sit down for this," I said.

EPILOGUE

Yarrow Glen's weekly farmer's market kicked off on Memorial Day weekend. The blooming wildflowers bordering three sides of the park now included an abundance of the town's namesake yarrow in white, yellow, and pink.

I finally had my table, which I'd positioned next to Baz's beautiful display of wood carvings. A microphone and speakers were set up for live music, but first the Sonoma's Choice awards would be announced.

I paced in front of our tables, unable to sit still. We'd only had two months to make an impression, so it was a long shot that enough people would've written our names for 'Best of' anything. I wasn't channeling any of my parents' sage advice this time, especially not *Good work is its own reward*. I couldn't help it—I really wanted to win one of the categories. It wasn't just for the sake of more business. People in town voted for these awards. Winning would mean I was being fully welcomed into the Yarrow Glen community.

Mrs. Schultz noticed my impatience. "Should we do our breathing exercises, Willa?"

The high-pitched squeal of the microphone saved me from the embarrassment of making moose-in-heat noises. The mayor's opening remarks projected across the park. I think I held my breath until she got to the awards announcements.

To my utter surprise, Curds & Whey won Sonoma's Choice for Best New Business. Archie, Mrs. Schultz, and I clasped arms, jumped up and down, and screamed in delight, as if our winning lottery numbers had just been announced. They pushed me out of their embrace to accept our award certificate. I had the urge to grab the microphone for a Sally Field–type Oscar-acceptance-speech moment. *You like me. You really like me.*

Instead, I blurted a thank you into the mic, shook the mayor's hand, and brought the certificate back to my team. Roman was there to congratulate me.

We'd talked on the night everything went down, and Roman explained his partnership with Guy. He told me that Guy lent him the money to renovate his tasting room in exchange for a percentage of the revenue over the next ten years. They had the deal in writing, and that's what Roman told Detective Heath when he questioned him. They only subpoenaed his accounts to make sure they had everything and that he was telling them the truth. Roman didn't tell me or anybody, for that matter, because of Guy's reputation. Neither of them wanted Guy's association with him to negatively affect the meadery. We'd both apologized—him for lying and me for suspecting him. Just as quickly, all was forgiven.

When they finished with the Sonoma's Choice awards, Baz said he had a special announcement of his own. He ducked under his table and rummaged through a box, hiding what he pulled out behind his back. He presented to me in dramatic fashion a cheese board he'd carved with my name and Favorite Cheesemonger engraved on it.

"Baz." I had to keep myself from bursting into tears.

"It's from the three of us," he said. "Just in case you didn't win a Sonoma's Choice award."

"Basil!" Mrs. Schultz scolded him. "We had no doubt Willa's shop would win," she said to me.

"Well . . ." Archie disputed.

"Regardless, we just wanted to show you how we feel about you," Mrs. Schultz said, looking a little teary-eyed, herself.

Archie and Baz nodded in agreement with Mrs. Schultz.

I was touched. "I should've gotten you something too. I couldn't have made it through these last two months without all of you. You too, Roman." I ran my hand over the walnut cheese board. "This is better than any award the town could've given me."

"You don't mean that," Baz said.

"Okay, maybe not, but I do love it. Thank you, guys."

We went in for a group hug and I waved Roman in to join us.

I couldn't believe it all worked out. I was accepted into this tight-knit community and I'd made four incredible friends who stuck by me during my troubles and my triumphs. Maybe I was right all along. Cheese *could* solve most of life's problems. Or at least a murder.

THE END

RECIPES

Gruyère-Slathered Croque Monsieur

Cheese on the inside *and* the outside of this sandwich won Baz over, even without his favorite cheddar. Nutty, oozy Gruyère blankets this simpler version of the French grilled ham and cheese, making it an easy cozy dinner.

Start to Finish Time: About 20 minutes
Serves: 2

Ingredients:
- Butter, for greasing the baking dish
- ½ cup Gruyère, divided (you can throw in some Emmental, too, if you want)
- 6 tablespoons heavy cream
- ⅛ teaspoon grated nutmeg
- 4 thick slices of your favorite hearty bread, like sourdough
- 4 oz sliced black forest ham or baked ham
- 4 teaspoons Dijon mustard

Instructions:
1. Preheat the oven to 400°F. Grease the baking dish with butter.
2. Grate the Gruyère (and optional Emmental) cheese and mix it with the cream and nutmeg.
3. Place two thick bread slices next to each other in the well-buttered baking dish. Put ¼ of the cheese mixture on one slice of bread. Put another ¼ of the cheese mixture on the other slice of bread. Top with the ham and Dijon mustard.

4. Put the two remaining slices of bread on top. Coat each top of the bread (the outside of the sandwich) with 1/4 of the cheese mixture, using up the remaining cheese.
5. Bake, uncovered, in the preheated oven for about 10 minutes. Switch to broil for a couple of minutes if the top isn't yet golden and bubbly.
6. Cut in half and enjoy!

Fontina & Friends Fondue

Sharing this warm, cheesy dish helped our brainstorming session. But even if you don't have a murder to solve, buttery fontina blended into this luscious three-cheese fondue is just right for sharing with friends.

Start to Finish Time: About 15 minutes
Serves: 4

Ingredients:
- 1/3 lb. fontina cheese
- 1/3 lb. Gruyère cheese
- 1/3 lb. Gouda cheese
- 1 tablespoon cornstarch
- 1 cup dry white wine
- 1 garlic clove, halved
- A hearty bread for dipping, cubed. (Day-old bread is good for this.)

Instructions:
1. Finely grate the fontina, Gruyère, and Gouda, combine in a bowl, and let it come to room temperature.

Once the cheese comes to room temperature, toss the cornstarch into the bowl of shredded cheese, coating the cheese thoroughly.

2. Rub the inside of a saucepan with the cut garlic. Discard.

3. Pour the wine into the saucepan and heat on medium until the wine comes to a simmer. Do not boil.

4. When wine is just simmering, reduce the heat to low and add a small handful of the cornstarch-coated cheese to the wine. Whisk until the cheese is melted. Continue this step until you've used all the cheese.

5. Transfer the melted cheese to a warm fondue pot so it remains at just the right temperature.

6. Skewer bread cubes and dip! You can also dip roasted vegetables, French fried potato wedges, or even small pickles—use your imagination!